Shadows Beyond the Darkness

Shadows Beyond the Darkness

The Eyes of the Shadows Series

S. K. BROWNE

FIRST EDITION

Book design by Publishing Push

ISBN 978-1-80227-266-6 (hardback)
ISBN 978-1-80227-264-2 (paperback)
ISBN 978-1-80227-265-9 (ebook)

Published by PublishingPush.com

Typeset using Atomik ePublisher from Easypress Technologies

Chapter 1

"Good afternoon, you are through to Rose Bud Primary school, Laura Winfrey speaking…"

"Yes, this is Mr Atkins office, how can I help you…?"

"Sorry I'm afraid he is not available at the moment as he is away at a conference until Monday noon. Can I take a message…?""Okay, I will let him know that you rang. Thank you for calling. Have a nice day."

Without delay Laura decided to type an email to Mr Atkins informing him of the telephone call when there was a sudden knock at the door. The door opened and in popped Sarah-Jane with a big smile on her face. "Hey Laura! How's it going?" Sarah-Jane enquired.

"It's going alright, I guess," Laura responded.

"Just a quick reminder; don't forget that we're going out for a drink to that new cocktail bar that just opened up on Fourth street," prompted Sarah-Jane, as she grabbed the file from the desk and walked out.

Laura's mind started to drift. She hadn't realised that the outing was today. She felt a sudden nervousness gripping her. Her palms became sweaty and she couldn't breathe. She regretted making such a solemn promise to Claire that she would attend, but knew that she needed to go. She thought to herself about all the things she would have preferred to be doing that evening. Laura was not sure what to do, but she knew that the decision was already made for her. She just couldn't let Claire down. She intended to perk up, stay loyal and be a good friend as well as a colleague. Her thoughts became bombarded with different scenarios to do with the invite for tonight. She contemplated going home to change but knowing that she was going out straight after work the option wasn't available to her. Laura glanced down at herself at what she was wearing and thought it was adequate for the evening. Laura had never once hung out with Emily and Sarah-Jane outside of work, so she wasn't sure whether they would truly like her on a social basis. As her mind wandered, the thought of not sending the urgent email message to Mr Atkins was niggling at the forefront of her mind. This brought her attention back to reality, as she knew that she needed to get her workload done and all emails sent before leaving the office for the day. Laura continued to write the urgent email and forwarded it to Mr Atkins. As she was sorting out all the files and paperwork, an email message came through stating:

"Good day Laura, could you please contact Mr Gibbons and make him aware that Mary is unwell and requires medical attention. Please contact him immediately as he needs to collect Mary and take her to the doctors."

Miss Riley

Medical team

Laura's hands began to tremble, as she was panicking for not only Mary but also for Mary's father. She speedily picked up the telephone and dialled his number from the files, whilst tapping her fingertips on the table impatiently. As the phone rang, Laura was praying in her mind that Mr Gibbons answered. "Hello!" came the deep, husky voice down the telephone line. Laura's breath was caught in her chest, as she didn't expect such a sexy baritone voice to penetrate through the telephone line. It sent shivers down her spine and melted her insides. Taking a deep breath, she explained what the call was regarding and what was required of Mr Gibbons. At the end of the conversation, she could not believe her foolish reaction to his voice, as the situation at hand was more important. She was kicking herself for behaving inappropriately like a childish school girl with a crush.

Laura sent a response to the email back to the medical team:

"Good afternoon, Miss Riley, I rang Mr Gibbons and informed him of the situation with his daughter Mary. He is on his way."

Laura. W

Laura completed all her paperwork and her filing in the nick of time before the loud, echoing of the school bell filled her office. She grabbed her belongings and headed towards the fountain area where she had agreed to meet with Claire. Laura tried her utmost best to paint a smile on her face, as she saw her best friend, accompanied by Emily and Sarah-Jane, approaching her. Although Laura knew that deep down, she was worried and really didn't want to go, she was not going to ruin it for the others. Claire and Laura got into Claire's car whilst Sarah-Jane and Emily led the way in their red ford fiesta car to the cocktail bar. On the way, Claire and Laura were held up at the traffic lights, momentarily losing sight of their colleagues ahead of them. As they tried to catch up, they must have made a wrong turn and ended up getting lost, as they ended up in a dead-end road that didn't seem familiar to any of them. Whilst they drove around in circles, trying to find a way out, they saw an oncoming vehicle with two handsome men inside driving in the opposite direction to where they were heading. They wound down the driver's side window and did everything they could to flag them down to ask for directions and were redirected the right way. When they arrived at the bar, Emily and Sarah-Jane were waiting in the car park for them. They had that look of what took you guys so long plastered all over their faces. As if reading their minds telepathically, Claire shouted, "We got lost! But we met two good Samaritans on the way, who kindly pointed us in the right direction."

When they walked into the cocktail restaurant bar, a waitress approached them and showed them to a table for four people, then handed each of them a menu. They all ordered a meal and a few cocktails. Whilst they were eating, they were having a girly chat, which carried on throughout their meal. Laughter filled the air, as they were cracking a few jokes and teasing each other about work-related mishaps. A few hours later, Emily and Sarah-Jane decided that they were calling it a night, as they were tired and had a long drive home.

"Come on, stay for one more drink, girls," Laura found herself trying to coax Emily and Sarah Jane to stay a bit longer, as she was really enjoying herself more than she thought that she would.

"We're so sorry Laura, as much fun as this is, and although we would love to stay a while longer, seriously we definitely have to go: we're both tired we still have a long drive home. But we could do this again real soon. What do you say, eh?"

Laura nodded her head and smiled at them, although deep within she felt disappointed and embarrassed to have asked and had been refused. Shortly after, Emily and Sarah-Jane exited the bar, Laura's boredom got the better of her, and she was scanning the restaurant out of interest. She couldn't help, but notice two familiar faces sitting at a table in the far corner. She reached out and touched Claire's hand to explain to her what she saw. After Laura had told Claire who she'd just spotted, Claire abruptly turned and stared in the direction of Laura's gaze. She then agreed that the men occupying the far corner table were indeed the two Samaritans who assisted them earlier on that evening. Just as soon as, they were about to look away, both men glanced over in their direction and immediately noticed them and smiled. The girls both smiled back and instantly glanced away without delay. Laura observed an awed expression on her friend's face, and Claire was blushing. Laura couldn't believe her eyes, as Claire had a boyfriend named Josh Barrett.

Josh Barrett was twenty-seven years old. He was of average height, had slim shoulders, beautiful brown eyes, and tanned skin and curly black hair. He had an amazing personality and a good sense of humour. He worshipped the ground that Claire walked on. It was clear how much he loved her but Laura was now wondering if Claire felt the same way as he did. Josh was so kind-hearted and helpful to everyone. He had strong religious beliefs and tried his best to uphold them. No matter what Claire wanted or needed, he would try his best to obtain it for her to keep her happy. In Laura's eyes, she thought that Claire should be proud of her partner's achievements and chosen career path. He had such a caring job. He was a general practitioner for the local GP practice in town. Confusion took hold of Laura, as she could not understand why her friend would not cherish a person like Josh, as any woman out there would thank their lucky stars to have a person like that in their lives. It made her wonder if there was something wrong in their relationship that Claire had not told her about.

She became even more infuriated, as she saw that Claire was now practically at the drooling stage and was ogling both men, although in fact, only one of them was looking in Claire's direction Laura was curious as to what Claire could see that had seized her friend's attention so significantly, and was making her behave so uncharacteristically. As she watched the affectionate glances continuing between Claire and the man, Laura noticed that the person that her best friend was interested in was somewhat handsome: of average height, slim, with neatly slicked-back light brown hair, a chiselled nose and beautiful lips. He was wearing black jeans, with a green loose-fitting t-shirt and he had a broad smile. But no matter how handsome he was, she was still angry with her friend for her behaviour. When she thought about it, she had to admit to herself that part of her felt a pang of jealousy that it was Claire who was getting all the attention. Laura knew she was being quite childish, but she was lonely. Dismissing the thought of jealousy and loneliness out of her head, she acknowledged that Claire's actions were still inappropriate as she wasn't single because she had Josh to think about.

Just when Laura was beginning to be fed up with her best friend's drooling and was about to glance away, her attention was captured by this muscular hand signalling for the waitress nearby. Regrettably, Laura couldn't help herself but to stare intently for a brief moment as this beautiful, handsome man whispered to the waitress. The waitress was practically falling over herself as he spoke to her. He was dressed in blue denim jeans and a black dress-shirt with the sleeves partly rolled up exposing black arm hair. He had olive skin, broad shoulders and sculpted muscles that bulged through his dress shirt, beautifully shaped lips, a dazzling smile that would capture the hearts of anyone, and not to mention his thick jet-black, straight hair. How she imagined running her fingers through his hair. He looked like a Greek God If God had ever created a perfect specimen this was it; he was the very definition of perfection. From where they were sitting, she couldn't see his eye colour, as he was looking at the waitress. All she knew was that he looked so much like a model. She watched as the waitress walked away swaying her hips trying to gain his attention, but failing miserably. He turned and stared in her direction as if sensing her intent gaze on him. His beauty had her captivated and he knew it. He gave her one of his dazzling smiles as he ran his long fingers through his hair. Laura froze as her body was betraying her without her telling it to. She felt the heat rise through her core. Her heartbeat quickened inside her chest. Her body temperature was becoming too much to bear. She had to get out of there or tear her eyes away from him. Scrambling her thoughts together her mind was telling her to look away whilst her eyes refused for what seemed like forever. She bit her lower lip as she looked at his lips, imagining what it would be like to kiss him.

She shook her head as if shaking out those thoughts. She had never felt like this before about any other guy that she had dated. They both continued to look at each other for a while before she finally managed to look away as she heard high heeled footsteps coming in her direction.

Suddenly, the waitress approached the table where Laura and Claire sat; holding a tray topped with two beautifully designed cocktail drinks accompanied with umbrellas, which she placed in front of them. Immediately, they queried who had sent the drinks as they hadn't order them. The waitress pointed in the direction of the two men whilst telling them that they were the ones to send them. Laura refused the drinks, but Claire accepted them, just before the waitress could retrieve the drinks to take them away. Claire raised her cocktail glass in a gesture to say thank you to the men who had sent them. Both men nodded in acceptance.

Claire tried to convince Laura to have the other cocktail, but Laura remained adamant that she did not want the drink, and didn't drink it. Laura was becoming agitated, as she was extremely disappointed in her best friend for behaving in such a disgraceful manner, when she had such a lovely partner. Laura decided that she'd had enough and was going leave, so she alerted her friend to the fact. Unfortunately, Claire couldn't understand why Laura wanted to go and why she was upset, so at first was a bit confused and reluctant to leave, as she was having a great time and thought Laura was, too.

Laura rose up from her seat in a huff and stormed out of the bar into the dead of night. What she did not realise was that she was slowly been followed not by her best friend but by one of the men. As she stood outside by the car awaiting Claire's departure from the bar, she was fuming with anger at her friend's behaviour. With trails of thoughts racing through her head at lightning bolt speed, she did not hear when the gravel crunched under the feet of an oncoming invader of her privacy. As her mind raced, the air was no longer odourless. The smell of spices, wood and masculinity invaded and attack her senses like a wild fire to dry bushes. She took a deep breath in and closed her eyes just for a brief second. The smell made her feel erotic and light headed, that her thoughts became wild and sensual. Instantaneously, she quickly opened her eyes and looked around, only to see a man of magnificent beauty in close proximity heading towards her. He walked with such grace. He had a charismatic smile painted across his face, as he approached her.

Laura immediately became aware of the fact that she was all alone outside with a guy that she didn't know.

However, for some reason she wasn't frightened at the thought, but only of her body's reaction to him. He was more beautiful than when she saw him in the partial lighting of the bar. He stood face to face with her now. At this point, her mind was scrambled, as she couldn't even manage to say a word, much less scrape a sentence together properly. Her knees felt weak, so she leant most of her body weight against the car, in the hopes he wouldn't notice. Furthermore, when he opened his beautiful mouth to speak, she couldn't help but noticed his brilliant white teeth.

"Hello, I'm Alex," he stated as he extended his hand to take hers in order to kiss it. Laura couldn't help herself; she just stared blankly at the hand outstretched directly in front of her, somehow not registering what the gesture represented. All that was going through her mind was how enticing and muscular his hands appeared. She started wondering if they felt soft and smooth. Her imagination got the better of her, as she began to foresee images of his hands doing things she should not speak about, much less to think of. His voice was smooth, deep and sexual, turning her insides into liquid fire. She could feel the pulse in her neck throbbing.

Laura automatically began to scan Alex up and down slowly under the streetlight, as if trying to paint a picture in her mind, whilst drinking in the sight of him. She felt like this would be the first and last time that she would ever set eyes on such beauty in all of her own existence. As she captured in his appearance and sweet aroma of him, her eyes stopped at his beautifully shaped lips. Her mouth became so dry that she tried to moisten her lips. He watched her intently as her tongue darted out of her mouth like a snake to lick her lips.

Something instantly stirred inside of him when he saw that, causing heat to surge through his body. His eyes darkened with desire. He could feel the forceful heat in his groin straining his manhood against his zipper. He let out a groan under his breath and took a deep breath whilst trying to block out what was happening to his body.

Out of curiosity, she wondered what it would feel like to kiss Alex, as she felt the temptation to reach out for him and do just that. Her hand instinctively touched her lips. Her cheeks were rosy, red as she gazed into his hazel eyes. As if reading her mind, Alex took a step closer to Laura as if drinking in the scent of her, feeling the urgent need to kiss her, but refrained himself from doing so. He waited to see if she would take a step back from him, but was shocked when she remained where she stood. Liking her bravery, he studied her reaction to him, and smiled seductively. For a moment, their eyes interlocked as if they were gazing into each other's soul. He had a wicked grin on his face. Staring into his face, she swore that she could see a flash of sexual hunger in the darkness of his eyes. It was there for a split second, and then his expression was unreadable, so she was unsure if her mind was playing tricks on her.

"I couldn't help but notice you from across the room. You're absolutely beautiful. I would like to get to know you. May I know your name?"

"Lau… I'm… I mean, my name is Laura," she stuttered.

"Pleased to meet you Laura," as he took her hand in his and kissed it lingeringly.

Laura withdrew her hand quickly as she felt the electricity shoot up her arm. She wondered if he felt it too. She could still feel the softness of his lips on her hand. The heat remained where his lips had been.

"I couldn't help but noticed that you looked upset earlier before you walked out the bar. Are you okay?"

"Yes, everything is absolutely fine and I'm certainly okay. I'm just ready to go home that's all."

"Would you like me to give you a lift home? I really don't mind. Plus, it would give me a chance to talk to you some more."

"I'm sorry but I'll have to decline your generous offer, as I would prefer to wait for my best mate."

Although Laura was tempted to accept the drive home from this gorgeous stranger standing in front of her seemingly to be requesting more of her company, which she also wanted to provide, she regrettably had to refuse for a few reasons. She did not want to leave Claire on her own and she wasn't sure whether or not her friend would be too intoxicated to drive. Laura knew that she would be the designated driver although she was honestly not in the mood to go behind the wheel of the car, but she knew that she had no choice in the matter.

Continuing their conversation under the glare of the streetlight, they were suddenly rudely interrupted by a staggering Claire singing, as she approached where they stood. Alex and Laura exchanged an apologetic glance then said their goodbyes. Laura assisted Claire into the car and hopped into the driver's seat. As they were leaving the bar's car park, Laura thought that she saw someone standing on the farther side of the car park next to a dark coloured vehicle. Whoever it was had parked under a big tree that cast its long shadow so that it pretty much hid them from the oncoming vehicles or passers-by. Visibility was next to nothing. Laura was unsure who it was, as not even their own car light could capture the image of the person because the figure withdrew themselves into the shadows to avoid being seen. Laura couldn't help but to wonder if when she was talking with Alex if that person was out there too, eavesdropping on their conversation and watching them. A cold shiver came over her. It definitely gave her the creeps to think that someone might have been watching her. What frightened her the most was that, at one point she was in the car park alone for a while, or so she thought when she first stormed outside.

During their drive home Claire and Laura were discussing the events of the evening. Apologies were exchanged from one to the other for not spending more fun times with each other, nor being there properly for one another at the bar that evening. Apologies completed; their chatter and laughter filled the car for a brief moment as they noticed there was a dark coloured BMWx5 jeep following behind them. Thinking nothing of it at the time when they were too engrossed in conversation Laura had said nothing. About fifteen minutes later, Laura realised that the same jeep appeared to have been following them for quite some time now. Explaining to her dearest friend what was happening, Claire told Laura to speed up just so that they could see if the jeep would do the same. As the car accelerated at a quicker pace, the oncoming jeep that accompanied them sped up too. Both girls looked at each other with fright written on the faces. They were hoping that the jeep would not speed up as well, but they were wrong, it did. Panic filled their very beings. Paranoia mixed with fright overtook them. They were not sure what they should do. Laura continued to drive Claire's car at a controllable speed although her mind was telling her to accelerate and push the car to its limits. She knew that she had never done that before and that she might, not be able to control the car at such a speed so she fought the urge to do so. They attempted to try and make out who was behind the wheel of the BMWx5 but couldn't tell who was driving the jeep as the windows appeared to be tinted. The only thing that stood out for them was the neon holiday logo stuck to the bonnet of the jeep. Déjà vu surged through Laura as she recognised the jeep. It was the same jeep that had been parked in the shadows under the tree in the car park at the cocktail bar earlier. No matter what roads the girls drove down, the jeep hurriedly followed.

Trying another tactic, Laura signalled for the jeep to overtake them but it didn't. It acted as though it would and so she slowed down enough to allow it to overtake but the driver instead tried to swerve into them. Out of pure instinct Laura sped up again and this time she didn't slow down. She realised that the driver of the jeep seemed to be playing cat and mouse games and their lives were in the balance as the prize. She couldn't fathom what would possess someone to do that. Sensing how dangerous this was becoming she decided that they should call the police. Just as Claire retrieved her phone from her pocket and was dialling the number, the jeep indicated and turned off down a dusty side road to their left at enormous speed leaving nothing but dust cloud particles in the air in its wake. Both girls inhaled deeply and exhaled a sigh of relief. They decided not to call the police in the end just in case it was harmless and unintentional. They began speculating that maybe the driver was intoxicated, lost control of their vehicle for a split second and could barely think straight. Besides, although they were petrified, they didn't make note of any vital information that the police would need, so they saw no point in pursuing it. Laura and Claire both thought to themselves that they'd most likely get into trouble with the police because they were drinking too, and they didn't need the hassle as they both worked in a school. Driving on to their destination, they continuously check to ensure that they were not followed again. However, although ridden with fear, Claire and Laura burst into hysterical laughter at themselves for been so foolish as not to realised that they had driven the shortest route to get to the dusty side road. This might explain why the jeep was automatically following them down every road they turned down. This was the shortest route home for them too, instead of taking the highway which would have been twice as long. They concluded that they were not followed at all.

Laura knew that this would become a re-occurring joke between them as to how stupid they were. Laura continued to drive on the main road, intermittently checking the rear-view mirror to make sure they were not followed, until she saw the turn off leading to their home. Their arrival home was a blessing that could not have come quick enough for Laura and Claire. She wanted the night to be over as quickly as humanly possible. Reflecting on the evening out there was a lot of it that she wished that she could erase without a trace, but she knew that it wasn't a possibility. Laura helped Claire out of the car and into their residence. She made some strong, black coffee for her friend and ensured that she drank it. After completion, she put Claire to bed.

Deciding to have a shower before bed, Laura quickly locked up the house and sorted herself out. When she was finished, she collapsed into bed from complete exhaustion of the whole day. She felt severely drained. Her body couldn't have moved again even if she wanted it to at this point, which she did not. As she lay there in the darkness staring up at the ceiling, her mind was pondering on the one good highlight of her evening. The image of Alex ambushed her thoughts causing a sweet smile to spread across her face until she was in full smiling mode. It felt infectious, dangerous but yet it made her feel great. She could not stop thinking about her amazing encounter with Alex as she lay there deep in thought she slowly drifted off to sleep with a big, bright smile upon her face. During her sleep, she entered the dream state of mind where she envisages herself in the near future of having a happy home and life with Alex. She could not help but imagine a life without him, and how devastated, she would be if that happened. He leant in to whisper in her ear. She could feel his hot breath against her neck. As he opened his mouth, an alarming sound that reminded her of her front door bell whisked her out of her sleep dragging her back to reality. She half opened her eyes in annoyance at the blatant disturbance. She could hear Claire shouting out to her to answer the door. This frustrated her even more as Claire was already awake and could do it herself.

Laura shouted out to Claire to answer the door, as she was not getting out of her bed because she was tired. Laura went back to sleep hoping that she could recapture her sweet dream but couldn't. Despite this fact, she slept anyway only to be hearing banging on the door downstairs as well as the doorbell ringing. Laura finally got up in a fury and went around the house hunting for her housemate Claire to give her a piece of her mind. She looked everywhere for Claire but couldn't find her anywhere. Her last hope was down stairs. As she hurried down the stairs worried about what could have happened to her friend, she remembered what Claire shouted to her earlier on that night when she was rudely interrupted from her beautiful dream, "Laura it's me Claire open the door."

Immediately that made her run to the door swinging it right open. Claire spontaneously barged her way into the house yelling, "Finally! What took you so long? I've been outside for over half an hour."

"What the hell are you doing outside at this time of night? Why did you not take the keys with you? You disturbed my peaceful sleep and I was having such a beautiful dream as well. I swear I put you to bed and tucked you in as you were legless, or was that just fake?" questioned Laura.

This made Claire stop abruptly in her tracks, turning speedily with a solid glare directed at Laura." Are you serious right now Lau? You are having me on, right? Why would you even think that I faked being drunk tonight? Anyways for your information, I got woken up by a phone call as someone came to see me urgently, mum. Is that a problem now? Do I need your permission now to go outside?"

"Don't be silly Claire, I just thought that you were too intoxicated to even hear the phone ring, much less to even stagger down the stairs to go outside. I'm sorry if I jumped to conclusion but put yourself in my shoes. You did give me a scare though when I couldn't find you anywhere in the house, plus don't forget that you zapped me out of my sleep. I was a little dazed for a while."

"Forget it Lau, it's okay. Truly, it's my fault for leaving the keys indoors and disturbing the beauty sleep that you truly deserve. It won't happen again. I hope that you can forgive me."

Claire flung her arms around her friend and kissed her cheek. They both looked at each other and smiled. "Would you like a cup of herbal tea, Lau, it's the least that I can do for you after everything?"

"Yes, I can't see why not," came Laura's response.

They both sat there around the table enjoying the hot beverages whilst reminiscing on the good times. They laughed at the silliest of things that they both had done in the past.

Laughter echoed in the house filling the air with such joy. It felt totally amazing to be extremely relaxed and happy again but all the amount of conversation would not stop Laura from wondering who had rung her friend on the phone and who Claire had to meet so urgently. Anyways she promised herself that she wouldn't ask her friend about this anymore. They both said their good nights and went to their beds hoping to get a good night's rest.

Chapter 2

Claire awoke with the most pulsating headache from her hangover from the previous night. Her breath stank of stale alcohol and tea. Her head was pounding relentlessly. She struggled to sit up on one elbow on her bed. She didn't want to move from that very spot because not only was she comfortable and warm, but also because her body was adamant that it wanted, in fact needed, to rest before the day's events. Her eyes were still battling to force themselves open, as her eyelids were still heavy with sleep. Her slender body cried out to remain resting, but her mind had already gone racing back to last night's events and what she had planned for today. Claire eventually found herself dozing off to sleep again so she lay back down, head against the pillow and covered her face with her slender hands. As she closed her eyes and drifted off, the ping of a text message came in. She rolled over with a groan, turned her head and stretched out her hand to the bedside table grabbing her mobile phone. Squinting as she read the message she read, please meet me tonight 8pm at Tom's Grill House in town. Come alone, I'll be waiting. George.

Claire responded so quickly without a second thought. Okay I'll see you there. Her heartbeat quickened inside her chest. She was now nervous. When she gave George her number last night although he told her that he would call her, she somewhat didn't believe him, she thought that it was just the drink talking.

Oh God! What had she done?

She lay there thinking whether or not she should cancel the meeting later on that evening with George, or whether she should just go, as a part of her wanted to see him again. What would Josh say if only he knew what she had been, up to. Battling with her thoughts, she decided that she would meet up with George as it was a harmless dinner, and they would only ever be friends. Thoughts of what she was going to wear started to fill her mind. The excitement spread through her body like a roaring fire. Her smile became much brighter, and anxiousness became the new feeling.

Moving quickly, she got off the bed dancing away in front of her wardrobe searching to see what she had to wear that would be suitable for her dinner date with George. Nothing there stood out so she decided that she would go clothes shopping and also get her hair trimmed, and her nails done as she had been meaning to do it for so long. Dialling the telephone number for the salon that she'd always attended for her pampering from time to time, Claire spoke to the receptionist whom she had known for years, promising to do her a favour in return, on the contrary that she manages to book both herself and Laura in for the same morning. Claire was elated when the receptionist informed her of the success in securing the two appointments she had requested. Thanking the receptionist again, Claire hung up the phone and smiled clutching the mobile to her chest. As she stood there in front of the open wardrobe doors, she wondered how and if she was going to convince Laura to accompany her. Knowing that there was more than enough time left before their appointments, Claire concluded that she would not disturb Laura's sleep until she was out of the bath because of the previous night encounter. Closing the wardrobe door, she slowly and quietly crept down the hallway to the bathroom at the end of the corridor trying her hardest not to wake Laura. She entered the bathroom silent as a mouse. Throwing off her nightdress, whilst walking towards the bath. She filled it with some refreshingly warm water and poured in some essential oil. Removing the last of her clothing, she caught sight of her reflection in the full-length mirror causing her to stop abruptly. For a moment, Claire stood there staring at herself with a broad smile on her face. She was quite pleased with her nicely toned body, big breasts and slender hips. Her confidence flew through the roof now as she thought of the perfect outfit to accentuate her breasts. She blew herself a kiss in the mirror and stepped into the bath.

During her relaxing bath Laura knocked on the door and asked her how long she was going to be as she needed to use the toilet.

"I have made breakfast if you fancy some," she added "Okay thanks," replied Claire.

Claire rapidly finished her warm relaxing bath and hopped out to get dressed and eat her breakfast, kindly prepared for her by her housemate, Laura.

"Lau, do you want to go and get a pamper session with me? This is my treat, to say thank you for everything you've done for me."

"To be honest Claire, I didn't have any plans to go out today all I was going to do was read a good book, drink a glass of wine and relax."

"Please Lau just you and me, like old times, before anyone else mattered."

"Alright, you've convinced me. Anyway, we haven't done this in a long time. We should take the opportunity."

Laura went to get ready so they could leave shortly. After Lau had her shower and hurriedly got ready, as she descended the stairs, she noticed that Claire was on the phone whispering to someone. The only line that caught her ears was, "I'll be there."

You know how they say curiosity killed the cat? I think that Laura is that cat in the firing line. Claire hung up the phone so quickly as if she had been caught red-handed. Laura didn't utter a word but she could see guilt written all over her best friend's face. She wanted to query what was wrong but she refrained from prying. At this point Claire was staring back wide eyed at Laura like a rabbit caught in the headlights.

"Are you ready to go?" queried Laura.

"Definitely," came the response from her friend who stood beside her at this point, car keys swinging in her left hand, releasing a breath she didn't realise that she had been holding.

Chapter 3

They drove in silence until they got to the mall in town. Exiting the car was the point where they began to chat to each other about what they going to have done first. They both decided that they would get the whole package, massage, manicure, pedicure, hair trimmed, facial and afterwards have a late lunch and then go clothes shopping. For every moment that there was an awkward silence, Claire wondered if Laura was going to question her and how much of the telephone conversation that she overheard.

The car park was quite full of vehicles which signified that the mall would be really busy today. As they entered through the automated doors inside, they saw it was crowded with a lot of people scurrying around doing their daily shop. There was a small fountain in the middle of the lower level where people often gathered and threw in coins to make their desired wishes before going about their busy day. Laura and Claire always made sure that whenever they went to the mall, they always make their wishes. The last time that they did that Laura had wished for true love to find her. However so far, she had been unlucky in love. Claire on the other hand wished for the latest designer bag by Micaada Moogli. Last Christmas Laura bought this as a present for Claire. Claire was so elated when Laura gave it to her. But then Claire had always been the lucky one; always getting just what she most desired, right from when she was young. Not even Claire could explain why she was so lucky, that's just how it was.

As Claire threw her coin into the fountain, she wished for her own fashion line and to be rich. On the other hand, Laura made the same wish that she always made - for true love find her.

As the hours flew by, they sat down hungrily in the café and ordered their lunch. They reviewed the events of their day whilst they ate their salmon fillets, side salad and croquette potatoes. They could not believe how quickly they completed the majority of things on their list except for clothes shopping. They drank a slush puppie, which reminded them of the first time they meet. As they were slurping on their drinks, they began reminiscing about that first encounter.

It was a boiling hot summer's day when Laura was working at her brand-new job at Rose Bud Primary School, as a receptionist to her new boss, Mr Atkins. Laura was trying figure out how to work the new program that was on the computer system as it was different to the system she was used to at her old job. She continued trying to figure out how to access the files using the new program but failed to do so. She became extremely frustrated and wanted to give up but didn't want to ask Mr Atkins to demonstrate to her what she needed to do, as she felt that, he would think she was incompetent for not being able to do such a simple task. Slumping back in her chair, she let out a big sigh. Just then, Claire walked into the office and after noticing the frustrated look on Laura's face, enquired if she was ok, and if she needed any help. Laura explained the situation and then found herself bursting into tears. Straightaway, Claire showed Laura how to work the systems and how to access the files.

While Claire was doing so, she also comforted Laura and explained what her first day of teaching was like and how similar it was, but instead she had spilled coffee on herself in front of the children and ran out crying and panicking that she might be sacked. Laura thanked Claire for the help and to show her gratitude she arranged to take her to dinner at the end of the day if Claire accepted the offer. The time finally arrived. They decided to go to Pete's café on the high street, near their work place. They ate grilled chicken sandwiches; garden salad and a slush puppie, which always gave Claire a brain freeze but still she loved it.

"Claire don't drink it so fast or you might get brain freeze."

"You're too late, Lau. It's already happening. Wooah! My goodness. I can never get used to this. It can't be helped, anyway as it's one of my favourites to drink.!" "Oh Claire, what we gonna do with you, eh?" Laura said with a smile.

Back in the present, Claire's alarm on her phone rang during the middle of their lunch. She immediately snapped to attention and asked Laura if she was ready to leave as she was finished with her meal. Laura nodded her head in response. They got up so quickly that it caused the chairs to scrape against the floor with a loud noise. The people occupying the other tables glanced across in their direction inquisitively. Lau and Claire both cupped their hands over their mouths and apologised for being a nuisance. They broke into a run as quickly as their legs could carry them. When they got outside of their favourite boutique, they came to a stop, looked at each other, and burst into hysterical laughter, then walked inside.

The woman, from the farther end of the counter strolled towards them with a crooked smile upon her face. Her face was smothered in layers of make-up, her thick lips painted with pink lipstick. She had beady grey eyes, long blonde hair and a pointed nose with a nose ring in it. She had long legs accentuated by pink high heels and she was wearing a pink and white short dress. Clearly, they could see that was the type of woman who really enjoys going to the tanning salon as she was almost orange. As she approached them her mouth opened with a screech.

"Can I help you ladies? I'm Dianne, the assistant manager here."

Claire described what she was looking for and the woman nodded her head as if acknowledging what Claire is after. "Right this way," she responded.

They followed closely through the aisles until they came to a beautiful rack of magnificent dresses in various colours, lengths and sizes with different styles. Claire's eyes were immediately drawn to a short black number that was hanging on the nearby rack. She searched for her size and retrieved it so she could take it to the counter. Turning back to her best friend and housemate, she attempted to convince Laura to treat herself to something nice. Laura gazed at her as if she was lost, although in fact she was visualising herself in a red dress she saw hanging there in front of her. It had a sequined pattern around the V-neck line, was quite fitted at the waist and would hug her hips then flare out at the end. It was a good length below the knees. In the end she decided to buy both the red dress and a blue skirt with a white silk blouse. Claire was so happy that she had her black dress for tonight's dinner with George. She wanted to confide in her friend but she was scared that Laura wouldn't approve. Deciding against telling Laura, they made their way back to the car park where they had parked their car, as they'd now completed all they had set out to do today. Getting into the car they turned on the radio. The DJ played some great drive-along songs. As the sounds echoed through the car, they sang along and giggled happily as they made their way home. The drive was easy going and straight forward. Within twenty minutes they were parked in front of their door on the driveway. They jumped out happily grabbing their shopping bags and skipping indoors.

Chapter 4

"Lau, I won't be in later as I'm going out to dinner with a friend for 8pm. I may or may not go and see Josh straight afterwards as I miss him. I hope that you don't mind been here on your own. If you want to you can call one of your other friends and meet up with them. I feel terrible to be leaving you here on your own though, as it was meant to be our girly night tonight where we watch a load of chic flicks, drink wine, order our takeout and eat lots of ice cream. I'm so sorry to break it. I hope that you can forgive me. Please be okay," begged Claire.

"Of course, that would be fine. I'll be okay. There's no need to be sorry. I don't think that I'll call anyone. I'll most likely read a good book and drink some wine. I haven't done that in a while. Infact I'm actually looking forward to it to be honest. No offence but the peace and quiet will do me good."

Claire just smiled and skipped up the stairs. She felt bad that she was abandoning her friend, but also even worse for lying to her and not telling her what she was up to. She just knew that Lau would not be understanding at all.

Leaping into the shower, Claire had a quick wash as it was already 6:00pm at this point and she didn't want to be late. When she emerged from the shower into the bedroom Lau asked her if she wanted her to do her make up or iron her dress just to be helpful. That made Claire felt the guilt surge through her bones again.

"It's okay Lau," was her guilty response.

Claire retrieved her dress that she had bought earlier and put it on. She put on her make-up, her earrings and chain and walk over to where she had her black lacey heels. Placing them on her feet she walked over to the full-length mirror in her room and looked at herself. Laura stood at the doorway of Claire's bedroom and stared at her friend admiring herself in the mirror and smiled. Claire noticed from the reflection in the mirror and asked.

"How do I look?"

"You look amazing, and I hope that you have fun. Tell Josh that I said hi, if you choose to go and see him. But wait, are you sure that you are not going out on a date, or meeting some new guy?"

Although Laura had a smirk on her face, there was still a seriousness to her tone. Claire stopped dead in her tracks with a guilty look on her face, instantly bowing her head and looking away for a brief second.

Composing herself she smiled at Laura and replied, "Lau, don't be silly girl. Josh is the only man for me and you know that."

Laura let out a breath that she didn't even know that she was holding. She didn't know what she was really expecting to hear from her friend, a confession? *Hmmm… that would be nice.*

Claire took one last satisfied glance in the mirror and hugged her best friend, and said goodbye before leaving the house.

Laura went off to the bathroom and had herself a long soak in the bath with some music playing softly in the background whilst she sang along to some Luther Vandross. The tranquillity made her feel serene. Finally, when she was finished, she put on some comfy pyjamas, went to the kitchen and grabbed a bottle of white wine, a wine glass and a chicken Caesar salad from the fridge. She grabbed a book that piqued her interest from the bookshelf in the lounge and sat down on her favourite armchair. She ate her Caesar salad and poured herself a glass of wine. As she placed the last mouthful into her mouth, Laura finally took a sip of her wine and opened her book. Smiling to herself as she basked in the serenity of the moment, she took another sip from the wine glass and smiled with contentment whilst savouring the cold, fruity taste in her mouth. Some hours in, whilst she read the romance book, she found herself getting caught up in the character's dramas. She thought that she heard a knock at the door, so she called out,

"I'm coming."

When she opened, the front door there was no one there. Closing the door behind her, she decided to go and check the back porch door, but no one was there either. But the outer netted door was swinging open and closed as it was off the catch, so Laura presumed that it was that she had heard, as it blew against the inner door. Reaching out her left hand she opened the porch door and grabbed hold of the netted outer door with her right hand.

Suddenly out of the blue she saw the neighbour's cat appear out of nowhere in front of her, meowing hungrily. It made her jump. Heart still thumping, she took the cat indoors and gave it some milk. When the feline was finished, she opened the door and let it out again.

"Don't scare me like that again she called after the cat."

The cat just continued its journey disappearing into the darkness. Laura shut both doors and resumed her reading and drinking of her wine. Engrossed, she vowed that one day she would find true, pure love no matter how long it takes. Her previous partners were useless. One used her for sex and the other for money. She thought she knew love then, but she was young and naive as she eventually realised that one of her previous partners was already married and the other was taking her money and gambling it away or spending it on prostitutes. Her heart was so torn it took her a while to recover.

Pouring herself another glass of wine, she started thinking about how lonely her life was at the age of twenty-three. She had not been out with anyone for a few years now and her confidence in her appearance wasn't at the greatest level. Bursting into full-blown tears, she cried her aches away for a while and vowed to herself that she would be okay. Picking her book back up again, she continued to read and enjoy her wine. When the bottle was empty, she took herself to bed and lay down on her back gazing up at the ceiling. She dozed off into a deep sleep. Easing into a dream state of mind her dream was soon invaded by Alex. It was like playing out the events in the book that she had just read downstairs. She saw the happiness that love could bring to her and it made her more eager for it to happen to her.

Chapter 5

Claire pulled up at Tom's grill house car park at 7.55pm. Looking into the mirror in the car she double checked her appearance and touched up on her red lipstick using the rear-view mirror. Suddenly she felt absolutely nervous but knew that it was too late to chicken out now, or was it? Sitting there in the car, Claire saw George emerge from the grill house looking around and checking the time. She presumed that he was looking out for her. So, she got out of the car and made her way across the car park towards him. Reaching where he was standing his mouth opened in awe as if dumbstruck.

"Hi Claire. Thank you for meeting me at such short notice. You look amazing. I wanted to see you again. I've booked us a table."

Blushing slightly, she stared at him and smiled shakily, feeling the nervousness drain away, whilst being replaced by anxiousness of where this might lead. For a while she hesitated thinking that she shouldn't have come but in a sense her curiosity got the better of her, enticing her in ways she couldn't explain even if she tried. Automatically, she courtesy and greeted him.

"Hey George. Thank you for the flattering compliment. You look good yourself.

Ready to go inside?" Claire enquired.

George looked so handsome standing there in black trousers and a crisp red silk shirt.

The shirt was unbuttoned a little from the neckline to the beginning of the chest, exposing some untamed chest hair. She wanted to touch it but had to fight the urge to. When they went inside a young waiter approached them leading them to their table. George couldn't stop himself as he kept staring at Claire, ogling her beauty, thinking what a lucky man he was tonight. He had been out with so many lovely women but none quite as beautiful as the woman sitting directly opposite him ready to share a meal with him.

"You know something Claire, I can't stop saying it, but you look so beautiful tonight.

And …"

He trailed off, piquing her curiosity once again as to what he was about to say. George could tell that she was keen to hear the rest of it so purposefully he changed the subject.

"And what?" She enquired leaning forward closer to him looking him square in the eyes.

She was close enough to smell the woody scent of his aftershave with a hint of lemon.

The smell was enticing. Little did she know he was drinking in the scent of her too? The fruity smell of her shampoo, the floral smell of her perfume.

George maintained the course of slyly digging for information without been abrupt by asking outright.

"Well, I must say if you had a boyfriend, he would be such a lucky man."

Claire was a bit taken aback by this statement and sat upright, leaning back against the booth, with her eyes averted elsewhere. Guilt rode her but she tried her best to suppress it as much as she could. At the sudden shifty movements, she made George felt a pang of jealousy towards a man he doesn't even know.

"Thank you for the compliment," she responded with a big smirk on her rounded face.

Claire purposefully dismissed the boyfriend comment because she knew that he was right as she was in a relationship, but she didn't know how to say it. She could sense that George liked her a lot and she didn't want to hurt his feelings, so she said nothing on that subject. Maybe it was wrong of her but for now until she figured out what it was between her and George, she would keep her relationship with Josh a secret. She was unsure that the relationship that she had with Josh was what she still wanted. The waiter approached their table,

"Hi my name is C.J, and I am your waiter for this evening."

George watched intrigued as Claire and the waiter engaged in a brief conversation. The way in which the waiter spoke with Claire was as if George was invisible. The waiter was clearly being flirtatious towards Claire which angered George a bit but he wanted to see the type of woman she was, as he knew that there was definitely something not quite right here. Her body language earlier on when they were both talking had been odd, but she didn't clarify nor did she explain anything to him. The most that she did was look away from him and that spoke volumes. She couldn't look him in the eyes thereafter and it made him wonder if there was someone else in her life who had her heart. Clearly George could see that Claire felt a little uncomfortable so decided to interrupt the conversation by asking for the menus that were still clutched in the waiter's hand. The waiter offered them the menus and apologised, getting back to his job at hand. "Let me know when you're ready to order."

George ordered a bottle of red wine and some grilled chicken, salad, spicy rice, and roasted sweetcorn for the both of them and Claire was happy with this. They sat there having a good conversation about their lives, their likes, and dislikes. The one bit of information that Claire failed to reveal was that she was in a relationship already. Although she felt terrible, she really wanted, erm…actually, she wasn't sure what she wanted, or what she expected to happen out of this date. Although her conscience was telling her to come clean with George about her relationship with Josh, she fought that urge with all her might.

`End the night at this point, you are threading on dangerous ground here' was the warning that kept going around in circles in her head. Continuing to fight that urge, she continued their conversation as they ate. After eating their meal, they ordered dessert accompanied by a dessert wine. Claire ordered a slice of chocolate fudge cake whilst George ordered tiramisu.

Although she was enjoying herself her mind drifted to thoughts of Josh. George reached and touched her hand and asked her if everything was okay. She nodded her head saying that she was enjoying herself, but that she really had to go. She expressed her apologies and stood up. He held her hand and begged her not to leave. Taking a long look at him made something stir inside of her, and this made her scared of what might be happening inside her. She saw a flash of naughtiness in his eyes, but it disappeared as quickly as it came.

Claire wasn't sure what to do next. A part of her wanted to leave and the other part wanted to stay and see where the dinner date led. Stay or leave was what she was asking herself at this point. With George watching her like that, it didn't help the dilemma she was facing. She decided that she would have one more drink then leave.

George suggested getting a taxi for her, but she refused. So, he walked her to her car. As they stood to say their goodbyes Claire leant in to kiss him, but he turned away and her lips brushed his cheek.

"If I'm going to kiss you again, I want you to be sober for this one so I'm sure it's what you want too," stated George although he desperately wanted to kiss her, too.

He had dreamt about her the night before and was looking forward to their first proper sober kiss, but he couldn't follow through as he wanted her to be thinking clearly and not under the influence of alcohol. Instead, he hugged her tightly smelling the sweet, fruity scent in her hair and kissed her on the cheek lingering close enough to the corner of her mouth as if taunting her to react. As he felt her shifting, he released his hold on her but not before whispering in her ear ` you are so beautiful'.

"Thank you for coming out to meet me tonight. Drive safely." "My pleasure. And I will."

"Claire, can you call me later and let me know when you get home?"

She got into the car and drove in the opposite direction to home. She decided that she was going to tell Josh what she was up to of late. She pulled up outside Josh's flat about fifteen minutes later, got out of the car and knocked on his door. He opened the door with a surprised look on his face but also was elated to see her as he had missed her dearly. He held her in his arms and kissed her gently increasing the pressure. His kiss deepened, as he kicked the front door closed behind her and took her to his bedroom, laying her on the bed. Josh could smell the alcohol on her breath. In fact, he could taste it on her lips. Restraining himself, he went to the kitchen and got her some coffee. As she drank the hot beverage, she kept apologising to Josh saying how sorry she was. He didn't understand why she kept apologising to him and crying. He became increasingly worried about her, so much so that he put his sexual desire aside. He could not bear to see her so upset and not be able to help. He took the cup from her hands and rested it on the bedside table. Holding her in his arms, he laid down with her, reassuring her that everything was okay, and that he wasn't going anywhere.

"I really wholeheartedly love you Claire, and I want you in my life. Please don't leave me if that's why you keep apologising. Let me take good care of you, my darling," Josh said in dismay.

He could feel the fear rising inside his gut, his heart slowly been strangled to death as he awaited her response. It felt like someone had stabbed him in the back with a knife, then twisted it slowly to open the wound, creating more extensive damage. His anxiousness was now evident as it felt like a good ten minutes before she said another word. It was the longest ten minutes of his life and he never wanted to experience that again.

"Why do you love me so much after everything I put you through?"

"You're very precious and special to me and to be honest with you, Claire, I can't see life without you in it despite everything."

She looked into his beautiful eyes and smiled. Reaching out her hand and touching his cheek, stroking it with her fingertips, she angled her head and kissed his lips. Feeling his love engulfing her body, she leant into him as if feeling weak. A sudden jerking motion took hold of her and she straightened up and ran towards the bathroom as quickly as her legs could carry her. Reaching the toilet, she projected out, vomiting up her entire dinner. He called after her thinking that she was leaving. Claire couldn't acknowledge him at that point, as the only thing she was thinking of, was to get to the toilet as quickly as she could before it all came spilling out on to Josh's floor. Luckily, she managed to make it in time. Josh raced after her only to have the door shut in his face. He listened from the outside with grave concern.

Finally, when he thought that Claire would be able to hear him much more clearly, he knocked on the door asking whether she was okay, his voice full of concern. He felt helpless as he was not sure what he could do to help her, but he wanted to try. He knew that he couldn't give her any anti sickness medication from his first aid bag as it's never good to mix alcohol and medication together. This made him feel helpless.

"Honey, is there anything that I can do to help you?" "No! I'll be fine eventually," yelled Claire.

Emerging from the bathroom after washing up, she told Josh that she would be making her way home immediately. Josh wasn't pleased with what he was hearing. He hadn't seen her in 2 weeks and now here she goes again walking out on him. He felt hurt that she wasn't even thinking to spend the night with him at all.

"You do know that it's not about the intimacy but about spending quality time, together, right? Don't feel that you're under any pressure to make love to me tonight. I just want to spend time with you, even if it's to hold you in my arms."

"I know, but I need to go home now. I want to sleep in my own bed."

"Well, I can't force you, and I give up trying to convince you. But you're in no fit state to drive home. I want you to be safe. Should I call you a cab to get you home? I don't mind driving your car over to you tomorrow," he said, sounding angry and concerned all at the same time.

"No thank you! I'm not that incompetent that I'm not able to drive myself. I drove here to see you, didn't I?" she bit back furiously.

Grabbing her shoes, coat and handbag she stormed bare footed out of the flat, slamming the door behind her. Josh called after her, but she ignored his plea to stay. Getting into her car, she made a call to George asking him to meet her at the cocktail bar in town. She started the ignition and drove off in haste causing the wheels to skid.

Chapter 6

George got out of bed and pulled on his clothes to go out to the bar to meet with Claire. When he thought about it, if Claire needed to blow off steam or cry, it was best to do it in private. Grabbing his phone, he rang her and suggested that she come to his place instead of meeting in the bar in town as that way they could have the privacy to speak without any disturbances. She quickly agreed. He gave her the address and directions of how to get to his place. He was sure that she sounded as if she was angry, upset or something. She told him that she needed to see him. He didn't know what the urgency was that she couldn't wait till tomorrow, but could hear it in her voice, so he agreed. Bracing himself, he wasn't sure if he would be able to concentrate solely on what she would be talking about without feeling sexually drawn to her. He wasn't sure if he could resist the urge again to kiss her. He had regretted it since turning her down earlier on that evening.

He was now kicking himself for making such a foolish suggestion as to bringing her to his domain. All he knew was that a damsel in distress somehow required the assistance of a noble knight, and he intended to be that knight, even if it was only for tonight. Quickly checking the cleanliness of his home to see if it was a good enough standard, he then decided to grab a couple of bottles of wine from the fridge in preparation, just in case they needed a drink.

After preparing everything, he heard a knock on his door. Striding towards the front door he could hear footsteps walking away, so he yanked the door open as quickly as he could. He called after her. She turned around her emotions unreadable. Convincing her to come inside, she sat down in the lounge looking all around her wondering why the heck did she even bother to call George in the first place after he turned away from her kiss earlier on tonight. She felt so embarrassed that she wanted to crawl under a rock somewhere and die. Telling herself that she wouldn't try that again ever in this lifetime nor the next. Claire couldn't believe how horrible the night had been. She felt jinxed as bad luck seemed to be coming her way full throttle. Feeling in turmoil of a catch twenty-two situation, she wasn't sure what she wanted to do. She was hoping that George could help her figure this one out, as he was part of the problem.

Surveying her surroundings, she noticed that this was a true bachelor pad as the colours were so masculine. There was no woman's touch to it whatsoever. Her mind began to wonder whether he had a girlfriend, lover or wife. She needed to know before it was too late. It was an urgent matter that needed to be solved. Could that be the reason for his refusal to kiss her earlier? Locked deep in thought George stood there staring at her trying to read the different emotions flashing across her face. The one emotion that stood out the most was embarrassment. He couldn't think what she had to be embarrassed about. She was a beautiful young lady with a lot to be thankful for.

Hold on a minute, where was her manners? Not even a hello and thank you for letting me come over. Usually that would not faze him, as the women who came to see him at home were always a quick fly by. There was no time for nice pleasantries just straight to the bedroom. After the deed was over, they would go home. Most of the time they'd go to a hotel room rather than come here. His mum always told him that he needs to find a nice girl and settle down. She wanted grand children before she died.

Nebissah Smith was a 56-year-old woman with the odd few silver strands of hair on her head. She was average height, long black hair, black eyes, and thin pursed lips. She was born and raised in Besiktas, Turkey. Her accent was extremely strong so there was no mistaking where she was from. George was her only child. She wanted more children but after having George, she was diagnosed with cancer of the uterus so had to have a hysterectomy. This had saddened her, but she had learnt how to accept what faith had brought her way. She was so grateful to God for his blessing. This mainly explained why she was always pestering George to have many children. Envisaging herself surrounded by lots of beautiful grandchildren, it was a dream that she wanted to be fulfilled.

` *Why this does bother him that Claire didn't say a thing to him so far since her arrival? He couldn't understand.*'

No woman had ever succeeded to have him at this point, where he cared enough to worry about how they are feeling. What was happening to his way of thinking, he couldn't fathom it out.

Occasionally, Claire would look up and stare at him without breathing a word and at this point he had expected her to come out with it, but she said nothing, but just looked away again, playing with her fingers, looking at her palms as if the answers to her mental questions would just appear there.

Regrettably, he would have to disturb her chain of thought, as he wanted to know why she needed to see him so urgently. He poured her a glass of wine and gave it to her. "Thank you," came her response before gulping it all down in one go. He watched deep in shock as she swallowed the wine as if it was water. As she raised her wine glass in front of him, signalling for him to pour her another, he obliged. At this point, she slowly sipped on the cold liquid, savouring it as if it was a comfort blanket.

Before he could say a word, she began talking without looking at him.

"I'm so sorry to disturb you at home. I had no intention to come here in the first place, but I must tell you the truth. Erm…. I'm not even sure where to start," Claire said apologetically.

"Okay, usually people would say start from the beginning but my suggestion to you is to start at the point that is bothering you the most."

"I shouldn't have gone out with you tonight without laying it all on the table to tell you that I have a boyfriend. His name is Josh and we've been together for four years now. I do care about him a lot but I'm questioning my feelings as to whether or not I still love him. The thing is our relationship has been on a rocky road for a while now, but he doesn't want to let me go. I feel like I owe him a lot as he gave me his heart and has done so much for me, but I just threw it all back in his face. It hasn't helped the situation that from the time I met you I have been physically drawn to you. Whenever I'm around you, I feel as though there is something pulling me in your direction. Before you say anything, I am sorry for landing this on you so suddenly and I should have told you from the beginning about Josh. I'll understand if you don't want to see me anymore. What I want you to know is, she gulped another mouthful of the cold liquid, then she continued… that I like you a hell of a lot and I hope that you feel the same. I'm not sure what to do next," came the confession as her words spilled from her lips to hang in the air between them.

For a moment, he stood there staring at her blank-faced and his mouth partially open. He could not process what Claire had said fully as part of him could not believe his ears. A part of him knew that a beautiful woman like Claire could never be single but he didn't want to believe it. He needed it not to be true. George walked towards the window, standing there peering through the window pane into the darkness. He stood there so rigid and distant.

"Please say something George! Cuss me if you want to. Tell me to leave but please don't ignore me. I'm truly sorry. I hope that you find it in yourself to forgive me," Claire pleaded feeling distraught.

Turning to look directly at her he said, "To be honest with you Claire, can I process what you just told me overnight and get back to you? I need time, after all you're telling me that you are taken," George said in despair.

"You can spend the night in the guest room if you want to and go home tomorrow. The choice is yours. It's quite late, and I'm worried about you driving home at this hour. Please stay. It will reassure me that you'll be okay. And a question - have you ended your relationship with Josh? I'm curious to know."

Ignoring George's question she snapped, "What's up with everyone trying to tell me what to do tonight, acting as though they care?"

She didn't mean to react so childishly, but she was disappointed as to the turn of events. She wasn't sure what she expected George to have said, but it sure was not that. She was hoping that he would have forgiven her straight away but how wrong she was. "I'm sorry for snapping. I'll stay the night, but I'll be gone early in the morning.

Chapter 7

A week later Claire and Laura were sitting on their front porch relaxing, having a slice of strawberry cheesecake and an icy cold glass of lemonade as it was an extremely hot summer's day. Despite sitting outside, they couldn't feel any wind blowing at all. The atmosphere was quite stifling. They sat there talking about work and life in general. Laura was telling Claire about the dreams that she had been having of late almost every night. The only information that she did not reveal was that they were of Alex. Claire noticed that Laura seemed to be putting a little weight on. It was falling in the right places. On her breasts, hips, bum and thighs, making her look more curvaceous.

"How fortunate you are, Lau," Claire protested, "that you aren't putting it on in the wrong places. For me, if I put weight on it goes everywhere. That's not fair. Thank God I haven't of late."

Claire felt a little pang of jealousy about how her friend was blossoming now. She wanted to remain the better-looking one in every way. 'Gosh!' she thought to herself, 'what's gotten into me, I'm not the jealous type. But everything is going so wrong for me and I don't know how to fix it yet'. Josh didn't want to speak to her now and she hadn't heard from George for a whole week now. She wasn't sure what to do next. Feeling like she was losing everything, she sunk into complete silence trying to contemplate how she could retrieve all she once had. She wanted to talk to Laura about it but decided it was best not to. Deep in thought, she was rudely interrupted by a phone call from George. Claire immediately stood up and went further up the driveway, for some privacy, and answered the call. Speaking for what seemed a moment she agreed and hung up. She hoped that he would be proposing to be more than friends as that is what she wanted.

Later on, that day, Claire got prepared to go visit George to see what he wanted to say. She got into the car and drove steadily to George's house.

When she arrived, he was waiting patiently by the front door for her. Getting out of the car, she warmly smiled and greeted him. She resisted the urge to throw herself into his arms. Her heartbeat quickened inside her chest as she looked at him. She bypassed him in the doorway brushing against him seductively as she walked into the house. George was wearing black knee length shorts and a white vest. His hair was still wet from his shower. She could smell his vanilla bath wash on him as the aroma taunted her nostrils. It was quite refreshing, she thought. He gestured for her to sit down around the pine dining table. He poured them some iced tea and then sat down. "You're looking lovely today," he said with a sensual smile.

Claire was wearing a short, yellow summer dress and white sandals with yellow sunflowers on them. Her hair was tied up in a ponytail. "Thank you," she replied with a cheeky smile.

"We'll talk over dinner if that's okay with you." "That's fine. I'm in no rush."

They made idle conversation until it was time for dinner. Claire began feeling nervous as the time drew nearer. Her palms were sweaty and her fingers trembling. Nerves were taking over her entire body by the time her meal was placed before her. It was presented well on a round white plate with a silver-rimmed edge. They had barbecue ribs, mashed potatoes, and steamed vegetables. The smell was enticing, taunting her nose whilst wetting her appetite. She took a deep breath in and closed her eyes for a split second. Unbeknown to Claire, George sat there admiring her, watching as she took her first forkful and placed it into her mouth. He couldn't stop himself from staring. As she opened her eyes, he looked away quickly before she could notice. As they ate their tasty meal, George steered the conversation in the direction he wanted it to go. "Thank you for coming over at such a short notice, Claire, I really appreciate it. I was hoping that we could discuss last week's revelation and clear the air. Firstly, if I had known initially that you had a partner, I wouldn't have approached you the way that I did that night. When I first saw you, I felt like there was something lurking in the wings. Like we could have something special hopefully, but to start this off with secrets and cheating, I'm not sure how I can forget that. Even though you and Josh are on rocky grounds you shouldn't have brought me into the middle of it the way that you did. To be honest with you, I think that you should have given me the choice as to whether I would still pursue you after knowing that you're taken. I wish that you had told me in the beginning, because now I feel as though I am part of the reason for you and Josh's problems. I am sorry if I am not telling you what you want to hear. I do like you a hell of a lot Claire, and I think that we could have had something special between us. However, despite the fact that we may not be together I would love for you and I to be good friends and be able to hang out from time to time. Please tell me what you think as that's the only way we could move forward and be on the same level," declared George.

Claire couldn't believe what she had just heard. She was hurting so badly she couldn't let George bear witness to her pain. Her jaw had dropped open in shock, but she now snapped it shut and straightened up. Putting down her fork and peering at him intently she said

"Well, I guess I can't change how you feel, but I appreciate you finally getting back to me in the end. " `Although it was a week later. Talk about leaving people wondering!' she thought to herself as it entered her mind. "However, I cannot see why we can't be friends, I suppose. I'm not sure where we go from here though, as I know that it was my fault.

Anyway, thank you for such a wonderful meal. I'm afraid I can't stop to have dessert, but maybe next time as I must dash now," she said hoping that he wouldn't hear the hurt in her voice.

She felt the tears sting the back of her eyes, threatening to fall at any moment. She swiftly stood up and said, "bye, we'll catch up" and walked out the front door without a backwards glance in his direction. George could have sworn that he saw tears welling up in her eyes. He wasn't sure, so he didn't pursue it to know if it was true. He felt terrible for telling Claire those things, but she needed a clear head to figure out where her relationship with Josh was going before anything could happen between them. He didn't want to be the reason for her leaving her partner. She needed to do this of her own accord. Fighting the urge to call after her, and pull her into his arms, instead he stuck his hands down in his pockets and forcefully kept them there. He was wondering how their friendship could sustain itself when they both felt the way they did. Knowing he couldn't act on it he dismissed the thought as quickly as it came.

`How the hell did I get myself into such a state at this hurtful, confusing point? What am I going to do now?' he thought to himself.

The hum of the engine of her car, the sound of slow jams on the radio playing out made her feel even more down. Feeling as if she was going on a downwards spiral, she accelerated more trying to get home as quickly as she could. It was quite dark outside by the time she got near enough halfway home. No longer threatening, but revealing themselves without choice, the tears began to fall as quickly as they formed. She sobbed hysterically with no end in sight. The car was swaying uncontrollably. She didn't realise until she saw the glare of oncoming headlights temporarily blinding her vision and heard the frantic beeping of a horn from an oncoming vehicle, that swung out of nowhere. There wasn't enough time to swerve to avoid the inevitable collision. The sudden impact sent her head banging against the steering wheel with a hard thud. Pain surge through her entire body severely and ferociously. She could barely move after such an impact. She felt the warm liquid flowing down, covering her face which was no longer the natural colour of her skin. It looked like a red painted artwork. A very sharp, excruciating pain was spreading through her entire stomach area. Her dress was absolutely soaking wet in blood. Weakness overtook her as her strength crumbled away. Her eyes were blurred, and her vision was distorted. Panicking she could not think what she needed to do. It was too much to bear, George's words replayed repetitively in her head hugging her like a comfort blanket. The pulsating pain from her injuries enveloped her body unremorsefully as it tore away at her nerve endings. She attempted to move her body but cried out loudly in agony. She felt like this would be it for her now. Thinking that she would die, she never envisaged that it would be in this way with no loved ones to hold her hands or be by her side trying to comfort her telling her that it would be okay.

A wave of dizziness hit her so suddenly, unfortunately as she closed her eyes to block out the feeling, she began slowly drifting into unconsciousness. The last face she saw was unrecognisable. The person seemed to be shining a bright light at her whilst trying to ask her, her name. She struggled to open her mouth to speak. Her name slipped off her lips into the air as a mere whisper. She opened her mouth again, "Laura, where are you? I need you," she slowly whispered whilst plunging into the darkness awaiting her arrival.

"I can't make out what she's saying even after putting my ear so close to her mouth, so we'll check her handbag after getting her to the hospital, so we can complete her medical papers," shouted the paramedic to her colleague as they radioed through to the nearest emergency hospital.

"Okay no problem," came the masculine response of the colleague standing closer to where the ambulance was parked. He grabbed hold of the gurney and headed towards where Claire lay seriously hurt and in urgent need of medical attention. He was puzzled as to how she had survived such a horrendous car crash, but was pleased to know that it wouldn't be like last week when he was at a crash site, and the patient died so horrifically that it still haunted him now.

"Come on new recruit, snap out of your daze. Now is not the time to be daydreaming.

Get your skates on, let's wrap this up and get her seen to at the hospital as quickly as possible," came the order that penetrated his thoughts from the senior paramedic in charge.

Glancing back around to the patient in front of her she said,

"Stay with me honey, try your best to stay awake. Look at me! Listen to my voice. Can you move? I'm going to examine you and check to see where most of the bleeding is coming from. What's your name? Do you remember?" asked Judith, senior paramedic and mentor.

Claire peered at her in agitation. She couldn't believe that the woman was asking her the same question again.

'My name is Claire. Are you deaf or something? Can you not hear me? Claire, Claire, Claire that is my name, she repeated in frustration. Don't look at me like you don't understand what I'm saying. I'm telling you my name so why do you keep on asking me?

Answer my question now, who are you? Where's Laura? What's happening here? Please don't touch me. What are you doing? Stop that! It bloody well hurts. Go away and leave me alone ple........'.

Everything went still.

Chapter 8

There was no movement in the branches and leaves outside as there was barely even a breeze. Feeling hot and miserable, Laura threw back her covers and sat up in her bed covered in sweat, thinking to herself whether or not she had opened up the window in her bedroom as she couldn't feel any air at all. Her room was so stifling, she remembered how hot and musty the day had been - the hottest day of the year so far according to the weather forecast that everyone, including herself, were praying for it to rain and cool down the earth's atmosphere to make it more comfortable for its occupants. Standing up, she strolled towards her window and drew back the curtains only to reveal a pitch-black night, humid and stuffy. She noticed that everything was at a standstill, unfortunately. Feeling like she was struggling to breathe, she decided to go for a swim in the pool situated at the back of the house, in an attempt to cool down, as she was restless.

As she was in the cooling water, she thought that she heard a noise and saw someone standing above her on the poolside. Her heart almost stopped in her chest as no one was supposed to be at home with her. Laura froze for a split second, with her eyes wide open trying to make out the figure standing there. Her mind was telling her to swim away as fast as she could, but her body just couldn't move. She was frozen with fear to the very spot for a moment longer than she wanted to be. She was not sure how she did it, but all she knew was that she had managed to get to the other end of the pool far enough away from where she thought she had seen the shadowy figure. She popped her head above the water to look to see if there was someone, but saw nothing. The glare of the back-porch light reflection shone enough to show her that there was no one there now. She snapped round to look behind her to make sure that she hadn't been followed. She was not sure how long it had taken her to swim that length, but all she knew is that it felt like a lifetime.

She didn't even remember swimming to the other end of the pool. As she was hovering there still in the cold water, frozen with fear and in frightened thoughts of 'what if' flashing through her mind a sudden ringing penetrated her thoughts zapping her back to reality. Her focus was now on the telephone ringing inside the house. She knew that she had to get to that phone before it stopped ringing. Although her body felt so weak, she pulled herself up and out of the pool, running with full-length strides towards the back porch with all the energy that she could muster. She didn't care that she had left all her belongings, such as her towel and radio, outside next to her shoes by the pool. As she approached, the back-porch door, she couldn't help but feel that something was wrong. She couldn't focus or register properly the details other than that she knew the phone was ringing, and she had to answer it. She ran straight inside, down the hallway and into the lounge and picked up the telephone receiver with a desperate need to hear a voice that was familiar to her. Panting and gasping for air to fill her lungs from all that running, made Laura feel exasperated.

"Hello Laura!" Came the weakened, strained voice down the telephone line.

"Say, something. I know that you're there. I can hear you breathing. woman," demanded the person on the other end of the line.

At first, Laura was so dazed that she merely recognised the voice of her flat mate, Claire Collins, coming through the telephone. She had to verify whom it was that she was speaking with. Although weak and in agony Claire was so taken aback by such a response, that she immediately was concerned for her friend.

"Laura, it's me, Claire! Is something wrong?" asked Claire so softly spoken; her voice suffused with grave concern for her friend's well-being.

Laura answered her friend so emotionless and distant, telling her that everything was all right, not that she believed it herself. Claire wasn't sure what she should do, but she knew that she had to tell Laura that she was in hospital because she got into a car accident on her journey home. After telling Laura the news, she finally had Laura's full attention; she could not believe what she was hearing. Claire went on to explain about the accident and that she believed that maybe she was exhausted and dozing at the wheel. Her unsureness puzzled Laura somewhat as Claire was coming across as being unaware of how she got into the accident in the first place.

She was unsure as to whether she had fallen asleep behind the wheel or if she did not see the oncoming vehicle approaching her, as it pulled out of the side road. The only thing that she seemed to remember clearly enough was swerving, the skidding of the tyres against the tarmac and the ultimate impact that sealed her fate as she hit her head against the steering wheel in the collision. Claire told Laura about the sudden jerking pain in her neck she had felt on impact, and the feel of warm liquid all over her face and body from the bleeding. She acclaimed that she could not remember anything else after that other than waking up in the hospital surrounded by doctors and nurses. Claire downplayed the severity of her injuries and reassured Laura that she would be okay, although she knew that there were some complications in her treatment. She refused to tell Laura because she didn't think it fair to burden her friend with her problems. She guessed that if she didn't speak of it maybe it wouldn't be true. Claire was scared shitless but didn't want anyone to know. Pausing for a split second, she stifled a cry as agonising pains hit her body again. As she silently winced in pain, Claire managed to disguise her voice well enough to tell her best friend that she should come visit her the following day, and that there was no point in worrying. Claire knew that there was a lot to worry about, but she could not bear to think of Laura being extremely worried about her. To justify her actions, she thought to herself that Laura sounded out of it, anyway.

Laura's heart sank to the floor as a big part of her wanted to go straight away to the hospital to be there for her friend, and the other part of her was scared to go back outside, just in case someone was out there waiting to attack her. Suddenly, the doorbell rang out and Laura clutched on to the receiver with dear life. She was grabbing the phone so tightly that her knuckles were as white as a sheet and the colour drained from her face leaving her pale. It was coming close to midnight and no visitation plans was arranged with anyone. "I know that you must be in a lot of pain and I'm sorry to hear that has happened to you but can you please stay on the line Claire, just for a brief moment, I don't expect anyone to visit me tonight and as you know I'm here alone, so if something was to happen to me then you can call the police right away."

Claire agreed, although feeling drowsy and faint, but still guilt ran through her very being knowing that she couldn't be there for her friend. As Laura approached the front door with the telephone clutched in one hand, she heard laughter and chatter outside the door.

Recognising who was outside her front door just by the chatter and laughter. Laura breathed a huge sigh of relief. She speedily opened the door to her mother.

Margaret Winfrey was a short, stubby woman, with beady eyes, long black eye lashes, and jet-black hair. Margaret presented like such a kind-hearted woman who worried about her daughter, and whether she was coping.

Laura was so ecstatic to see her mother that she leapt into her open arms. Her mother held her close in a warm embrace, savouring the sweet moment. As Laura's thoughts drifted, she remembered that Claire was waiting on the telephone. She quickly put the receiver to her ear and reassured her best friend that it was just her mother, and not to worry. She added that she intended on visiting Claire at the hospital in the morning and rang off.

"What are you doing here so late mum?" Laura enquired in disbelief as she replaced the receiver.

"Can't a mother visit her only daughter if she feels the urge to?"

"I'm really elated to see you mum. You've always had perfect timing even when I was really young. But seriously what are you doing here, and for that matter, why did you come so late?"

Laura remembered a time when the neighbour's children used to bully her and take advantage of her, and her mum got there in the nick of time to save her, except for one dreadful, unforgettable occasion, which could never be erased from her deepest memory.

* * *

Angela Woods was a butch looking woman with short, dirty blonde hair, smoky grey eyes, and tobacco-stained teeth. Everyone knew her as a loud-mouthed woman who constantly shouted no matter what. Every time she was in close proximity, she always stank of tobacco and coffee: tobacco was always her cologne and coffee were constantly her mouthwash. It was a despicable combination of fragrances that assaulted the senses. She didn't really give a shit what her daughter and son got up to. In secret, she enjoyed a fair bit of drinking of alcohol. All she seemed to care about was when her ghastly children would be going out to terrorise the neighbourhood children, so she could get some peace and quiet to consume her alcohol and smoke to her heart's content.

Her son and daughter John, and Jennifer woods always appeared scruffy and unkempt whenever they were at home. They didn't care for anyone but themselves. They bullied everyone around the neighbourhood. They used foul-mouthed language, swearing just like their mother. Laura could recall that she was their main target and she could not figure out why. She wondered whether it was to do with the way she looked. At the time, she was a scrawny little thing, who wouldn't squash a fly. She was always kind-hearted to everyone no matter who they were. Confused as to why they picked on her every day, Laura came to the realisation that it seemed to be a fun activity for the Woods children.

Jennifer was model-like although she was short and slender, with grey eyes and blonde hair and beautiful features to be honest. The people in school, especially the senior boys, took a fancy to her. Typically, she was the type of girl that boys would queue up just to ask her out on a date. Jennifer was extremely popular with her peers, which left Laura puzzled as to why Jennifer picked on every day. Knowing that she didn't possess such beauty, and no one took a second look in her direction, confused her even more. People kept telling her that she was as thin as a rake and needed to eat more to gain weight. Complaining a lot about what she was experiencing from these bullies to her mother was a regular trend on a daily timescale. Her mum's response was always,

"Don't listen to those terrible remarks, just always be kind to them."

Laura tried her utmost best to remain true to herself by showing nothing but kind- hearted qualities, but it made no difference. It just seemed to rile up Jennifer even more, and John was no different in this matter. He didn't put a stop to the situation; instead, it was continuously fuelled by him, which in turn caused Laura even more anguish. He assisted in the name callings, the pranks, the fights, making Laura feel less than nothing.

Laura did not know what she should do; all she knew was that she wanted, in fact needed, the bullying to stop. It was extremely scary to know that she must go through this horrible ordeal every single day. At one point she was beaten so badly that she wished that she would have died, so she would not have to face up to the Woods siblings ever again in this lifetime. This was the one time that Margaret was unable to save her from such a beating.

The doctors at this point were unsure as to whether Laura would survive the next twenty-four hours, much less to the next seventy-two hours, as she was laying there in a coma. Severely beaten into unconsciousness, the doctors were fearful. Intensive care unit doctors attempted and tried all that they could medically, and announced that the rest of the healing was down to Laura, and her will to survive.

Family and friends were encouraged to continue to talk to Laura and motivate her to regain consciousness. The recovery process took three months before Laura was back on her feet again and discharged from the hospital with a referral to a therapist to discuss how she felt.

The Woods children were sentenced to complete one hundred- and eighty-days community service. No one understood how the two children got off so lightly after the crime that was committed on Laura. Being of juvenile age the law unfortunately could not try them as adults, so instead was lenient in its judgement. For Margaret it was the lesser end of justice, as she believed that the law was not harsh enough on these two unruly children to teach them a valuable lesson. She would have settled for five years imprisonment so that they would have had plenty of time to reflect on what they had done.

John Woods was now twenty-nine years old, a short, slightly overweight guy with dirty blonde hair, grey eyes, and no fashion sense. He didn't care for anything and anyone except for his sister Jennifer. To be honest both Woods siblings would protect and defend each other to the ends of the earth and beyond. He worked as a supermarket assistant locally, re-stocking grocery items, customer service, cashier and assisting with home deliveries from time to time.

Despite his tough exterior, he loved his job and mainly enjoyed meeting, greeting, and assisting the public. In secret, he had a softer more caring side that he rarely revealed unless he was at work or looking after his sister. The thing that was so strange to Laura was why they both picked on her so badly. Time after time, she could not understand if she had done or said something wrong to them that was forbidden. The more she asked the perpetrators for a reason, the more they bullied her, until one day she ceased to ask anymore. The bullying was continuous throughout the whole of high school. All of this made her life very miserable, traumatising, and fearful to the point where she was resisting going to school. Eventually, she got used to it in the end. Her mother Margret had tried her hardest to put a stop to all the trauma that Laura was facing. Margret only managed to succeed in the last year of school after the Woods children were excluded. They were forced to move away to the countryside to reside with their uncle Bobby, after their mum, Angela passed away. Rumour had it that she died of alcohol poisoning, but others said she had died from lung and throat cancer, and last but not least some people said that she committed suicide by overdosing on sleeping tablets and as a result suffered a heart attack. It was said that John and Jennifer were the ones to discover the mother's lifeless body. *'How sad and disheartening it must have been for the Woods siblings.'* Feeling the need to be there for the Woods siblings but not being able to fulfil that need was the ultimate damper as she was too terrified to approach them. It was not certain what response she would have encountered from these now grown-up siblings under the circumstances. Feeling heartbroken for them, Laura finally figured out what could be done. No matter how hard she tried, there was no way that she could contemplate what it would be like to lose her own mother. All in all, her mother was her world, and life without her would be a devastating ordeal not worth facing. Drifting away, from the thought of her own imaginative anguish, she focussed back on the emotional task at hand and decided to write a letter to John and Jennifer to express her deepest condolences. After completion of the letter, Laura took it to the supermarket where John worked and left it with his supervising manager. Tears stung the back of her eyes as she wrote the letter of sympathy and they eventually streamed down her face and onto the paper.

Dear John and Jennifer,

I know that this letter would not change your circumstances, but I hope that it provides comfort to you both. I am so sorry for your loss and I hope that you guys will find peace of mind eventually. I cannot begin to understand what you both are experiencing, but I can only imagine the agony you must be facing. My heart aches for you. I send my deepest condolences to you and the rest of your family. I know that you both don't like me, as you proved that each and every day you put

me through hell, but despite that fact, I am here for you both, whether
you need to talk or a shoulder to cry on.
May your dear mother rest in peace.
Laura Winfrey

"So how are things here?" came the question that would penetrate her daze, bringing her back to reality once again but without precision of focus to the person that stood before her. She could see her mother's mouth moving but found it difficult to regain focus for a moment. *'What the hell is happening to me? My whole world is falling apart. And now my mind is going What do they call it again… bonkers is it? Or something like that.'*

"Laura! Honey I'm talking to you. Are you okay?"

Laura didn't seem to register what her mother had asked about, but she recognised the worry and panic in her voice. Margaret couldn't understand what was wrong with her daughter. Laura looked blankly at her mother as if she couldn't recognise the woman standing there in front of her. With her eyes wide open, Laura had a terrified look on her face. Margaret watched as the colour drained its way out of her daughter's body. Laura was standing there pale-faced, giving the impression that she had thought that she had seen a ghost. Her body was frozen, her limbs could not have moved no matter how much her brain told her to. The questions that were been asked of her flew through one ear and then shot out the other. She could not utter a word nor answer any questions. She stood there staring at the window on the farther side of the lounge behind where Margaret stood. Confusion and fright took hold of Margaret as she wondered what the hell her daughter was looking at so colourless. As she turned to investigate in the direction of where her daughter was staring, Laura screamed out aloud and grabbed hold of her mother so tightly as if to prevent her from seeing what had struck the fear of God into her, whilst in the process partially restricting her mother's breathing capacity.

"Honey! I can't breathe," Margaret choked out with a cough. "You're scaring me! I'm really worried sick about you now. What are you staring at? Was someone there?"

Margaret held Laura by the shoulders and shook her until she was looking directly into her eyes. "Whatever is going on with you, sweetheart you do know that you can talk to your dear old mother, right?"

Laura just nodded her head in acknowledgement as if half registering what was said to her. Margaret just held her close in a warm embrace until she felt Laura relaxing in her arms. Her voice was like tremors as she shakily said, "Thank you."

Although not understanding, Margaret kissed her daughter's forehead in acknowledgement.

Releasing her daughter, she went to the kitchen to prepare some hot drinks for them both.

Laura sat at the kitchen table dumbstruck. Her mother was busily trying to make them some hot tea, whilst attempting to ask her daughter to explain what had happened earlier on in the lounge. Deep within, she knew that something had frightened the life out of Laura, but she couldn't admit that, not to Laura, nor to herself. Margaret was scared that if she did admit it, that it would take over and she refused to allow that. Margaret felt the need to find out what had happened to scare her daughter, or why Laura was so speechless now. Nothing made any sense to Margaret at all, but what she didn't know was that Laura herself was confused, too.

As Margaret carried the hot cups of tea to the table, she noticed that her hands were trembling. Placing one cup of tea in front of her daughter, she ordered her to drink it whilst it was still hot. She sat down placing the next cup in front of herself. Prayers patrolled inside her head as she hoped in her mind that Laura would snap out of the trance she clearly appeared to be in and come back to her. Margaret wanted Laura to be able to confide in her and tell her what was going on. No matter how much she tried to encourage Laura to open up, her instincts told her that Laura evidently would not tell her anything about what had happened. Well at least not tonight. Working on gut feeling alone, she decided not to pressure her daughter, but only to comfort her daughter as much as she required.

Chapter 9

Morning arrived without Laura closing her eyes to sleep all night. She attempted to get some rest as her mother, Margaret, instructed but it was impossible. Her eyelids were heavily laden with sleep, but her brain would not shut down. Firstly, she could not stop thinking about Claire being in hospital after what was said to be a horrific accident. She was a bit angry with her friend to lie to her and tell her that it is mere cuts and bruises knowing that it was much worse than that. However, she forgave Claire, as she knew that she was only trying her best not to let Laura worry too much about her.

During the night when she couldn't sleep, she tried to call back Claire at the hospital but the nurse who was on nightshift duty answered.

"Hello St. Sandringham Cross hospital, Nurse Adams speaking. This is Wedge-wick ward. How can I help?"

"Hi, my name is Laura. I was just calling for an update on my friend, Claire Collins, in room nine. I can't sleep since she told me that she had an accident. Although she told me not to worry about her, I can't help but worry. Am I making sense?"

"Yes, you are making sense. I understand what you mean. Are you a relative, Laura, or a friend you said?" Nurse Adams enquired.

"Friend and house mate," Laura quickly responded. "Listen I know that you have a confidentiality policy but please ma'am, I need to know, to prepare myself in the morning for what to expect."

"I'm so sorry Laura, although I would like to be of some assistance, I can't reveal much information. Heads up! All I can say is brace yourself. I am so sorry; I am not trying to be rude but the emergency buzzer for help with CPR is ringing and I have to go. Bye," Nurse Adams said apologetically and replaced the receiver.

Laura did not even get a chance to say goodbye nor a thank you before she heard dialling tone in her ear. She was left to wonder who needed CPR and would the hospital team manage to save the patient? She was also wondering what the nurse meant when she told her to brace herself. Did that mean that Claire was extremely critical. She didn't understand. When she spoke to her friend earlier Claire had said she was fine and not to worry.

"Oh God! I hope that was not Claire who needed CPR last night," Laura exclaimed.

At that thought she leapt out of bed. She picked up the phone and tried to call the ward but got no answer. Instant worry and panic took hold of her. There was a need to get to the hospital as fast as she could. She tiptoed down the hall into the bathroom, closing the door behind her. She didn't want to wake her mum who had stayed over last night. She got into the shower as quickly as she could and washed herself. Although her shower was refreshingly good, she didn't stay in long, switched off the tap and got out wrapping herself in her bath towel. She got dried up and dressed in under ten minutes. Laura hurried down the stairs, and wrote a note, and left it on the kitchen table for her mum so that she would know where she is. Sometimes, when necessary, Laura would use their local cab service, not that she liked to. She rang the cab station and asked them to send her a cab urgently as she had to get to the hospital quickly. The controller dispatched the cab straight away and within five minutes was outside her door.

Grabbing the bag with the essentials she had packed for Claire the night before; she exited the house locking the front door hastily. The cab was yellow with black stripes across its body. The make was a Vauxhall Astra. When she got inside the car it reeked of tobacco and stale coffee. The smell was off putting and brought back bad memories that Laura would prefer not to remember, but there was no time to exchange cabs. "Good morning driver; St. Sandringham Cross hospital please and please take the quickest, shortest route possible," she demanded impatiently.

The cab driver was an undistinguished looking guy, with a square-looking jaw line, stony faced, with big brown eyes. He appeared as though he was in his late fifties. He had dark ginger hair with a bald patch, ginger eyebrows and had a long beard. He was slightly overweight with a beer belly like a bear. He looked like he could do well to with a good shave and a hot bath. His teeth were slightly stained from smoking tobacco. He had a strong Scottish accent which was hard to understand.

Although she requested for him to hurry the driver still drove at his own pace and chit-chatted all the way there. Pulling up outside the hospital, she got out of the car and paid the driver after grabbing her belongings. She hesitated for what seemed like a brief moment, then made her way towards the main entrance. She entered the main entrance lobby heading for the lift for the seventh floor. When she finally found it she saw the doors were about to close. "Hold the lift," she shouted.

The young girl inside the lift, had managed to stop the lift doors from closing so that Laura could get inside. The girl queried the floor Laura needed then pressed the button for her.

"Thank you darling,"

She noticed that the girl was attached to a drip stand with a bag of fluids and a bag of antibiotics hanging down from it, with two tube lines connected to a cannula in the young girl's arm. When the lift got to the fifth floor it stopped and opened and the young girl limped out. Laura noticed and asked her if she needed help to get back to wherever she was going.

The young girl was 5'3inches, with short brown curly hair. She appeared quite pale in colour. She had big brown eyes and her eye lashes were long and neatly curled. She was wearing a hospital gown with a shawl draped around her shoulders. She appeared to be around fifteen years old.

With a gorgeous smile, she said "Yes please lady. My name is Amie. What's yours?" "Oh! I'm Laura, pleased to meet you. I hope that you get better soon."

"Thank you, for your good wishes and thank you for your help."

Laura and Amie slowly walked down the corridor until they got to Amie's room. She followed her inside and helped her back onto her bed before the nurse popped in to check on

Amie. "Bye," they both said to each other just before Laura walked out again, heading back to where the lifts are. Glancing towards an interlinking corridor she abruptly stopped. She could had sworn that she saw a familiar face walking with a companion. For a moment she wanted to shout out his name, but she didn't bother just in case that it wasn't him. She didn't want to face the embarrassment. Doubts was crawling into her mind. '

What if he doesn't recognise me and just blanks me? What if that isn't his real name?

Who was that beautiful woman he was walking with, so engrossed in conversation? It couldn't be him, could it? Alex is that really you, she wanted to shout but chose not to.'

The opening of the lift doors interrupted her chain of thoughts. She walked inside and touched button seven.

Arriving at the seventh floor, she approached the nurse's station in a rush to ask for her friend Claire. "Hi, I'm here to see Claire Collins. Could you please point me in the right direction?"

A sweet young healthcare assistant obliged showing her the way. "This is her room, but my boss says that visiting hours don't start for another hour yet. Your friend has been transported by the porters to go for some extra tests so you will have to wait in the family waiting room. Would you like a cup of tea or coffee while you wait?" she asked Laura.

"Yes please, a cup of tea with two sugars would be lovely."

The healthcare assistant skipped off and in what seemed like less than five minutes returned with a hot steaming cup of tea and a cheese sandwich. Laura thanked her and took the items from her hands.

Sharon, the healthcare assistant, walked away with a smile on her face leaving Laura to eat her sandwich and have her tea whilst waiting for visiting time to start. Laura hadn't realised how starving she was until she took her first bite of the sandwich. Acknowledging that she hadn't had any breakfast whatsoever she ate all her sandwich and her tea with a packet of crisps that she had brought from home. Feeling much better, she leant back in the sofa and rested her head against the back rest. Although sleep began to creep up on her, she tried her best to fight it, but failed miserably. Laura didn't know when her eyes closed but was awaken what seemed to be a long time later by Sharon stating that Claire was back in her room from her tests.

"I saw you sleeping earlier, and I couldn't wake you up until I knew that your friend was back in her room. You seemed so tired. Not changing the subject but … Pausing for a moment as if weighing out the options of whether to ask her a curious question. Who's Alex? You were calling out his name in your sleep?"

For a moment, Laura stared blank faced at her. The thing that shocked her and caught her off guard wasn't the fact that she had dreamt of Alex; it was more the fact that even when she should be focussed on Claire and her condition, he could still bombard her mind and take over her thoughts even in a hospital. She was appalled at the revelation of knowing that this man had taken over her train of thoughts and her life. "Oh! He's just a guy I know, Laura said, embarrassed, her cheeks turning rosy red. She felt like she could crawl under a rock somewhere, curl up in a ball and die.

"Well from the things that you were saying and the way you were reacting it seems to me that he is certainly more than a friend" Sharon said with a cheeky smile.

Sharon left her outside Claire's intensive care room door and went back to resume her duties. Quickly, she opened the door and walked inside and was shocked and emotionally torn at what she saw there.

Chapter 10

Standing on the inside of the doorway, Laura couldn't believe her eyes. It was difficult to gather her thoughts and get her confusion in check. Her head felt very light and wavy as if she were about to drop. Her eyes suddenly felt hazed as if she couldn't see anymore. Cold sweat ran down the side of her face. Her heart felt like it had stopped beating. At this point tears were streaming down her face at breath-taking speed. Her voice felt trapped, as if she was been strangled; the lump her throat felt bigger than a tennis ball.

How can I get my head around this? I just don't understand. Was it that I dreamt that I spoke to Claire? I'm not going crazy, am I? This can't be my friend's room, who rang me to say that she was okay and not to worry. But if I dreamt it, how would I know that she was in hospital, the room number, the floor? Why would she lie to me about something this serious?

Finally realising why, the night duty nurse informed her to brace herself, Laura dashed back out of the room into the corridor as if she had seen a ghost, finding her voice at last as she cried out aloud, "My God!" causing the health care assistant Sharon to look around in confusion. This couldn't be the room, no way could she believe that. She swiftly walked down the corridor, not taking a second glance backwards. "Are you sure that this is Claire's room?" She cried hysterically, tears streaming down her face.

Immediately Sharon did a double take, walking speedily towards where Laura stood, with her hands clasped around her face, trembling severely as she wept the tears of sorrow for her friend. Extending her hands to Laura, she gently patted her on the shoulders in acknowledgement to say' it's alright'. "Of course, Hun. I wouldn't lie to you. I know that it looks scary but I'm a hundred percent sure that I took you to the right patient."

Before Sharon could continue what, she was saying, Laura collapsed to the ground on her knees in disbelief, tears pouring down her face as she wailed noisily in pain. "Oh Sharon! I feel so terrible. I don't know how to help her. I feel useless," she revealed openly, hoping to get an idea of what she is required to do.

Crouching down beside her, Sharon assisted her back up to her feet. Holding her hand, she led Laura back to Claire's room, whilst reassuring her that all she needs to do was just to be there for her friend as and when she needed her.

"What do I say to her?"

"Whatever you want to say to be honest with you. I would like to believe that she can hear you, although they say that the brain is at a low base level. Speak to her the same way you guys communicated to each other before the accident. It will help."

Reluctantly nodding her head, Laura acknowledged what was been said to her, although she was fearful of what it meant she would have to do for her friend. Déjà vu was slowly setting in, entrapping her into a drowning state of mind – this is what it must have been like for her mother when she had been in a coma as a child. Reaching out to grab the handle of the door, her fingers trembling shakily, she opened the door so slowly, peeping inside as the door revealed more and more of the horrific scene there in front of her.

Suddenly, for some reason unexplained it felt as though she was staring directly at herself lying there in a coma, with tubes, wires all connected to beeping machines, cast and bandages surrounding her, connected inside her, holding her in a prison. Clueless as to what's going on in the world around her, Claire lay there so still, fragile and helpless. Rushing to her best friend's side, in sheer panic, Laura crouched down by the bedside watching in horror as Claire appeared so lifeless as only the machine was breathing for her at that very moment.

With every breath from the machine Laura's stomach tightened as she watched on helplessly: there was nothing that she could do to ease her friend's pain. She wished with all her heart that Claire would have a speedy recovery.

If only I could trade places with you Claire. I'm so sorry that you are going through this and there's nothing that I can do to help you. Please don't leave me. Don't you dear die or I swear.......

The sound of the alarm on the intravenous drip machine snapped her out of her drifting thoughts. A nurse came barging into the room within a split second before Laura could register and gather her thoughts clearly. She silenced the loud, screeching alarm and changed the drip bags with professional ease. After disposing of the empty drip bags, she took up the medical folder and was documenting what she had done for Claire. She wrote quickly whilst checking the other machines and Claire's vital signs, blood pressure and SATS. Replacing the folder back in its holder she turned her head in Laura's direction and asked if there was anything that she needed.

"I'm okay, thank you. All I need is for Claire to get better quickly to be honest."

Her voice coming out as a mere whisper at first but then gathering strength, she had a quizzical look on her face that froze the nurse in her position as she could sense that Laura wanted to talk or ask something. The nurse stared in Laura's direction, with her thin hand resting akimbo on her slender hips, shifting uncomfortably from foot to foot impatiently as she waited for Laura to speak. It felt like she was wasting her time so the nurse kissed her teeth, thinking that she had a heck of a lot more patients to care for and she had a tight schedule to keep if she wanted to finish and leave on time to go home, so she turned and was about to walk out of the room when Laura mustered up the courage to finally speak.

"Before you go nurse, can I just query as to why Claire is in a coma and why she looks as though she's in severe pain?"

Just the thought of Claire being in pain made Laura's heart sink to the floor.

"I'm sorry but the consultant and the surgeon would be the best people to explain her medical status and her treatment. The most that I can say to you is that your friend has been through a tough time. She's in intensive care and we are doing our utmost best to ensure that she recovers well, and to provide the right medical treatment for her condition. I am not sure if she can or cannot feel any pain but we give her pain relief at regular intervals. And besides, we check on her every 15-30minutes as recommended. We log the times in which her medication should be administered. Your friend is in safe hands."

The nurse hastily touched Laura's hand as if sensing the doubt in Laura's mind. If you are still in doubt, don't hesitate to either request to see the doctors looking after Claire or wait and speak to them on their ward rounds. Before Laura could say another word the nurse briskly walked out of the room closing the door behind her without a backwards glance.

Looking back at her dearest friend, her only true friend Laura began to talk to her, telling her what they would do and places they'd go when she recovers. She didn't know what else to do. She felt uncomfortable sitting there watching her friend fight for her life while she was unable to help her. She felt absolutely out of place and useless. Laura felt the guilt rushed through her as the desperate need of escape was rising inside of her. Forcing herself to sit there, she reached out and held Claire's hand whilst telling her how much she needed her to wake up. Suddenly, Laura began to wonder where Claire was driving from before she had the traumatic car accident and why Josh wasn't here by her side already.

`So many unanswered questions. Hmm...'she thought to herself.

She picked up her phone and rang Josh to inform him of what had happened to Claire. His phone rang for what felt like forever.

"Josh Barrett's phone, how can I help?" came a feminine but posh voice, so polite.

Laura was taken aback by this and was puzzled as to why someone else was answering Josh's phone. Who the hell was she? And where is Josh?

"Hello!" Came the voice again to interrupt her train of thoughts. "Can I speak to Josh please, it's important?" Laura said urgently.

"Sorry but he's busy at the moment, so would you like to tell me what it's about, and I'll give him the message?"

"No, I wouldn't like to, but can you tell him to call Laura as soon as possible please. It's a matter of life or death."

"Okay, I'll tell him as soon as he's finished."

"Thank you," replied Laura, with gratitude to the stranger on the other end of the line.

Laura ended the call and was hoping that Josh would get the message straight away and call her back immediately. As if hearing her thoughts, her phone rang after what seemed like ten minutes.

"Hey Laura! Janice said that you called, and you said something about life or death.

What's wrong? Are you ill?" Josh worriedly asked. "No, I'm okay. It's ..."

Losing her words, she took a deep breath. "Laura, honey what's the matter?" Asked Josh lovingly.

"It's... it's Claire. She's hurt in a bad way, Josh. She's in hospital in intensive care. I don't think that she's going to make it. She was in a car accident on her way home," Laura choked out between her sobbing.

"Is this one of Claire's lying schemes to try to get me to talk to her and forgive her?" Said Josh angrily.

"What! What the hell are you talking about? I'm very serious. This is no joking matter. What do you mean by forgive her? Forgive her for what Josh?" cried Laura in confusion.

"Forget that I said that Lau. It doesn't matter now anyway. Just tell me what hospital she's in and I will swing by after work."

Responding straight away, Laura gave the details to Josh and rang off. Standing there confused from the telephone conversation which took place mere seconds ago between herself and Josh, Laura looked at Claire in disgust for a brief moment and thought to herself, whether it had anything to do with the secret meeting after their cocktail rendezvous, or anything to do with the secret phone call that Claire had been so shady about. She hoped in her heart of hearts for Claire's sake that she hadn't messed up her relationship with Josh as she'd be an idiot to let such a good man go.

As she stood there hovering over her friend like a guardian angel, she picked up the medical folder and began to read it to try and understand what exactly Claire's medical diagnosis was, as she was adamant that she had spoken to her friend last night and she was fine then, so none of this scenario made any sense to her at all.

Claire Collins born July 27th 1982. Involved in a traumatic car accident. She has bruising and lacerations to her face and back. She has extensive bruising on her liver and kidneys. Fractures consists of: 3 ribs right-side 2 left side. Proximal tibia fracture with soft tissue damages (nerves, ligaments surrounding the area). She also has a fractured ulna from the sudden direct trauma she encountered. Patient has severe intractable pain, dizziness with confusion upon first treatment, low blood pressure, skin pale and showing signs of anaemia. She has a dislocated shoulder and knee joint and a pene-trating wound due to abdominal injury on impact. Upon examination blood appears in urine, difficulty breathing, severe abdominal pain and chest wall pain (intercostal neuralgia). Also has uneven surface over skull contour indicating fracture. Signs of internal bleeding on the brain and bruising.

Surgery performed three am to release pressure on the brain and to repair fractures and to stem the internal bleeding. Patient unconscious and in coma state. Breathing tube inserted to aid breathing as right lung punctured from broken rib and SATS levels are too low. Pain relief given at regular intervals.

Half the diagnosis didn't make much sense to Laura as it was medical jargon but she knew in her heart of hearts that the doctor, or Josh, would be able to explain it to her in a more simplistic format to relieve her confusion. There were too many tubes inserted in her friend's body. She wanted to pull them all out and take her friend away from all of that trauma but knew that she wouldn't be able to help as she was not medically trained. The machines started making a weird rhythmic song, but that didn't appear to be anything of concern to the medical staff on duty, as no one came in again for a while.

More often than not, when the nurse came in all she did was to administer pain relief and antibiotics prescribed by the consultant and to change her IV fluids. They also checked on her vital signs and ran tests. On one occasion a phlebotomist entered the room to take some bloods from Claire. She told Laura that it was to check Claire's FBC, U&E'S, and LFT'S, liver profile, iron and glucose levels. Laura watched on because none of those made any common sense to her other than iron and glucose levels. All she did was to nod her head in acknowledgement. When the phlebotomist had completed her duty, she excused herself from the room carrying several bottles filled with blood to send off to the hospital lab for testing.

Sharon entered the room to collect a urine sample from the catheter bag dangling on the side of the bed on a framed hook that kept it in place. Afterwards she spoke to Laura with grave concern for her well-being and told her that she needed to go and get some fresh air and grab herself a bite to eat as she had been there all day, and would be no use to Claire without strength. "To be honest with you, Laura, Claire is unaware that you're in the room so you can excuse yourself for a while. Your sister is in capable hands. We'll look after her."

The word sister was the only thing that stood out from what Sharon had said to her.

Why would she make such a mistake as to call her my sister? I can't recall ever saying that Claire was my sister to anyone. I wonder what made her think that. We don't look the same, do we? I suppose that it's okay for them to view her as my sister. After all we live together, work together and we get along like sisters do.

"I'll go and get some fresh air in a short while. I'm not hungry but I will try and eat something, I promise. Oh, and by the way Claire is not my blood sister but I suppose I see her not only as a best friend and flat mate. but as a sister. too."

Laura spoke like a child that had just been scolded.

Sharon had to smile at the response that she got from Laura. "Mmhmm... whatever you say, darling. Sorry." Her hands in the air as if surrendering. She knows that she meant well, as she wasn't trying to be bossy, or anything; she just cared too much about the people she met and that had always been her downfall.

Despite this, there was something about Laura that made her feel that she had to protect her, look out for her well-being as long as she was on duty when Laura visited Claire. It was just like mothering her. Laura had been through a lot and as a result from time to time appeared to be lost and confused.

"Before I go, just to let you know that they're going to come and change your friend's bandages, clean her wounds and change her tubes in about fifteen minutes and at that point they won't allow you to be in the room whilst they do this. This process takes about half an hour to forty-five minutes as they also swab the wounds to ensure that they aren't infected, anymore. As you know your friend is on a course of antibiotics, so the doctors have to know if it is working and if not, then they will prescribe a stronger one in order to clear the infection so that it doesn't get worse and cause more complication. Maybe you could use that window to go and get your fresh air and eat something. Just a thought. Anyways, I got to go before they wonder what's taking me so long."

"Okay, thank you, Sharon, I definitely will," Laura reluctantly replied.

Exiting the room Sharon went about doing her daily rounds. Laura leant back in her chair and thought what she would do if she lost Claire. She could not contemplate life without her best friend. Claire was her sanity, her fun and company. In every aspect of her life now Claire had always been a part of it somehow.

You can't think like that, girl. Don't jinx it. You've always been a positive thinker so why are you being so negative now? She's not going anywhere. She can't otherwise......

Confirmation between three members of staff outside Claire's room door reminded Laura that the care plan treatment was about to take place. As she took up her handbag the staff walked into the room. One member was pushing a steel trolley containing a lot of sterile medical items and equipment. The other two members had a stethoscope each hanging loosely around their necks. The male doctor appeared vaguely familiar, but she couldn't place where she knew him from, unfortunately. They both gazed at each other with some sort of familiarity as if recognising that somehow their paths had crossed before but unfortunately couldn't place where or when. The female registrar standing next to the nurse asked Laura to leave so that they could do their procedure. She explained what they had to do and said to her to come back in forty-five minutes. Laura just nodded her head in acknowledgement and took up her handbag and walked out of the room, praying to God that whatever the procedure entailed that all would go well for Claire. Reflecting on the expression on her friend's face, it still did not take away the unshakable feeling that she had regarding whether Claire could feel any pain. She refused to go too far away from the hospital just in case Claire needed her, so purchased a container with a portion of chips with two battered fried sausages, smothered in tomato ketchup and a freezing cold bottle of orange juice. With her food items in a bag she walked out of the hospital cafeteria and into the cool breeze of the afternoon in the hospital grounds garden area. Plonking herself on a bench situated between two beds of flowers she inhaled and exhaled quite loudly. She felt exhausted but didn't really want to leave her friend behind. Not sleeping well, the night before had taken its toll on her body, and the emotional turmoil that her friend's horrific trauma was putting her through was draining her at breath- taking speed. Her eyelids felt heavy at this point as the cool breeze wrapped its arms around her as if serenading her to give in to the urge to sleep. A loud growl made Laura jump, making her snap around to see if there was an animal or someone there with her. Noticing that there was nothing there she laughed to herself as she heard the growl again and this time feeling the rumble in her stomach. "Okay, okay. I hear you the first and the second time!" she giggled.

She took out the container with her food, opened it and commenced eating, not realising how hungry she was until she put the last bite into her mouth. The feeling of satisfaction flowed through her body. She drank some of the orange juice and packed away the rest. Checking the time on her wristwatch she realised that she still had another fifteen minutes left before it was time to go back upstairs to the seventh floor to sit with Claire.

Hold on one cotton picking minute. Where the hell is Josh?

Don't be so paranoid! I'm sure that he's still at work. I'm certain that he would be here if he could. Snap out of this negative paranoia. It's no good.

Sharon was right. The fresh air and a bite to eat worked wonders on Laura as she felt rejuvenated. She was ready to go back up to Claire's room, but the time wasn't up yet for the procedure to be finished. It felt like the time was dragging. The deepest oceanic blue eyes that she had ever seen came back before her like a pair of precious gems not wanting to be forgotten.

Oh god! I know who he is now, but his career change doesn't make any sense at all.

How could I forget him when he excited me just seeing him work his magic?

Smiling broadly at her realisation she couldn't believe it. Thinking that she would never in her entire lifetime see him again she had fought her fixation on such a handsome creature. A schoolgirl crush buried after years of struggling, she moved on with her life. Not that any of her other relationships worked out. They were never him. They couldn't replace him. What a sight for sore eyes. She was in shock. She thought that she would never, ever set eyes on him again. Her heart beat quickened and her breathing became a little erratic. Oh wow!

Chapter 11

Freddie Laurent was a tall, athletically-built guy with broad shoulders, rippled muscles, and the deepest oceanic blue eyes that you had ever seen. He had black hair and a tanned skin. He worked in his father's plumbing business at the time she knew him. He was called out to fix a leaking kitchen sink pipe when it had flooded out their kitchen. Margaret was furious over another problem that needed fixing in their home. She was struggling with life as a single mother; it was difficult and very hectic. Laura was going through hell at school and it was hard to get the bullying to stop. It frustrated her and she needed the bullying to vanish so she could get a break. At the time Freddie was seventeen years old when he first stepped foot in the Winfrey's home. His dad, Greg Laurent, was stuck on another job and couldn't accompany Freddie to this one. Laura could recall when she opened the front door the awe she felt when she saw the magnificent beauty standing in front of her. His French accent was to die for. He walked in so gracefully. She had never encountered anyone so polite before as the only thing that she knew and was experiencing at that time was just pure bullying. Because of this she didn't think it humanly possible to find someone that was genuinely kind-hearted until she met Freddie. He was a God sent to guide and advise: he had overheard her talking to her mother about her ordeal, and suggested to her what she should do to help herself and aid her situation. His advice to her was to take self-defence classes as he knew someone who could teach her what she needed to know.

"Personally, Laura… did I get your name right? I know that self-defence would do you some good. At least it would help you to protect yourself."

"I think that it's just another way to promote violence by putting a label to convince oneself that it's just a protection ploy," protested Laura.

"Although you have a good point and it can be viewed like that it also has its benefits and it will save your life. I was like you once, and I was bullied severely by the senior boys at school. The last straw for me was when they attacked me so badly that I needed physiotherapy to help me to get my feet operative again; I couldn't walk for a while. The strain it took on my mother, the tears she cried each day and the fact that I nearly lost my life put things in a clearer perspective for me. My older brother Timothy, he's a karate instructor. He heard of my ordeal when he returned from his tournament and decided to teach me how to defend myself. I was chuffed about that because it helped me throughout the rest of my school years. Don't leave it too late. I'll leave you Tim's details, okay. Use it if you want to do so," said Freddie.

"I'm glad that it worked out well for you. I'm sure without classes that it'll work out well for me, too. They'll get bored and stop I'm sure," stated Laura unconvincingly. "I hope they get bored of me now," whispered Laura under her breath as she prayed that the bullies would, crossing her fingers behind her back hoping no one would hear and notice.

Walking up behind her, Freddie whispered into her ear, "I hope so for your sake that you get your wish."

Wide eyed she stared at him, mainly shocked that he had heard her whispered prayer.

Taking her hand, he pressed his brother, Timothy's number into her palm and his own personal number and whispered, "call me anytime even if it's to talk."

Spinning around too quickly, she stumbled as she hadn't seen when he crept up behind her after her mother exited the room, but held her balance before embarrassing herself in front of their plumber. "You startled me!" She yelled in a high-pitched squeak of a voice.

All Freddie could do at that point was laugh hysterically. This caused Laura to laugh too as she knew her reaction was ridiculous. They both stopped and stared at each other in appreciation then quickly looked away. Freddie excused himself and went to the kitchen and investigated and completed the job he was called out to do in the first place. After he finished the job, he said his goodbyes to Margaret, and then said his goodbyes to Laura with a wink and a dazzling smile. Automatically she winked back and smiled as she waved her hand to bid him farewell. She thought that he was sweet. He was the subject for discussion the remainder of the day between Margaret and herself. Margaret thought that he seems very lovely and told her daughter that guys like that are hard to find. Out of curiosity, Margaret had to ask the question that was bugging her. "Laura darling! Not changing the subject, but do you think that you should take any of the self-defence classes that Freddie was telling us about?"

"I'm not too sure to be honest, mum. I need time to think about it. You'll be the first to know what I decide I promise. Oh, by the way mum, you have to remember though, I'm no Bruce lee or Jackie Chan," giggled Laura.

"I know that sweetheart. I'm not asking you to be, but whatever you decide I'm behind you one hundred percent."

They exchanged a hug and smiled at each other, expressing the love they both felt towards each other.

Later on, that evening, Laura decided that it wouldn't hurt to give the self-defence classes a try as she stared intently at the scribbled numbers on the wrinkled plumber's receipt paper that Freddie had written on earlier in the day. Although this went against what she believed in, she picked up her telephone and dialled Timothy's landline number. The phone rang until just when she presumed that no one would retrieve the call, she was about to hang up and replace her receiver when a deep male voice answered.

"Hi Tim speaking, not been rude but who's this please?" the voice abruptly fell through the line more like a command.

Nervously, she quietly spoke with a low tone of voice. "Hi I'm Laura Winfrey. Your brother gave me your number earlier on today."

"If you don't mind telling me, which one of my brothers gave you my number and why?" he asked out of curiosity.

"It was Freddie. He said that you would be able to teach me self-defence to help me protect myself from the neighbourhood bullies. They beat on me every day and I don't understand why." She explained in as much detail as possible.

"Hmmm… I see." Timothy mumbled that Laura had to strain her ears to hear his response.

"So, would you be able help me please, sir, as I'm in a desperate situation?"

"Well, I guess that I might be able to help you before I go on my holiday," Timothy replied sympathetically.

"Thank you so much, sir, but is there a cost and what venue do I need to attend and when?" she said with gratitude.

"You are coming to Laurent's gym in town on Moubreh Street, next to Tasties bakery shop, at ten forty-five tomorrow morning. Please wear loose, comfortable clothing. It's fifteen pounds per session for an hour's training. If you're still interested, then be there on time please." Timothy informed her.

"Alright sir, thank you. Have a good night and I'll see you tomorrow." replied Laura, cheerfully.

"Good night, Miss! Catch ya tomorrow."

Laura stood there staring at the phone for a while after the conversation had ended between herself and Timothy wondering why she was willing to discard her feelings towards such violence. Just as she replaced the receiver there was a knock at her bedroom door. This startled her, and had her mind wondering if her mother was eavesdropping on her telephone conversation, or whether she had listened on the telephone situated downstairs in the lounge. If this was the case, she wouldn't be very happy and couldn't wait to grow up, leave school then branch off on her own to live her life. This wasn't the first time that she was suspicious of her mother, but couldn't prove it, so said nothing regarding the matter. Plus, she was under her mother's roof so extended her respects all round no matter the circumstances. She loved her mother dearly and didn't want her to feel like she was being accused. Wanting to ignore the knock at the door but knowing that it wouldn't be the wisest choice at that very moment, she leapt to her feet, breaking out into a half run towards the closed door that separated her from her mother., who had been knocking for what seemed like ages, as she could sense the impatience surfacing through the way her mother called her name from the other side of her bedroom door. She opened the door halfway, the telephone numbers clenched in her fist behind her back, answering her mother in the politest manner. "Hey mum! Is everything okay?"

"Oh yes dear! Just letting you know that dinner's ready so make your way downstairs to eat while it is still hot."

Without responding she slipped the crushed piece of paper in her shorts pocket, sidled through the half open door and darted out and down the stairs with enthusiasm, ready to feast on her meal as quickly as possible so that she could go back to her room and call Freddie, just to update him. Unfortunately, things didn't go to plan because after eating her delicious dinner, her mother told her to shower up and get ready for bed immediately. At that point she hatched a plan as to how to get the telephone call accomplished without getting caught out.

She hurriedly excused herself from the dining table and said her good nights and rushed upstairs. The plan was to switch on the shower in the en-suite bathroom leading off her bedroom, while keeping an ear out for her mother's footsteps creeping up the stairs.

This is so deceiving. I shouldn't need to sneak around like this. I suppose the reason for this now is because it's a guy, and mum said that I'm too gullible and vulnerable and I trust people too easily. Or is it because he's nice looking and I like him? Or maybe it's because he showed an interest in me? Don't be silly girl, he was only been polite. Oh well! Whichever it is I haven't the time to work it out. If I'm making this call it has to be now or never.

Laura picked up the phone and extracted the crumpled receipt paper from her pocket and punched the numbers into the telephone keypad after making sure to lock her bedroom door. After a short pause, the phone was ringing. Just as she was about to bottle it and hang up Freddie answered. She went mute for a short while. Trying to tell herself to speak before he hung up, thinking that it was a prank call. Forcing the squeaky 'hi' out of her voice box she finally whispers his name.

"Is that you, shy girl Laura?" asked Freddie in a cheeky manner. "Yes, it's me."

"What's wrong? Is everything okay with you?" he asked with concern in his tone.

"Sorry to bother you so late, I just wanted to say thank you for today and to let you know that I rang your brother earlier on this evening and I booked a session with him for the morning," she said proudly.

"I thought you was dead set against self-defence as you made it crystal clear to me today," he teased.

"I know, okay, it's just going to be a taster session and if I like it then I'll continue but if not then I'll cancel," explained Laura.

"At least you've considered what I said, and you're giving it a try, so be proud of yourself because I am. Let me know how it goes tomorrow. I'll be looking forward to your call tomorrow," revealed Freddie.

"Okay, night, I'll call you tomorrow when I can," stated Laura. "Night, Lau!" said Freddie.

Laura hangs up the telephone receiver and made her way into the shower and had a refreshing wash. She put on her nightdress and tumbled into bed. Clicking off her bedside light she closed her eyes feeling exhausted. *He's proud of me. Wow! He's so so… hmmm… Stop it. Don't tread in dangerous shark infested waters. You'll be eaten alive.*

Finally, she dosed off into a nice peaceful deep sleep so relaxed with no care in the world as she was looking forward to the next day. It was the first time that she had ever been looking forward to the following day.

Chapter 12

The next morning, Laura woke up feeling nervous and unsure about the previous night's decision to book a class with Freddie's brother. Pondering as to what made her convince herself to give it a try, she concluded that it must have something to do with Freddie's argument as to why he believed that it would do her some good to learn. A part of her wanted to see if self-defence could help her or not?

Perk up girl! You were the one who made the call to Timothy. No one twisted your arm or put a gun to your head so just get on with it. The next step now is to build up the Dutch courage to tell mum what I decided. I hope maybe she'll be proud of me for taking the leap forward., Sometimes mum can be unreasonable and I don't agree with her, but I love her lots, though, despite that. Anyway, I'm so thankful that it's the summer holidays so I get a breather from those horrible Woods siblings. I suppose that if it wasn't for them being on holiday down in the countryside with their uncle, I would have had the worse summer ever.

Leaping out of bed, and gliding across the carpet, she skipped into the En-suite bathroom leading from the bedroom.

Removing her garments, she stepped into the shower, turned on the water and stood under it as it sprayed down all over her body from head to her toes. She closed her eyes and raised her head allowing the water to wet her face as her mind wandered towards the event ahead for this morning. Wanting to cancel the appointment but feeling that everyone would be disappointed in her for chickening out instead of giving it a try first, she grumbled under her breath. `*I swear that it's my choice, whether or not I choose to do this. Grrrrr... Oh well! I suppose that I'll try it, I think, protested Laura.*'

Laura felt so indecisive.

"Life is never fair to me; I wonder why? she said aloud, irritably.

Kissing her teeth, she attempted to try and enjoy the rest of her shower, or what was left of it, she knew that she had to be as quick as she possibly could. After showering, Laura clambered out feeling lazy and deflated in momentum and towel dried her hair and skin. Then she got herself dressed and ready in comfortable clothing for her trial self-defence session.

Tying her hair back in a ponytail, she exited the bathroom and went downstairs to have her breakfast. Just as soon as she got there, her mother emerged from the kitchen silently, startling her with her loud "good morning" greeting, accompanied by a crooked smile. This made Laura feel uneasy, but she pasted a smile across her face and said "good morning" cheerily to her mother. Whilst they sat at the dining table conversing and having their breakfast, Laura thought that it was the perfect time to announce her decision to try out the self-defence classes.

"Mum, I've come to a decision. I'm going to give the self-defence classes a try and see how it goes from there." `Not that I want to.' Were the words echoing through her mind?

"Oh, and when did you decided this, madam?" asked Margaret abruptly with her eyebrows raised.

Laura was taken aback by this response and had to stare at the woman sitting opposite her at the table, pondering what it was that she'd said that provoked such a terrible response. It wasn't at all what she had expected. Sometimes, her mum could be so kind and loving and other times very unpredictable, getting angry and possessive for no apparent reason whatsoever. Most times that her mother behaved in such a way, she restricted her from leaving the house and confined her to her bedroom for hours on end. She didn't need to do anything wrong, as just breathing was sometimes enough. She couldn't contemplate the reason for her mother's behaviour at these times and sometimes it scared her. Acting like nothing had happened, and before Laura could answer the question Margaret began to sing a different tune as to how wonderful she thought it was that Laura was using her initiative and trying to help herself to become more equipped to deal with the bullies. This gave Laura mixed feelings as on one side she was ecstatic that her mother was proud of her and on the other hand confused as her mother at first seemed to object to her doing the self-defence classes. "What time do you have to be there for?" asked Margaret with a scowling attitude.

"Ten thirty, Timothy told me when we spoke," replied Laura flatly.

"Okay! Well, it's nine o'clock now, so you'd better get your skates on if you're going to be there on time."

"Yes mum!" replied Laura as she hurriedly ate the last bite of her breakfast.

With a grate of the chair against the tiled floor, she swiftly stood up, grabbing her plate and teacup in a rush and almost dropping the teacup back onto the table. Laura's heart was in her mouth as she felt the heavy beating of the pulse in her neck. The big lump that formed in her throat spoke volumes. Quickly she glanced at her mother apologised and made her way towards the kitchen sink where she placed the dishes, washed, and dried them as quickly as she could, then packed them away in the cupboard. As soon as she was finished, she partially turned around, and she could have sworn that she had seen an evil and angry look plastered on her mum's face as she stared at her intently. It made Laura feel very uncomfortable to be glared at like that and made the tiny hair strands on the back of her neck stand up. Trying to ensure that she wasn't imagining things she turned around properly, leaning against the countertop, only to be greeted with a warm smile and a look of joy plastered all over her mother's face. It caused her to believe that maybe her mind was playing some kind of a trick on her.

When she had completed the washing up, she approached her mother, gave her a hug, and said her goodbyes before putting on her trainers and exiting the house. Arriving at the bus stop without a second to lose, Laura got on the nine twenty-one bus going five stops before getting off at the nearest train station. She entered the station and waited on the overcrowded platform for the arrival of the train with people commuting to work. When the train pulled in at the platform, Laura boarded the train and sat in a seat by the doors opposite a lady not looking much older than her own mother. In fact, there was a fair bit of resemblance to the lady's features and appearance that somehow puzzled her. Laura contemplated before creasing her brows together in fury as she would have liked to think that her mother finally trusted her. The similarities were so close to her mother's and that made her wondered why, as she knew of no sister of her mum's. *I left mum at home so it doesn't make any sense.*

The middle-aged woman was wearing a pink floral scarf wrapped over her hair and down the side of her face where it was criss-crossed over her neck and shoulders. Her blouse was black and pink with three quarter length sleeves that flared with frills at the ends. She was wearing black full-length trousers with plain black, flat shoes. Her eyes seemed to be somewhat part focussed on Laura's every move, although it was still a little difficult to tell if the lady was full on staring at her as she was wearing oval shaped sunglasses dark enough that you could hardly see her eyes. Laura tried to avert her attention to elsewhere on the train, as she listened to the music belting out of the red earphones that she had placed over her ears after she left home. Although enjoying her music, her mind kept rewinding back to this morning's encounter with her mother's strange, confusing reaction to her news. Although it was in her thoughts, what plagued her most was who the commuter was that was sitting opposite her. Looking far beyond the train as possible to zone in on a different focus, she didn't realise when the lady got off the train and at which stop. She scanned the train frantically, but saw no sign of her. Giving up, as she reached her destination, she exited the train and headed out of the station towards Tasties bakery. As she got closer, she felt her heart thudding in her chest. Her palms felt clammy and sweaty. The closer she got to the gym the more nervous she felt. She checked her wristwatch and realised that there was only two minutes left to go inside and find the instructor to alert him to her arrival.

Suddenly, before Laura could pull the door, it was flung open and a man stood in there staring intently at her. He looked to be about thirty-five years old although she couldn't be sure, with blonde hair, grey eyes, and of average build. He was wearing a white karate pants and robe tied with a black karate belt. He startled Laura, as she didn't expect the door to be flung open like that. Gathering what was left of her nerves and voice she introduced herself. She queried whether or not he was Timothy. He nodded his head in a gesture to say yes, invited her inside and led her to his small office where he tried to find out more about her situation, and fill in the relevant documents. Laura couldn't help but noticed that he looked nothing like his brother Freddie. His voice was quite deep.

Fifteen minutes later, they had a brief conversation about the session timetable, rules and commitments expected of each other and then Timothy introduced Laura to everyone in the class. Shortly afterwards, Laura prepared herself for the session. She felt so scared that she wished that she was somewhere else. Despite that fact, she conjured up the rest of her inner strength and steadied herself for what was to come. He taught them some basic exercises and stances but he kept having to assist Laura with everything as she was no good at any of it. She felt so embarrassed and ashamed, that she wanted to crawl under a rock and die. The next step was some blocking techniques, but she just couldn't grasp any of that, either. Maybe it was that her beliefs wouldn't allow her to pass the starting point. The feeling that she was left with was anxiety and annoyance.

'God! Why can't I get this, or is this not for me?'

"Laura are you still with us or are you drifting into your own world? asked Timothy. "Oh! I'm so sorry. I'm still with you," responded Laura, apologetically.

"Okay then, can I have your full attention now please? Plus, you need to concentrate if you want to learn anything out of today's session," advised Timothy sincerely.

For the remainder of the session, she tried to put one hundred percent into her efforts. It wasn't too bad to be honest, but when it was finally over, she was so elated. The decision was already in mind of what she was going to do about the self-defence classes. "Can we talk?" asked Timothy.

"Yes sure! What's up?" asked Laura curiously.

"I think that if you want the best out of these sessions, if you choose to continue that is, then you would need to focus and apply yourself more than you have today. Besides you have to truly believe that this is the step you want to take, because if it isn't then I can't see any reason for you to torture yourself over the summer holidays. I suggest, you hook up with friends, have fun and enjoy your summer. But if this is what you want then I'll help you as much as I possibly can before I leave again for an international tournament in September," said Timothy, truthfully.

There was something peculiar about Laura that made him feel that he had to help her if she permitted him to, but the decision had to be her own. He would not be forcing her to do the classes. Timothy's heart went out to Laura in the predicament that she faces on a day-to- day basis at school with those horrendous bullies. No matter how he felt she was just another client amongst the list, she was an unforgettable client.

"Thank you, I appreciate your thoughtfulness and advice sir. I'll think about it and let you know my ultimate decision. Also, sir I just want to thank you for your patience with me today as someone else would have given up on me by now or criticised me, but you didn't and for that I truly appreciate it from the bottom of my heart," she revealed openly and honestly.

They said their goodbyes and Laura left the gym feeling exhausted with her mind in a turmoil about quite a number of unresolved issues. Hoping that a conversation with Freddie could be of some use to her in helping her to decide as to what she should ultimately choose to do, she decided that she would call him. She wondered if that was the real reason that she wanted to call Freddie or if it was just so that she could hear that beautiful, alluring French accent again.

'I wish that I possessed a magic wand that could chase all my pains and fears away; stop all the bullying that I endure at school. If I did then I would magic myself off to some place exotic for a long, long time. How I wish, I really wish….'

Laura lifted her head upwards to the sky and whispered a prayer,

"Please God help me to survive the remainder time left of school. Grant me that miracle"

There was a delay on the trains when Laura arrived at the station intending to make her way home, so she sat down to wait on the nearby bench on the platform. As a solution to try and ease her mind from the exploding turmoil of various confusing thoughts circling around in her head Laura turned on her mp3 player and placed the earphones into her ears. The music was turned up loudly to block out her own thoughts, but instead worked to cancel out the outside noises because she didn't hear when the announcement bellowed through the speaker to say that the train, she needed was fast approaching the platform. Her mind was so far afield that the train pulled up to the platform and was just about to close all the doors. Swiftly, she leapt up in time to notice that the train was directly in front of her and was about to close the doors to depart. Shouting out in desperation, "wait please" drawing the attention of the platform station officer, who was just about to signal the all-clear to the driver, to prevent the train doors from closing so Laura could climb aboard. "Thank you, sir," she whispered as she hurried onto the train.

"No problem, but be more aware next time," the platform station officer said, sternly.

'What's going on with me lately? I don't seem to be with it. Whatever it is I need to get a hold of myself before I completely lose my mind.'

In the seat next to her sat an elderly gentleman, who was staring with a look of grave concern plastered across his wrinkled face. Although she was listening intently to the music playing through her earphones, she noticed the changed look on the passenger's face and the fact that at this point he was looking directly at her. Confusion filled her mind, for what seemed like a split second, then it registered with her what her last thoughts were. At that point her mouth fell open as it filtered through her brain, the echo of her own voice, saying, 'what's going on with me lately? I don't seem to be with it.'

No wonder he's looking at me like I'm crazy. I just got a lot on my mind that's all. If only he knew what I'm going through, he would sympathise and understand why I'm like this. Although, I don't want pity, just a solution to my problems.

Laura mentally blocked out the old man sitting next to her and scanned the carriage looking for her mother's double, but saw no sign of her at all. When she had reached her destined stop, she rose up and got off the train taking a deep breath in, to counteract the feeling of suffocation.

Reflecting back on the events of the morning made the air quite stifling. Her head was pounding and her mind was feeling as though it would explode. 'He's right. I do need to have fun this summer and stop thinking about the what-ifs.'

Swallowing her thoughts, she hopped on the bus home singing aloud to the music that bellowed through the ear phones. Tapping her feet to the beat and bopping her head, Laura felt uplifted and joyful, not that she had anything to be joyful about. With that said, she vowed to herself that she would create some really happy, good memories from the summer holidays.

"Mum, are you home?" called out Laura when she walked into the house.

There was no answer, so she kicked off her trainers and ran upstairs to her bedroom to call Freddie to tell him as promised how her day went. "Bonjour! I mean Hello," came the familiar French accent through the telephone line.

"Oh hi, Freddie! It's me, Laura." "Hey! How are you?"

"I'm fine to be honest," she said with a smile. "So …,. tell me," Requested Freddie.

"Tell you what Freddie?" I don't understand.

"How did the self-defence class go? My brother is amazing right?"

"Arghh…. Yes, he certainly is. He was so kind and thoughtful. He is truly amazing," Laura said in agreement.

Freddie grunted as Laura spoke so highly of his brother. He wished that she was talking about him like that.

'What the hell man! Get a hold of yourself boy. Are you nuts or what? You only met her once.'

All Laura knew was that the eeriness of silence was unbearable. It felt as though the line had gone dead and Freddie annihilated from that moment's existence. The urge to double check and call out to him surfaced. She half yelled his name out. He answered her without hesitation, but in his mother tongue. "Bonjour Laura! Oui, mademoiselle. Je suis……"

Cutting off his ranting, "Huh! I don't understand a word of that, other than my name."

"I'm so sorry Lau, is it okay for me to call you Lau? I just lost myself for a split second."

'I understand more than you think because I seem to be doing a lot of losing myself lately.'

"It's okay, Freddie. It's totally fine."

"I don't mean to interrupt you, but you were telling me about the session with my brother."

"Well to be truthful with you, as interesting as it was, I hated it with a passion. I feel that I just went there to embarrass myself severely, as I couldn't do any of it, nor could I focus. Your brother was so patient with me, but although he offered to help me if I wanted him to, I just think that it's best I just abandon the thought of self-defence being the key skill that I need. Freddie, before you say anything, I just want to say thank you so much for helping me."

"Wow! You seemed to have made up your mind completely already, so I'm not going to try and convince you of why you should do the classes, as the decision is yours to make.

All I can say is at least you gave it a shot and it didn't work out, sweetie. Just know that I'm here for you, no matter what, day or night just call me."

"Thank you for respecting my decision. It is nice to know that I can count on you.

You're a good person. Maybe we could meet up and hang out sometimes if you want to, that is," stated Laura.

Without hesitation he answered, before she changed her mind. "Yes of course, that would be awesome."

With a hint of disappointment in his voice, Freddie revealed that he had to terminate their call because he needed to help his dad with a job. Before he hung up the phone, he bid her farewell as he said "Au revoir… I mean goodbye sweetie".

A little disappointed that he had to go, she said goodbye and replaced the receiver. ` *He called me sweetie. I can call him day or night if I can outsmart mummy. Still, I can't believe that he wants to hang out with boring me. Yesss….*'

A contagious smiled slowly crept across her face filling her with joy. With her eyes closed she shimmied across the room humming to a tune she had heard earlier on her way home on her Mp3 player, feeling happiness spread through her body. Suddenly when she turned around the happiness she felt and the smile she had across her face dissolved rapidly, as there in front of her stood her mother with a quizzical look on her face, hand in the air as if preparing to knock on the opened bedroom door. Laura could have sworn that she had locked it behind her before making the telephone call. She was usually so attentive to details like that so she was puzzled as to how the door got open, when and how long was her mother had been standing there and if she had heard any of the conversation? Although, irritated that her mood was ruined in that moment by the intrusion of her mother again, Laura tried to appear as though she wasn't angry about the interruption.

"Oh! Hi mum. I didn't realise that you were home. When I got in, I called out to you and got no reply at all."

Margaret had this patronising look on her face, as she said, "Really now? So why is it that I didn't hear you call out then?"

"I'm not sure mum, but I did call out to you."

Margaret didn't answer back but instead walked away with her hand on her hip, looking angry. Laura, still had no idea why her mother had come to her bedroom door in the first place or why she seemed to be so, angry. Not unless it was another ploy to spy on her and eavesdrop on yet another conversation of hers as she'd already suspected her mother made a habit of doing. Laura couldn't build up the courage required to throw the accusation in her mother's direction.

`*If it's just coincidence and mummy is innocent, she would without a doubt kill me.*

She would never let me get away with that. She would punish me for the rest of my miserable life and I can't have that.'

Shortly, after Laura collapsed on to her bed feeling quite jaded and deflated; her appetite had disappeared along with the joy she felt earlier before the unexplained 'mummy dearest' interruption. Although, Laura knew how thin she was her appetite didn't budge at that moment, vanishing like an amazing magic trick with detrimental repercussions. Falling into prayer, Laura wished to she could gain weight and grow up to be much more beautiful than she was at that moment, so that everyone who despised her, bullied her and called her names could eat their own words. Also, she prayed for the bullying to completely stop as she was so fed up of enduring such traumatising ordeals. She wanted, in fact, needed for it to be all over. The warm tears filled her eyes and rolled down her cheeks. Over the years there was so much pain that she had bottled up inside herself that it was an open wound fester oozing bit by bit. The horrible experiences, the beatings, the name callings that she encountered on a daily basis at school had severely traumatised her emotional, mental, psychological and physical state of mind. Laura had never felt more grateful for the six weeks school holiday, because the Woods siblings were out of town.

`Lord please I beg of you, to help me find a solution to my traumatic problem. I don't think that this is the reason for me living, is it? Save me please. I need you...'

After sobbing her heart out in prayer, she felt a little better at having off-loaded her problems onto this higher being that she undoubtedly believed would eventually save her life. Before long Laura was drowning in the depths of her thoughts. Her mind was so far adrift that she didn't register that she was exhausted to the point that she fell into a deep sleep, until several hours later when her mother woke her and informed her that there was someone awaiting to talk to her on the telephone, and that she was unsure who it could be as the caller never told her their name. Laura crawled out of bed lazily and slowly crept to the phone on the corner table. Just when she reached for the handset, she automatically looked in the direction of her mother, only to see that she was now sitting on the edge of her bed with her arms folded on her chest and looking curiously in her direction. Laura's heartbeat quickened. She could hear the rush of blood in her ears. Her palms were becoming sweatier. Her mother staring at her like that made her feel very uneasy. Finally, Laura put the handset shakily to her ear and squeakily said hello. From the distance Margaret could barely make out the caller's voice so she got up and walked closer to Laura pretending that she was using the mirror on the wall as if she got something in her eye. Laura watched wearily, knowing that her mother was snooping on her conversation. Laura acted as if she hadn't noticed what her mother was trying to accomplish and had a brief conversation with the caller whilst her mother leant against the wall staring blankly at her the whole time. Margaret's facial expression was unreadable. The only thing that Margaret could gather from the conversation was that her daughter was agreeing to meet up with this guy to hang out the following day and, according to the information she overheard, and the remaining five weeks of the summer holidays. All she could think in her head was that Laura had a lot of explaining to do.

Margaret stared at her daughter intrigued as to why Laura appeared to be extremely excited about this arrangement. She had to know who Laura was planning to meet and why?

Margaret was ready to pounce on her daughter to extract the necessary information she needed.

As soon as Laura replaced the receiver, her mother began firing question upon question her way so that it muddled her brain, as she didn't know which question her mother wanted her to answer first. Noticing that the questions that she was being asked were getting more and more intrusive, Laura decided to outsmart her mother by answering only two of the cleverly constructed questions, as she couldn't handle the interrogation. The ones she chose were 'who was it, and the why did they call?

"Mum… mum… mother! Stop for goodness' sake. Not being rude but how could you expect me to answer any of your questions, if you don't give me an opportunity to answer?"

"Well! Get on with it then. I'm listening." Her hands akimbo as she barked out her demand. Fright crept through Laura's bones but she couldn't back down now. She had to do it. It's either now or never. She plucked up the courage and began answering the questions as swiftly as she could before her mother became more irritated.

"It was Freddie, mum. He wanted to know if I was okay and whether I'm free to meet up and hang out tomorrow and the rest days of the summer holiday, if I don't have anything else planned."

Laura was cautious as to what details she shared with her mother as she saw her mother raising her eyebrows at her with an emotionless expression on her face.

"Oh, I see. I thought that he worked in his dad's plumbing business so what does he want with you? Doesn't he have jobs to complete?"

"Yes mum, he works helping out his dad. But his dad is giving him the time off to enjoy the summer holidays before going back to finish his course at college in the Autumn."

"Okay. Fair enough, but don't go thinking that all of the days of your summer holidays will be spent idly with that boy. Take that as your warning, girl. Anyway, your dinner is in the microwave. By the time that I was finished cooking, you were sleeping."

"Alright, thanks mum."

Laura kissed her mum on the cheek and thanked her, not only for the dinner, but for letting her go out with Freddie the next day. Margaret stared at Laura for a brief moment, opened her mouth as if wanting to say something more, but then snapped her mouth shut, turned and walked out of the bedroom with a sour look on her face without a backwards glance. Not so much as a 'you're welcome' or a 'bye' escaped from her tightly shut lips. The bedroom door was left wide open clearly displaying there was no privacy or boundaries when it came down to Laura. It was hard to get over the childish display of her mother's behaviour from her mind. Laura felt appalled and could only wonder about what happened to the adult that was supposed to be the responsible one in the house, whose duty was to teach her right from wrong, and nurture her the right way. Sometimes she felt like a possession, not a daughter. She felt trapped most of the time by the very person who was supposed to love and protect her. She dare not confront her mother about how she felt at home because who knew how she would react to the accusations.

If she was honest with herself, she was elated to have something to do and someone close to her age to be around who liked her, someone who really wanted to spend time with her. To be fair she craved the attention from him. It was not a want but a need to be in his company. Something about him made her feel alive and she wanted more of it. Even though she had only experienced just a fraction of it, and she wasn't used to people being kind to her without an ulterior motive, she needed more of this kindness to cleanse her tortured mind and heart. Laura hoped that relaxation and happiness around Freddie was imminent. Already she felt comforted by just talking to him and had noticed that he had a good caring side to him and was quite friendly, not to mention being extremely handsome.

`He couldn't just be pretending to care about me, could he?`

There she went again. Paranoia setting in. Mind on definite overdrive, overthinking everything. But she couldn't blame herself because she had been through hell and was still going through hell. She was just waiting for it to ignite again after school resumed. She was drowning. Unable to keep her head above water and needed a way out fast. She wanted to be able to breathe and live more freely without worrying about which beat down was next. She wanted… in fact it was a need to survive, to live and breathe without restriction, experiencing the freedom of it all. Laura couldn't wait to get to know Freddie more on a personal level.

She wanted to know everything about him. He had her intrigued, captured like a deer caught in the headlights.

A thought crossed her mind that she must look lovely for her meet up with Freddie the following day. She walked over to her wardrobe and had a sneak peek at her summer outfits, hoping to see the perfect one to wear. She saw a red and white heart patterned crisscrossed halter neck dress that fall just below the knees that she hadn't worn for a long time. Laura decided that she would wear this. She thought she heard her mother's footsteps coming in her direction, so she quickly closed the wardrobe door and dashed out of her bedroom and down the stairs into the kitchen to warm up her dinner left in the microwave. Although she had no appetite, she forced herself to eat as much as she could before her mother had a go at her for not eating. She couldn't deal with the nagging in her head. There was always a consequence and she knew that her mother would use any excuse to prevent her from meeting up with Freddie and she couldn't have that. It was the only thing that she had to look forward to that was exciting. As soon as she was finished eating, Laura scraped out the remainder of the food into the rubbish bin and washed and dried her plate and high-ball glass and packed them away into the cupboard. After Laura had completed that task, she entered the lounge and switched on the television. Lucky for her, her favourite television programme was showing as a double bill of episodes back-to-back. It felt great to lounge about for a while. She folded her legs underneath her in the armchair and got herself much more comfortable. A scene she was watching on Ally McBeal set her mind adrift, pondering about what she hoped her life could be like. Laura was continually exhausted from experiencing the traumatic overload of it all. A large number of the times, Laura could recall feeling unhappy and she wanted it to change for the better. Sometimes when it got too much, Laura often asked herself if there was any point in living such a miserable, lonely life with hardly any friends at all. The other students at school were scared to befriend her because they assumed they would become the next target for the bullies. They didn't want to take the chance of being the next victims of the physical, mental, emotional, verbal and psychological abuse that Laura faced daily. More often than not Laura got this jittery feeling like her mother loved it when she is totally needy and truly dependant on her, and that sickened her as to why her mother could be so evil.

'Maybe I might be wrong, you know. Imagining things yet again. What if I misjudged the situation? Most of the times mummy attempted to save me. She couldn't have a hidden agenda now, could she?'

It was moments like these that made her wish that she had a father and knew how to find him if he was still alive out there somewhere. In fact, her mum never spoke of him at all, and she was too afraid to ask anything of the sort. Sometimes she often wondered if he was around, would he protect her from those bullies. Her mind was in tatters trying to figure out things beyond her control.

'Have I ever walked past him in the streets? I have never even glimpsed or seen any pictures of him.'

With her hand cupping her mouth, Laura gasped at the thought as it was a possibility. She felt deflated as what little energy she had left she could feel it draining away from her body.

Often, she saw other people with their dads laughing and joking and wished that she could have even a fraction of that. She was so envious of these people although it was wrong to feel that way.

'Was it me? Did I do something wrong? Did you not love me enough to stick around?

Why did you leave us? You… Oh God! You… didn't want me. You didn't love me either.'

Tears streamed down her face at record breaking speed. She sobbed and sobbed hysterically into the palms of her hands until there were no more tears left to spare. Laura thought about calling Freddie to talk this out but suppressed the thought as quickly as it surfaced because she knew that her mother would never allow her to call him at this time of night no matter what the circumstances. So definitely she would have to wait till lunchtime tomorrow to see Freddie and speak to him if necessary. Laura rose up from the sofa as if she was someone possessed, grabbed the television remote from the coffee table and switched off the television. She replaced the remote back on the coffee table and flounced out of the lounge and climbed the stairs to her bedroom where she showered and got herself prepared for bed. Shortly, after putting her nightwear on she clambered into bed. Laura lay there in the dark, staring at the window curtains, hoping that her energy would return by tomorrow before she met up with Freddie.

Chapter 13

Laura hadn't realised when she had drifted off to sleep other than when the following morning the bellowing sound of the alarm clock at top volume on the bedside table shot through her ears with a tune she loved. She reached out and clicked the snooze button, hoping to sleep for an extra ten minutes or so as she still felt exhausted and lazy. Laura knew that she needed time to start getting herself dressed and prepared for her meeting with Freddie but she couldn't move just yet. As soon as she was drifting back off to sleep the alarm rang out again, making her groan aloud, so she dismissed it this time and lazily crawled out of bed and made her way towards the bathroom to shower up and brush her teeth thoroughly. When she was finished, she tried on the red and white heart printed dress and looked in her full-length mirror. Laura decided against wearing this and took up her pink three-quarter length trousers, white floral chemise vest and white sandals and put them on and was satisfied with the way she looked in the mirror. She blow-dried her wet hair and added some hair oils for moisture before brushing her hair and drawing it up in a neat ponytail at the nape of her neck. Before closing the wardrobe door, Laura grabbed her pink handbag from the inner hook and exited the bedroom. She went in search of her mother around the house but couldn't find her anywhere, so she decided to eat a slice of toast and drink a glass of apple juice. When she was finished, she wrote a note on a crinkled piece of paper and secured it to the refrigerator door for her mother to find when she returned home. Laura quickly rang Freddie to let him know that she was making her way to their agreed meeting place. The conversation was polite as usual, and brief. After the call she replaced the receiver and exited the house, closing the front door behind her. It felt like someone was watching her, but she continued walking anyway without looking back. The bus journey was shorter than Laura had anticipated to her desired destination. She was a few minutes early and was trying to put her nerves in check, feeling more anxious and overly excited than she should have. But a slight bit of fear crept in as she wasn't hundred percent certain how she should behave in these circumstances.

`Oh boy! Here he comes. Hmm… I got to get a hold of myself before he thinks that I'm a psycho.'

Laura took some deep breaths to try and suppress her nervousness. As he got nearer her heartbeat quickens. She swore that she could hear it loudly, so she was adamant that perhaps Freddie could hear it too. He looked drop-dead gorgeous in his baby blue t-shirt and black jeans. He was also wearing blue and black Nike trainers. His hair looked wet from his shower and had a sleek, silky, soft textured appearance to it. She felt the urge to run her fingers through his hair but decided against it. Her palms were sweaty so she automatically wiped them down the sides of her trousers. Thank goodness her hands were clean. The pulse in her neck was beating rapidly as the blood rushed through it. She could feel a lump forming in her throat as Freddie looked at her and smirked as if he knew the effect he was having on her body.

"Hello beautiful. You're looking breathtakingly sexy."

Swallowing loudly Laura smiled, "Arghh…. Thank you Freddie, you look absolutely gorgeous, too."

The heat rose in her cheeks turning them rosy red as she stared into those magnificent oceanic blue eyes.

"Thank you for meeting me today. I hope that you can ice skate as I thought you would enjoy something like that."

"You're welcome. I should really be saying thank you for inviting me out to spend time with you. To be honest I haven't been ice skating since I was seven years old, so I'm quite rusty on it, so there's your pre-warning before I embarrass myself and you all at once."

"That's okay. I'm no expert either but the aim is to have some fun so we'll do just that."

Fiddling with her thumbs she asked, "If I fall will you laugh at me?"

At first, he burst out into laughter but then realised that Laura had a serious look on her face. To lighten the mood, he teased with a smirk on his face, "No way sweetheart, I'd be the first to catch you if you fall. You have my word."

Freddie placed his hand on his heart as if making a pledge of allegiance. Laura didn't know how to take that statement Freddie made so she buried her head in her hands feeling flushed. She was unsure what he meant by that statement as it could carry more than one meaning, but she refused to ask him to clarify what he meant. The way that Freddie's eyes surveyed her, she could have sworn that she was melting. Her whole body felt so hot under his gaze. The air was stifling as the sun blazed down on them. The heat all over her body didn't help the situation either. The way he looked at her, as if she was the only person in the world that mattered, accompanied by the smell of citrus scent of his cologne mixed with soap made her head feel dizzy. She needed to catch her breath and she needed to do it fast.

`Now is no time to get mushy on him. Just get a hold of yourself.'

His eyes lingered on her lips for a brief moment, darkening with desire. He stared at her intently, watching the way her body reacted to him, then smirked. He reached out his hand and she placed hers in his as they walked about seven minutes to the ice- skating rink, situated down the side road. He pulled the entrance door open and held it for her to enter like a gentleman. He rented both of their skates to match their outfits. Laura chose white figure skates and Freddie chose a black ice hockey type ice-skates. After putting on their skates, hand in hand they stepped on to the ice, flawlessly. Neither one of them realised that they automatically entwined their hands until they felt the shock of electricity shoot through their palms forcing them to withdraw from each other immediately. They looked at each other as if silently asking 'was it me or did you feel that too?' Whilst Laura skated Freddie looked on amazed as he saw how happy she was. Her smile was radiant which made him smile, too.

They talked and laughed so much that Laura's cheeks felt sore. She could not believe how much she had remembered about skating. Freddie teased, "Oh is that how rusty skaters skate? 'Cos right now you are skating like a pro, Lau."

Immediately Laura smiled and stuck out her tongue teasingly at him. She felt so filled with joy that she couldn't thank Freddie enough for giving her a taste of what life could be for her. All she wished now was that she could skate all her troubles and turmoil behind her and go forward towards the joy and the laughter that was clearly waiting for her. Freddie noticed the different emotions flashing across Laura's face especially the sadness as if she was battling with her thoughts. He approached her and led her off the ice into a private corner table where they could talk without airing their business to the general public. The ice rink was bustling with lots of people, with their friends, families and children. Freddie turned and looked at her with grave concern. "What's wrong Lau? You look upset. Talk to me."

"Don't laugh, but there's some things about my mum's behaviour that's bothering me a lot."

"Like what exactly?"

"I think that my mother always eavesdrops on my telephone conversations. It seems like she is spying on me like a detective staring at me intently like a hawk around the house. Sometimes it feels as though she doesn't love me. One minute she is fine and instantaneously she becomes so angry and vicious that it scares the living daylights out of me."

"Maybe you're reading it the wrong way. She's your mother; how could she not love you? That doesn't make any sense. I think that she's being overly protective as you're her daughter and she wants the best for you. Give her a chance. Have you ever tried talking to her about how you feel?"

"To be honest with you Freddie, no I haven't. I've never given mummy any reason to not trust me at any point in time, so something doesn't make any sense at all to me."

"Well, talk to her and see what she says about it."

Freddie stared at Laura intrigued by her revelations, but couldn't help the feeling of concern that rose in him. He tried to think of what he could do to help her with her situation. "Freddie, could I tell you something else? But you might laugh at this one. You know what… my mum creeps around the house like a ninja. I swear to you. You can't even hear when she's walking around most times other than you would look and see her standing there looking intently at you. To be honest she could be here somewhere looking at us right now." That came out in a whisper like Laura was scared that she would be overheard. Freddie felt uneasy by that revelation. He wanted to tell Laura that her mum sounded creepy but he couldn't. He didn't want her to think that he was disrespecting her mother.

At this point Freddie couldn't hold back the hysterical laughter choked up inside him. He stuck his head back and laughed aloud drawing the attention of the nearby customers and staff members. Laura looked at Freddie bemused and burst out laughing too as she replayed her last statement to herself. Shortly after they handed in their ice skates, put their shoes back on and headed through the door into the open air. He conjured up a plan to cheer her up. He decided to take her to his favourite place in town where he thought they made the best hotdogs and hot chocolates. When they got there, they sat at a table and the waitress took their orders: two hotdogs and two cups of hot chocolate with double cream, marsh mallows and chocolate dust. They ate their hotdogs and drank their hot chocolates whilst having a good widespread conversation where they laughed and joked around. Laura was enjoying the time that she was spending with Freddie so much so that she wished that it didn't have to end, but knew that it had to at some point. She indulged herself, savouring every taste of her hot chocolate, agreeing with Freddie that it was the best she had ever had, as she enjoyed every sip that smoothly glided down her throat. Freddie watched Laura under hooded eyes as she drank, inadvertently closing her eyes when she sipped the warm liquid. She thanked him for sharing his favourite place with her and for making her day so filled with happiness. He just nodded and smiled that dazzling smile that kept making her breath catch in her chest. Finally, when they were finished, he escorted her home so that he knew she had got there safely. They made small talk all the way to Laura's residence. It was the most fun that she had in a very long time and was overly thankful to the guy that stood before her. She was no longer nervous or anxious around Freddie as he was definitely good company, a gentleman in the making all the way. Laura was truly looking forward to the next day when they could meet up again. They said their goodbyes and he walked away leaving with the notion that he had accomplished what he had set out to do in the first place. Calling out after him, Laura expressed what a wonderful time she had with him earlier and how much she was looking forward to the next day. Freddie raised his hand in acknowledgement and smiled, shouting back, "me too Lau."

Laura opened the front door and walked inside. She could hear the television bellowing through the lounge door and knew that her mother was home and watching television programmes. Margaret had this tendency to turn up the volume full blast, loud enough to wake up the dead. Anyone would have thought that she had hearing problems but Laura knew better; that her hearing was sound. In fact, her mother's hearing was sharper than a razor blade which is why she could eavesdrop so well. Approaching the lounge Laura braced herself just in case her mother might be in a bad mood as the majority of times that she watched the television that loud was to drown out her anger or whatever demons she needed to exercise. Laura wanted to talk to her mother as well about her concerns and also to tell her about her afternoon with Freddie because she knew that her mum would ask her anyway. Laura slowly entered the lounge and greeted her mother, only for her mother to be unreceptive towards her like she did not care. Margaret appeared to be angry and concerned about something but Laura was unsure about what it could be. Despite her mother's bad mood, Laura built up the courage and told her mother about the fun afternoon she had with Freddie.

Margaret was impassioned. She leapt up and hugged her daughter tightly expressing how please she was that Laura was happy, had lots of fun, and how proud she was to have a daughter like her in her life. Seconds after hearing such loving words from her mother Laura's worries faded away like dust in the wind. This made her reflect on what Freddie said about her mother loving her and acknowledged that he was right. She couldn't help it but smile at the thought. Margaret patted the seat next to her on the sofa without saying a word, signalling for Laura to sit down next to her. Laura understood the gesture and made her way to sit down next to her mother. They watched television for the remainder of the afternoon, interacting with some game shows shouting out the answers at the screen. It felt incredible to be in a more relaxed environment at home with her mother, as for the past few days the atmosphere in the house was quite tense that you could literally cut it with a knife. It was uncomfortable and daunting and Laura had confined herself to her bedroom reading books, or writing diary logs for that day to avoid any confrontation with her mother. They had an enjoyable evening together and Laura could not stop her loud laughter and was feeling really happy. Later, feeling exhausted she said thank you to her mother and bid her a good night.

Laura climbed the stairs and went straight to her bedroom where she got herself washed and prepped for bed so that she could rest well before her next excursion with Freddie, as she had no clue what he had in store for them the next day.

Throughout her summer holiday on and off, Laura and Freddie met up and had an incredible amount of fun doing many activities with some being more chillaxed than others. Over time they got to know more personal things about each other. Although Laura would have loved to spend each day with

Freddie, there were days that her mother would not permit her to because she was in a mood and decided to confine Laura to the house like a prisoner locked up for illegal activity. Margaret didn't care that this caused Laura to get upset. The reason was that her daughter was hanging out too much with this plumber boy. Laura could not understand what the problem was, because she had found someone who liked her for being herself and was quite fond of hanging out with her. Finally, within herself she was happy being around Freddie as he was such a positive friend in her life, so it was quite confusing that her mother should try stop her from enjoying this. No matter if she sulked around the house or cried about her confinement it didn't make any difference to her mother as she never changed her mind. Her mother was as thick skinned as an alligator with a heart made of stone sometimes. Her telephone privileges on these days were revoked so she was unable to inform Freddie that she would have to cancel. So, Freddie would go to their agreed meeting place and not see her there. Freddie felt concerned and visited her at her home to make sure that she was alright. But Margaret would always be the one to answer the door, refusing to let Laura conversate with Freddie or permitting any entry into the house. It was hard to comprehend what was going on, but nevertheless Freddie kept on trying to obtain Margaret's trust towards him as he only had her daughter's best interest at heart and nothing more.

There were other occasions where Freddie would be allowed inside the house when Margaret was in the best of moods. Occasionally, he would stay for dinner or lunch as Margaret would insist. They would all have a good laugh together, enjoying each other's company. Margaret would make it known to her daughter that she thought that Freddie was a positive, lively young man with flare and a good persona.

"You've got a great friend here, my Lau."

But then other times she would contradict herself and when they were alone would say as warnings things like, "Young men like that cannot be trusted. They're only after one thing."

Nearer the end of the summer holidays Laura and Freddie hung out a lot more with each other for lengthier periods of time. They became so close that she was introduced to Freddie's family at his home. She met his mother, dad, two brothers and his younger sister. For the first few times that Laura went to Freddie's house she felt shy and reserved because it was just so unreal how kind, caring and welcoming they all were. After a while she warmed to them, feeling more and more at home each time. The shyness dissolved so quickly and confidence stepped into place. This was her home away from home. Her sanctuary, her escape and she'd be always grateful to Freddie for it.

Greg Laurent was a forty-five years old man, who was a workaholic but still found time to spend with his family. He had grey eyes, dyed blonde hair with streaks of black strands, average height and had a lethal smile. He was self-employed and owned his own plumbing business called Laurent and Sons; although all his sons had different interests, they stood firmly by him. He was very plain minded with his thoughts, concerns and opinions. He appeared to be a brilliant, loving father and husband.

Melanie Laurent was forty-three years old woman with piercing blue eyes, jet black curly hair. She was of average height with a strong French accent. She was absolutely beautiful. Laura realised that Freddie got his stunning features from his mother's side. She was also a business owner of the local bakery in town. She was well known for her trade. She had this loving, warmth that shines through her personality. She adores all her children and always made sure that she was always there to support all four of her children despite work commitments.

Timothy was the eldest son, a twenty-six years old karate instructor. Peter the second son was twenty-three years old with features just like his father's and worked in his dad's plumbing business. Freddie was the third child and Tiffany was the youngest. Tiffany was a sweet young girl the same age as Laura. According to her family, Tiffany attended the school closer to home. She was the mirror image of her mother. Tiffany and Laura, over time, became very fond of each other. They viewed each other as the sister they each never had.

They often would get together when Laura would visit their family home and do girly things such as skylarking with make-up, fingernail painting, styling each other's hair and so forth. They both wanted to do sleepovers but were not permitted to do so. Margaret was not keen on the idea of having anyone over and she wasn't going to allow Laura to have a sleepover at Freddie's home even though she was reassured that her daughter would be in safe hands.

Laura continued to be the studious daughter that she was expected to be. She didn't want any arguments and tension at home between her mother and herself.

Instead, when she visited Freddie's, she would make the most of the time she spent there. She valued her time with Freddie a lot, more than she cared to admit to herself. It was always a pleasure to be around that family. Eventually as time went by, she developed deeper feelings towards Freddie but she didn't want the way that she felt towards him to affect their friendship. She couldn't bear it if a rift was to drive them apart. It was hard to imagine life without Freddie in it. She was fearful that maybe Freddie only liked her as a friend and nothing more so she kept the way she felt to herself as she couldn't handle any rejection at the moment, not after all the trauma she had faced for years at home and at school. She needed one solid thing in her life that would always be there as her source of comfort, her go to when things got tough. There were times that she would catch Freddie staring intently at her in awe, with a sincere look in his eyes so soft and tender. There was an unwritten message in the way he looked at her. He would linger a while longer as if deep in thought as he stared at her before sharply looking away, but not before gracing her with a dazzling smile. Each time he did this she would feel a tug on her heartstrings and her body would feel as though she was melting on the inside under the intensity of his gaze. Laura often wondered if Freddie knew what he was doing to her. She didn't understand what it was she was feeling each time he looked at her, but she basked in the feeling. It was exhilarating and made her feel alive.

She didn't want it to stop; in fact, she wanted more of it. Whatever it was that was making her feel that way, she figured it was the best feeling ever. She never felt this way for anyone before and it scared her a little as she didn't understand it well enough. Sometimes she felt tempted to talk to Freddie about it but changed her mind each time as she couldn't muster up enough courage to do it.

`Does he know and is he just teasing me? I wish that he would kiss me. In my dreams his kisses are addictive, they set my body ablaze. I want to know if in reality a kiss, not just any kiss but his kiss, could cause my body to react that way.'

As Laura sat there deep in thought as she reflected on a time when Freddie spontaneously showed up at her doorstep and asked her mother if she would permit Laura to accompany him to the cinema. Initially, Margaret flatly refused to allow Laura to go but after much convincing agreed to let her go with Freddie. Oh, how elated she felt. Freddie was quite pleased with his efforts to convince Margaret and thought that maybe she was finally beginning to be accepting of him. Laura remembered getting ready in record breaking time before her mother changed her mind. Freddie thanked Margaret with the sincerest gratitude. They went to the local cinema across town to watch the latest comedy film that had just been released. They bought their popcorn, sweets and drink to share together. They both thought that it would be more intimate that way. They watched the film indulging themselves in their goodies, each other's company and the laughter. Each time their hands met, they would glance at each other and smile. As soon as the snacks was finished Freddie reached out in search of her hand and held it. The gesture made her look at him shocked but she didn't pull away as she had wanted this for quite a while, although she felt scared and shy. They continued to watch the film in dead silence other than the eruption of laughter at the funny parts of the film. This still didn't stop questions running through her mind and speculative answers about what was happening between them. When the film had concluded they remained seated savouring the intimate moment between them before it vanished. The look on Freddie's face changed as if he was battling with his thoughts. He kept shifting around nervously in the seat and then said, "Laura, I erm… I just wanted to tell you that this was one of my favourite summers ever. I truly enjoyed spending time with you. The laughter we shared and most of all the connection we developed in relation to each other and not to mention your company is fascinating. Just wanted to say thank you for allowing me the pleasure to get to know you and be around you. I hope that this won't be the end of what we have. You are very special to me and I want to be here for you, protect you and keep you happy."

Laura's heart was thudding so fast inside her chest, listening to Freddie's confession. She couldn't stop smiling. She felt uplifted, happy and loved when she was with him. If this was what love was, she was all in. she wanted it desperately to wash away all the trauma, all the pain from her life, her heart, her mind. "The pleasure was all mine. I should be the one thanking you for giving me such good memories and the most amazing summer ever. You opened my eyes and showed me that there are truly genuinely kind, caring and loving people in the world beyond the evil ones. You boosted my confidence in myself and for that I will always be grateful. This definitely can never be the end."

Laura could feel the stinging at the back of her eyes, the build-up of the tears as they threaten to fall and now, she wasn't sure how to stop them. Tears were streaming down her face although she tried to fight it. Freddie stood up and pulled her gently to her feet and put his arms around her in a warm embrace. Laura was tense and resistant as she hesitantly fought the urge to lean into Freddie's embrace. She was scared that she would never want to let go and she didn't want to come across as clingy at all. Lowering his head, he whispered in her ear, "it's okay my darling, I got you. I always got you. I promise that I would never hurt you. You can trust me."

The warmness of his breath against her neck sent tingles all over her body. Without Freddie to lean on she would have crumpled to the floor as her knees felt wobbly. It didn't take much convincing before Laura leant in to Freddie's hard chest, wrapping her arms tightly around him as she listened to the strong steady beat of his heart. He was alluringly sexy. The smell of his woody cologne was overpowering her senses. Her head felt light. He was temptation on strong, muscular legs.

'*Damn! He's driving me crazy. What's wrong with me?* What *is this that I'm feeling?*' He buried his face in the nook of her neck as he inhaled the floral scent of her sweet fragrance. There was something different about the way he held her tonight.

'*Was he… does he feel what I feel? Can he read my mind? Snap out of it, girl. No one ever wants you. Stop fooling yourself.*'

Laura held on tighter just in case all this would be gone by the morning, not that she wanted it to. Freddie noticed and squeezed her a little tighter. The way they held on to each other as if it was their final goodbye, as if they would never meet again. Freddie couldn't get enough of the smell of her. He drank in the scent of her, like it was his lifeline. He buried his nose in her hair and inhaled deeply the smell of the exotic hair oils she had administered only hours ago when she was preparing herself before leaving home. The smell of the coconuts and herbs was exhilarating to his senses. He lifted his head and tilted her chin so that she was looking directly into his gorgeous blue eyes. They were a darker shade than they are normally. There was desire and hunger shining through. He stared at her longingly as he moved his head closer shortening the space between their lips.

'*Is he going to kiss me? Oh God. I think he's going to kiss…*'

His lips felt sensational. They were soft and gentle as they caressed hers. She let out a soft moan against his lips. This ignited the fire stirring in him. He was restraining himself and Laura was making it harder for Freddie to keep control. This was her first kiss, and she was getting lost in it. Laura snaked her hands around his neck and placed her fingers through his hair as she grabbed hold pulling his head closer to deepen the kiss. Just as he threw caution to the wind and was responding to her passion, the doors burst open rudely interrupting the display of affection between the two of them. A grumpy, craggy looking woman holding a dust pan, broom and some rubbish bags came barging in.

"Arghh... excuse me the film is over. Get out! So, I can clean this place up. Now be gone."

That was enough to ruin the mood. She needn't say anymore. They released the embrace and apologised to the woman who seemed like she was having a bad day and walked out hand in hand. Laura's mind set adrift with thoughts of the early sensual encounter with Freddie. She wondered how far he would have taken it. She wondered if she was dreaming and, in that case, she didn't want to wake up. 'Would it happen again?' As if sensing her thoughts he said, "It wasn't a dream."

Freddie took her home as promised, but not before asking her to meet him the following day. Without hesitation Laura agreed and nonchalantly walked into the house. Freddie stood there watching her until she closed the door shut behind her. A few hours later the phone rang. Laura picked up the receiver and answered, "Hello."

"Laura it's me! I just wanted to update you on a few things. Remember what I told you about my grandmother?"

"Yeah, I do. Why what's wrong?"

Laura could hear the panic in his voice. He took a deep breath in and exhaled loudly through the phone. "She's not doing so great, Lau. Everyone's in a panic. She's still so poorly and mum's quite emotional wondering if she will lose her mother. I'm so upset right now and it's taking its toll on me because I wish that I could help her. Why do I have to feel so helpless, Lau?"

"I'm so sorry to hear that she's taken a turn for the worse."

Freddie choked back the tears. "It's not your fault, Lau. Unfortunately, it's the laws of life," he said sadly with a sniffle.

"Why don't you go and be the carer for your grandmother Freddie, for your mum? I believe that you would make a good carer," Laura joked".

Freddie smiled sadly, "if I did, would you consider coming with me? I don't want to leave you behind. It would be so hard."

Laura's heart stopped for a brief moment as she digested what Freddie had just asked of her. "I wouldn't be able to. I'm so sorry my mother would never let me."

"Okay, fair enough, I understand. But answer honestly. Would you miss me, Lau, if I went?"

"Yes of course! Without a doubt."

"I'm elated to hear it, because I would certainly miss you more than I can explain." "Does this mean that we're not meeting up tomorrow?"

"No! We are still meeting up I promise. Good night, Lau. I got to go. Catch you tomorrow because mum needs me right now."

"Okay. Bye. Please give my love to your family especially your mum."

Laura spoke to her mother Margaret after the phone call ended and informed her that Freddie asked her to meet with him the next day. She held her breath as she prayed that her mother would approve. Laura was ecstatic and couldn't wait to see Freddie again so that she could be there for him. Be his rock, his moral support, his comfort like he'd done for her and still doing.

* * *

The next day Freddie was his usual cheery self, full of life and vibrancy. This shocked Laura because she'd expected that Freddie would have been in a dampened mood, but it was quite the opposite.

"Hey handsome. How are you doing?"

"I'm as well as to be expected under the circumstances."

"How's your family holding up, especially your mother? And is there any change in your grandmother's condition?" she asked with grave concern.

Laura could see the hurt reflected in Freddie's eyes. "There is a slight change, but nothing major, I'm afraid. Mum's heartbroken and scared at the moment. Anyways today is about us spending some fun time together, so I'm taking you to my favourite place to unwind and think. It's extremely special to me, so I hope that you'll love it like I do."

He picked up the picnic basket of treats that he had brought with him to meet her.

They walked on through the park in a comfortable silence. At first, Laura thought to herself, why is the park is so special to Freddie? But as long as she was with him, she didn't care where they were as long as they are together. He was very special to her, and she wanted to tell him about the way she felt about him, before it was too late. Surprisingly to her, Freddie turned off the path, veering left through a bushy pathway. Laura followed closely behind Freddie. At the end of the pathway was a nice green clearing with a babbling brook running through the middle of it, leading into a swimming pond. The trees shaded over the water creating a sense of privacy that if someone wanted to wade in and bathe, they could without worrying about being seen. The sound of the running water over the stones was quite soothing. It was paradise. It was serene and peaceful with the wild flowers kissing the ground around them, with the birds chirping in the trees. The view was absolutely spectacular.

Finally, she understood why Freddie found this place so special. He laid out the picnic blanket and unpacked the hamper which contained freshly baked bread, cheese, grapes and various fillings. There were juices and a variety of snacks. Laura was shocked that despite the circumstances he had found the time to put together something this spectacular. She felt special and knew that this place would be precious to her, as well as the boy sitting down opposite her on the blanket. They tucked into their delicious feast and talked about a lot of things - everything except their pressing worries. They laughed and joked around.

"Not many people know about this place. I'm always down here thinking, relaxing when I'm not busy, so you know where you can find me if I'm not at home. This place could be your sanctuary too, Laura, as it is mine. I'm willing to share it with you," he laughed, as he gave her shoulder a gentle squeeze.

"Thank you, it will be. After all, it is a very special place, so who could resist?" She looked at him just as she said those words. "It'll always have a special place in my heart, just like you have already."

Freddie looked at Laura gobsmacked at the revelation in her words. He couldn't believe what he was hearing. He thought that he was the only one that felt that way, and often wondered if Laura loved him the way that he'd fallen in love with her. He had contemplated telling her many times, but he was waiting for the right moment. He shifted next to her after they had finished eating and held her in his arms so lovingly. He reached out and cupped her face with his hand tilting her chin upwards so that she was gazing up into his eyes. He leant down and kissed her so gently, his lips just barely brushing hers. He stopped and looked at her; he still couldn't believe his luck. The way she melted in his arms, the bedazzled looked she had on her face full of pure, raw emotions. "God, you are so beautiful," he said, with his voice so husky.

He kissed her again this time with a bit more pressure. It was full of hunger, the need to be closer. He teased her lips with his tongue making her open her mouth to him. She moaned against his lips, succumbing to the moment. She put her hands around his neck, snaking her fingers through his silky soft hair at the nape of his neck holding him closer with need. Freddie deepened the kiss plunging his tongue into her mouth so skilfully as their tongues danced in unison together creating a swirl of heat through their bodies. Laura could feel the heat rising, setting her core ablaze. She didn't understand what she was feeling but she loved it. Her body felt weak, she clung to him for strength as the intensity of the heat skyrocketed through her body. His lips were soft, his kiss demanding. He kissed her harder and deeper giving into his desire. He was slowly losing control. The taste of his lips was like nectar, so sweet and addictive. She just couldn't get enough of him.

"J'adore, Laura, Mon Cherie," he whispered against her lips. Then kissed her again.

"I love you too Freddie," she said breathlessly when they came up for air from their passionate kisses.

Her brain was a bit scrambled. Those kisses had turned her world upside down. He was the first boy that she'd ever kissed in her life. There was something about this time that was so different. His kisses were more intense. The strangest but excitingly intense feelings overtook her body filling it with unadulterated pleasure. She was quite shocked that she knew what to do; her lips seemed to work of their own accord -they instinctively knew just what to do. Thanks to movies and observing people on the street, at least she didn't embarrass herself. She cleverly following his lead to match the fluidity of his movements.

Touching her fingers to her swollen lips, she thought to herself,

'Wow! That was… was too good to be true. Should I try it again? Am I in a dream? If so don't wake me up anytime soon. Leave me in this sweet moment with my first love. My first love? I like the sound of that. Yes mine, all mine forever and a day.'

To test the theory, she reached out and kissed him again. He groaned against her mouth. He was so close to losing his self-control with her. He was so receptive it made her heart flutter. The beats were so erratic, Laura was unsure if it was possible to ever slow them down again. He chased hot kisses down her neck and her collarbone, lingering in the sensitive dip of her neck. Everywhere that he touched and kissed her left a heated sensation behind. She let out a moan as she called out his name. It was like sweet nothings to his ears. He groaned again as her hands caressed his chest and his stomach. Freddie chased kisses along her cleavage. He could see the nipple buds straining against the material. His fingers expertly caressed them through the material of her top. Laura leant her head back and gasped as another moan escaped her beautifully shaped lips. She was like putty in his hands. And he loved it. Freddie knew that he had to stop at this point otherwise he wouldn't be able to keep his self-control anymore. He wanted to make love to her but he knew that it wasn't the time or place. Not for her first time. Breaking off the kiss he asked, "Wanna join me for a swim in the cooling water?"

"But I didn't bring any swimwear with me." "Neither did I." he teased.

"Erm… maybe I shouldn't. I'll just watch you from the bank whilst you swim. As tempting as it sounds, I'll pass."

"Then join me then if it's that tempting," he replied as he lifted his shirt, removing it to reveal an impeccable torso. He was sculpted in the right places; his muscles were well defined. He was astonishingly gorgeous.

"Woah! You got a nice body, baby. I really like it," she said with confidence although she blushed.

Freddie turned and gave her a cheeky grin in appreciation, then dropped his pants.

Laura covered her eyes and looked away embarrassed even though she was battling with the urge to look at him standing there in all his glory. When he walked away towards the water, Laura couldn't resist staring at Freddie between half splayed fingers. She watched as his muscles flexed all over his back.

Freddie waded in and began swimming. "Come on in baby. The water is refreshingly lovely."

The temptation Laura felt over road the first initial answer she said. So, she removed her top and her skirt and head towards the cooling water. Laura didn't notice the stillness of Freddie as he had stopped swimming and was now staring in her direction. He stared at her intently, with a pleasing, mischievous grin across his face. As soon as Laura waded into the water, she couldn't see Freddie at all. She was looking anxiously around for him and began to panic. Freddie crept up slowly pretending to be a shark hunting its prey, and popped up behind her from under the water. He held her in his arms once again, as he kissed her neck.

Laura felt the urge to pound her fists against his chest but couldn't. With her body so tense at first, slowly she relaxed under his touch and leant into his solid muscled chest. The way that he held her so lovingly she didn't want to break that.

Freddie whispered in her ear, "You are so gorgeous. Do you know that baby?" as he peppered her neck with little kisses, causing her to giggle. Grunting they broke the embrace both looking a little disappointed to let go. They swam around chasing each other back and forth for a while, splashing water at each other in a playful manner as they laughed aloud, enjoying every moment of their time in the cooling water. Their laughter filled the air, along with the chirping of the birds, the rustling of the cool breeze through the tree branches. Time drifted by unbeknown to them as they were caught up in the bliss of the moment. This was the first time in a long while that Laura felt really free from monitoring eyes. Almost everywhere she went it felt as though someone was watching her. Often, she felt uneasy but decided against telling her mother anything. It could just be her own paranoia, she hoped.

Laura tried to get on with her everyday life as if nothing was completely and utterly wrong.

'*Who was she kidding, eh!*' Something plagued at the back of her suspicious mind but she dares not be inquisitive. In the pit of her stomach Laura could feel that something was definitely wrong. What it was she was unsure. Every day was torture from bullies. Her mother was acting as though she was a burden most of the times with her confusing, and strange behaviour. Freddie broke her trail of thoughts when he threw water at her face. Laura swam after him but couldn't catch him, so she faked a pulled muscle in her right leg. At first Freddie stared at her with suspicion and concern but then swam back to her side to help her. Laura sneakily lightly tapped him on the shoulder and swam off as fast as she could.

"Hey! Clever clogs. Nice try but you're not getting away that easily," he sneered behind her, before swimming after her.

In his heart he made a wish that this moment would continue for the rest of his life.

He truly loved her and wanted to be with Laura. She was a ray of sunshine that made his day, every time he saw her. He wanted the life that these happy moments with Laura promised. It was an unspoken solemn promise that he hoped to fulfil for the both of them. They were so happy together and he didn't want anything or anyone to jeopardise that. He knew now that he needed, in fact had to, protect the love of his life. But Freddie knew that it wasn't that easy to accomplish. Too many obstacles stood in their way but he was not going to go down without a fight. He would trade his life for hers if it meant that she could live happy and in peace, even if that meant it was without him as bitter as that might sound.

As the sun was setting in the sky, reality sunk in, so they came out of the water and got themselves dressed. They packed up the picnic items and placed them back in the picnic basket, including the blanket. Laura tiptoed over and placed a soft kiss on Freddie's lips and smiled loving at him. It tugged at his heart because he knew that as much as he loved her, there was a lot that they needed to overcome before being completely free to be together.

Laura turned and began making her way out towards the path to exit their sanctuary with Freddie close beside her as quickly as they could. When Laura was halfway home, Freddie felt the urge to express his undying love to her, letting her know how much he loved and wanted to be with her. In turn Laura expressed her love for Freddie and sealed it with a passionate steamy kiss. Breathless they both came up for air. Panting quite fast from their kiss. "Lau, I could meet you tomorrow for 12:30pm, at our sanctuary, don't forget. If you want to bring swimwear or a change of clothing with you. I'm going to surely miss you Mon Cherie. Until tomorrow when I have you in my arms again where you belong."

"I'll miss you too honey. I can't wait for tomorrow."

Freddie did his usual gentlemanly deed of escorting Laura directly to her front door, said his goodbyes and waited for her to go into the house, but not before Laura, taking one last glance in his direction with a gorgeous, heart racing smile, before closing the door behind her.

The next day couldn't come quickly enough for Laura. She was getting impatient. The excitement was too much too bear. Laura was counting down the hours as they went by. She was unsure when she fell asleep, but woke up as soon as her alarm sounded. She got out of bed and packed her rucksack with her swimwear items and rushed to get herself washed and ready for her encounter with Freddie. Afterwards, Laura zoomed out of the house after telling her mother she was going to meet up with Freddie again. She left earlier than expected to surprise Freddie, however, before she could get to her destination the bus she was on got caught up in slow moving traffic near enough at a standstill, due to an accident where a pedestrian got ran over by a truck carrying bales of hay. As much as Laura felt sorry for the pedestrian and wished them a speedy recovery, she was getting quite agitated as the time was drawing near when she was due to arrive and meet Freddie at their sanctuary. She had less than five minutes to get there and she was still at least twenty minutes away. Laura was getting worried and hoped that Freddie wouldn't think that she wasn't coming. *'Freddie, you must be there by now. I'm on my way darling. Just give me some time.'*

There was no way of letting him know that she was delayed on the bus and the reasons why. She was praying hard that he'd wait for her.

Unbeknown to Laura, Freddie was not waiting at the sanctuary for her to arrive.

Instead, he had turned up at her house to tell her that there had been an emergency and he had to go back to France to take care of his grandmother who was still unwell. As he knocked on the front door, he could just imagine the sunken look that would be plastered on Laura's face and it broke his heart. He knew that he owed her the courtesy of telling her face to face.

However, as a just in case measure he wrote a letter to Laura to let her know what was going on and how one day he would come back for her so that they could be together. The opening of the door distracted his train of thoughts. Margaret seemed to be in a huff as she addressed him, but Freddie ignored her irritation and smiled his most dazzling smile.

"Hi, Margaret, is Laura here?" he asked with urgency.

Margaret creased her brows together and stared at him intently from head to toe. "How could she be, when she went to meet you?" she rudely asked.

"I went there first but she wasn't there."

`Oh Mon Cherie, where are you? I wanted to see your beautiful face before I leave. I need to say goodbye to you and explain myself. I didn't want you to believe that I'm walking away from us, but this is exceptional circumstances. I promise that I will never forget you and I will one day come back for you. I'll write to....'`

The honking of the horn behind Freddie revealed a car parked in front of the driveway. There was a man sitting in the driver's seat with the window rolled halfway down looking at Freddie with impatience, reminding him that they were pressed for time to catch his flight. Freddie wanted to wait around for Laura but knew that he couldn't. His father was quite insistent that they got a move on.

`Oh no! Laura where could you be? Hopefully you'll understand that I couldn't wait.'`

"Please can you give this to your daughter for me? I have to get going now as time is of the essence. Please could you tell her that I said that I am very sorry to have let her down today? Please tell her that I had to leave for France to take care of my sick grandmother and try to help her recover. Let her know that I'll be back as soon as I can and that I would miss her more that I can explain," he sniffled as the tears rolled down his face.

Feeling heartbroken Freddie wiped away his tears and extended out his hand with the letter perched between two fingers towards Margaret. Margaret grimaced but still accepted it. "Okay, no problem. You go, I'll give her your letter when she gets back. I wish you a safe flight and your grandmother a speedy recovery," she said with a strained smile across her face.

After reluctantly handing over the letter, Freddie dragged his feet as he walked away slowly towards the parked car, as if hadn't wanted to leave, but knew that he had to.

* * *

Finally, Laura arrived at their special place and searched for Freddie but he was nowhere to be found. She felt saddened by the fact, but decided that maybe he might be held up in traffic, too. She waited until the sun was setting but still there was no sign of Freddie. Her mood felt dampened, tears filled her eyes and her heart felt like it had been ripped out of her chest. Choking on the sobs the tears kept rolling down her face one after the other with no sign of stopping. Her crying was hysterical as she couldn't believe that he couldn't even have the decency to tell her to her face that he didn't want to be with her anymore, that he'd changed his mind about meeting up with her again. He had made her feel so happy, loved, special and safe, but now she felt cheap, used and unwanted. A discarded feeling took over her and she didn't like it.

`He ambushed my heart. Tricked me into believing I was someone special. He fooled my senses, overcrowded my mind and dreams with constant thoughts of him but didn't mean it. Why was I so stupid as to allow him to do that to me? Am I that gullible? Did he not love me?'

Screaming aloud she shouted into the air as it carried off in the wind, "why me?

Always me. When will I learn not to trust so easily?"

Scraping together what little energy she had left she washed her face and made her way back home. When she arrived, she went straight to her bedroom threw herself on her bed and cried her eyes out. Margaret heard when Laura got in and went upstairs to check in on her. As she approached the bedroom door, she could hear her daughter crying and was concerned.

"Laura honey, what's the matter?" asked Margaret half believing that she had an idea already.

"He didn't show up mum. He made me believe that he would and then he failed me," she cried.

"Typical guy, dear. That's how they are. I'm so sorry darling. Maybe it's for the best," Margaret said slyly, already knowing the real reason why Freddie didn't show up to meet her daughter, but refusing to tell her or give her the letter as she was glad that Freddie was gone from her daughter's life.

The days, the weeks, the months and the years was a struggle for Laura to mend her broken heart and become stronger. She barricaded her heart as she grew up away from prying guys who tried to get her attention as she blossomed into a beautiful, curvaceous young woman. She shielded herself from more hurt and anguish. It had now been eight years since she'd last seen Freddie, but felt as though she was much stronger to continue living life without him. Laura was considering possibly dating again.

Chapter 14

"Are you okay Miss?" asked the stranger as he stood there facing her, looking so battered.

Zapping back to the present, she responded with a baffled look on her face. "I'm alright sir, why do you ask?"

He looked at her so strangely as if she had taken leave of all the senses she'd obtained at creation. He was puzzled as to why such a beautiful young lady looked like she was carrying the whole world upon her little shoulders.

No way, you can't tell me she cannot feel her tears.

"Forgive me for prying my dear, but is it that you're feeling sad about a loved one here in the hospital?"

He watched on so intrigued to see what her reaction would be. Laura buried her head in her hands and nodded her head signalling 'yes' to the stranger.

"I'm so sorry, my dear, I hope they have a speedy recovery. I'll pray for you."

The puzzled look vanished from his bloodied face and it was replaced by sincerity and sympathy. Now he understood the reason for her tears and the look of distress that was written in her eyes. "You look heartbroken my dear, so trust in god and he will put it right."

This made Laura's head snap up as if she got a slap to the face and she gazed at him blankly.

What the hell was he talking about? Heartbroken but why would I be heartbroken? I just don't get it.

Just as soon as he said that he smiled at her and bid her farewell. Laura called after him and said thank you and asked if he was going to be okay, recognising and registering the blood all over his t-shirt, his hands and his face. It was somewhat dried in and flaking, which told her that it was a while ago since his injury, or injuries it seemed. He walked with a limp and a slight sway as if he was about to collapse but didn't. He held himself up as firmly as he could with the little strength that he could muster. He waved at her and said that even though she had her own heartbreak to contend with, he could see that she still worried about others. "You're an angel," he yelled out to Laura before disappearing through the A&E entrance automated doors.

Laura wondered what had happened to the stranger that she she'd just been talking to. She prayed in her mind that he would be just fine. She thought that he must be in a lot of pain of his own, but stopped to check on her instead before attending to his own needs.

How kind she thought. At least good people exist in the world now, but not when I was growing up.

She raised her hand to stroke her cheek and realised exactly what made the guy stop to check on her.

What! How could I not know? It doesn't make any sense to me. No wonder he was staring at me so strangely, like if I've gone insane. Have I? I was bloody well crying and didn't even know. What a fool I am! Why the hell would I be crying though? I don't understand.

A sudden chill washed over her as the sun began to slowly set over the horizon. She wrapped her arms around herself and shivered for what seemed a brief moment. It was springtime so Laura didn't think that she had needed a cardigan to wrap around her when she left home. Now she felt the chill in the air she wished that she had brought a cardigan with her. She didn't plan on being out all day but couldn't bear to leave Claire long enough to go home and get it. Also, she was in no hurry to return home despite her mother being there, especially after her experience the night before, when she was alone at the house. Realising that she had sat there for what seemed like to be an hour and a half, Laura thought to herself that the healthcare assistant most likely believed that she had gone home. Without even a second's thought she got up and grabbed her handbag, juice and the rubbish from her sandwich and began making her way out of the hospital gardens. Eventually, she stopped by the bin near the main entrance and disposed of the rubbish.

With that done, she walked through the automated doors towards the lift. Her mind drifted on to Amie and wondered if maybe she should pop in and see her; see if she needed anything. Yes, she thought, she would definitely do just that. She stepped into the lift and pushed the fifth-floor button. When she arrived at the fifth floor the lift door opened with a ping and she stood there half frozen not sure if she should go visit or just go straight to Claire's room. Perhaps Josh might be there by now she thought. He better be. That way Claire would have someone sitting with her until she returned. Plus come to think of it she would need a shoulder to lean on, just in case.

Stop thinking so negative girl. She is not dying. She would wake up eventually. She has too.

As the lift doors were about to close, Laura snapped out of it and made her way down the children's ward corridor in search of her new found friend, Amie. Fast approaching the room, she paused at the doorway, not knowing what she was going to say or talk about. She popped her head in but saw a few people already in there with Amie. They looked like they were having an interesting conversation as Amie seemed engrossed in it. She burst out laughing, but winced in pain as reality kicked in for her, reminding her that her injuries were still there. A brown-haired lady rose to her feet and sat next to her by her bedside and cuddled her asking if she was okay. Laura presumed that the lady was Amie's mother as she could see the resemblance. At this point Amie was in extreme agony, but it still didn't stop her from seeing Laura at the door through teary eyes. She signalled for her to come in, but Laura promised her that she would pop by the next day when Amie was less in pain.

"I'll call the nurse for you, okay. Please feel better," she mouthed quietly.

Amie smiled the best she could before Laura turned and walked away to the nurses' station to inform the nurse sitting behind the desk about Amie. After she had done that, she then turned and headed in the direction of the lifts. When she arrived at the seventh floor she hesitated before pushing herself towards Claire's room. Sharon was just on her way out of the room when she almost bumped directly into Laura.

"Hey! I thought that you decided to go home as to why you were gone for such a long time. Are you okay? Did you eat as I advised you to?" she asked.

"Oh no I'm still here for a while yet. Yes, I did eat, thank you. How did the procedure go? Any change?" queried Laura.

"No change, I'm afraid. The procedure went as well as expected," Sharon told her with an apologetic smile on her face.

"I have to go now, duty calls. I'm finishing my shift in two hours if you want a lift home as you said that you didn't drive here. I'll check in with you at the end of my shift," said Sharon.

"Okay, thank you. You are too kind," responded Laura.

Laura entered the room, and was ecstatic to see Josh standing there by the bedside. He didn't look as though he was pleased about something. He appeared remorseful and guilty but he kept his thoughts to himself.

She walked up to him and hugged him, and said, "I think that she would pull through this. Claire is tougher and stronger than we give her credit for. Don't you think?"

"Yes, yes sure she is ... Definitely," replied Josh.

"I can't stay too long though Laura, as I'm on call tonight. Claire wouldn't even know that I'm here," he said, boldly. "She wouldn't give a damn either as she doesn't love me anymore," he mumbled under his breath, so Laura couldn't hear it.

"I understand your position Josh. It's okay to feel helpless, hurt and in despair. Plus, what could you do if you're on call? Someone has to do it otherwise sick people would continue to suffer in pain."

"Are you okay though? How are you holding up, as I know how close you two are as best friends," asked Josh in concern.

"Ermm.... I'm broken, I'm still in shock but I can only try my best to be here for Claire."

"Even on her intensive care bed she has people who would stand by her side and remain loyal to her. Ha! Ha! Ha! It's a shame she doesn't know the meaning of such qualities. She doesn't possess this inside of her at all," he added with a sinister laugh.

"Josh! What are you babbling about? What do you mean by what you just said?" asked Laura curiously.

"It doesn't matter, Laura. It doesn't matter."

Josh spoke like a broken man who had lost his world somewhere and didn't know where to search to retrieve it. He seemed so distant towards Claire but was trying to put on a brave act in front of Laura. It felt to Laura like Josh was forcing himself to be there and she couldn't bear to watch the strain on his face anymore so told him,

"The shackles are released, so whenever you are ready you can go back to work. For what it's worth, you are a kind hearted man and I hope that you find whatever it is you are searching for."

Reassuring herself through motivation she tried to make Josh believe what she was about to say.

"I'll be here with her, so I will keep an eye on her to the best I can. When you're ready to come back and see her and find out more about her condition don't hesitate to call me as well as calling the hospital."

Josh gazed at Laura in shock, as he'd never hear her speak like that before. She was always so calm and level headed. He assumed that she was being over protective about Claire, as after all, they are best friends as well as flat mates. He couldn't get irritated with Laura because she had always been so sweet to him. Also, she is a good friend and he'd be damned if he'd let Claire ruin that too. Time after time when he needed someone to confide in, she was the point of contact and she'd always been there without fail and vice versa.

Josh wasn't sure whether to walk out or stay a while, until he was beeped on his pager. He stood there in two minds with Laura staring at him wide eyed, with those beautiful big eyes she had. He truly loved Claire but a couple of weeks before their last encounter, things felt as though they were going belly up between them. Claire didn't appear to be happy. He hardly saw her and they hardly spent quality time together. He couldn't contemplate as to why this was, because Claire refused to have a heart-to-heart talk and he couldn't force her to speak to him. What sealed their fate was that last encounter, when Claire spontaneously dropped in on him all dressed up in a mini black dress. She stank of alcohol and grilled food. She kept apologising to him, but he didn't understand at that point as to why until after she left and he reflected back on a night when he went out with some work colleagues to the new cocktail restaurant bar in town. What he saw was enough to break any strong man down. He didn't approach Claire at the time, instead he tucked himself away in the corner where he sat and watched from a distance. The more he watched the scene unfold the more it ripped him apart. He couldn't believe that his girlfriend was cheating on him. He couldn't ditch his colleagues and boss as it was a work celebration that had been pending for a while. He put on a brave face even when all he wanted to do was to crawl under a rock and shrivel up and die somewhere, but instead he had to pretend like he was enjoying the evening. That night was enough to seal their fate but unfortunately despite everything he still loved her.

Perhaps it's not enough anymore so it's time for me to let go. Our relationship is no longer built on solid qualities such as love, trust and honesty. She betrayed me and that cannot be changed. It seems like I wasn't enough for her, no matter what I've tried.

Everything that she'd ever wanted I've given her and more.

Some part of Josh knew that if he was to forgive Claire, the trust would never return and how can a relationship survive on one way love alone?

The jokes on you, you idiot!

He felt so frustrated and angry. He couldn't be there anymore. Wanting, in fact needing, to escape, he grabbed the work bag and was ready to storm out of the room. Laura sat there observing his battle with himself. Not knowing what was going on inside his head, she remained as silent as a church mouse. A part of her knew that it had to be something to do with her best friend, Claire, as it always was. She stood up and approached where Josh stood facing the window peering outside.

"You know that if you need to talk then I'm here for you anytime. There's no rush, take your time and whenever you're ready come find me," explained Laura.

Afterwards she patted him on his shoulder, and was just about to remove her hand, when he quickly reached up and grabbed her hand keeping it in place. They both turned and looked at each other. He opened his mouth as if about to say something to her but somehow refrained himself from saying whatever it was that he wanted to say. Closing his mouth again, he squeezed her hand in a gesture to say 'thank you' still leaving his hand over hers until he finally let it fall away, back down to his side. Laura sat back down with her mind in worry not only for Claire, but for Josh as well. Feeling drained from all that thinking she leant her head back against the wall and closed her eyes almost drifting off to sleep.

Josh leant against the window sill, day dreaming with his eyes focussed on Laura as she eases into a light sleep. He could hear the change in her breathing as it became more relaxed and deeper. It was time to make his move but he just couldn't do it. He knew this was the time that Laura needed to go home and rest but he couldn't offer her a lift as he was on call and could be paged at any given moment for an emergency, and he couldn't leave her stranded. Going forward he approached Claire's bedside and said his goodbyes. Then he approached where Laura sat sleeping, crouched down to her level and woke her up, to query how she was getting home. In a daze, Laura explained that the healthcare assistant had offered to give her a lift after she completed her shift, so she'd be okay. In reassurance she raised a lazy hand and touched his cheek and smiled. "You really are sweet, don't worry about me tonight. I'll be alright. Good luck with your on-call duties my friend."

Josh smiled back and rose back to his feet. Picking up his stuff, he kissed Claire on the forehead and turned to walk away.

Suddenly, when he got to the door, he could vaguely hear a weakened voice saying, "Please Josh don't go!"

Chapter 15

Pitifully, Josh walked out of the hospital room. He wanted to stay with her but knew it wasn't possible. He had to leave. He needed to leave. Continuing his way out of the main entrance, he stood outside the doors in the cooling breeze torn between leaving and staying.

He inhaled and exhaled so deeply. His mind was in a scramble, but before returning to work, he needed to get it fully focussed before he makes a detrimental mistake, tonight. All he could see before him was that puppy-eyed look. Her eyes spoke volumes. She had that look of 'I need you'. Or is he fooling himself again.

She couldn't, could she?

It took a lot for him to force himself to continue his journey. He popped into his car and started the ignition. The engine roared to life with the readiness to cruise the open roads to take him to his destination. Although his mindset was on the destination ahead, he couldn't get the image of her erased from his head. Just as soon as Josh had switched off the engine to go back upstairs, his pager went off with an emergency bleep. Using the car phone, he called the number written on the pager screen. The person on the other end of the line exchanged the important details that he required about the patient and where he needed to be, then ended the call. Collecting the information, Josh entered the postcode into his GPS and drove off as quickly as he could. His previous thoughts had to be buried as far as he possibly could shove them, as this was not an appropriate time. Josh arrived at the destination in less than ten minutes. He assesses the patient and her injuries. Based on the injuries he made a swift and effective decision taking into consideration the patient's current and previous medical history. After his diagnosis of the patient Mrs Jones, he explained to her in simple format what her injuries were and what the plan of action needed to be. Despite the fact that Mrs Jones was unhappy with his decision, as she hated hospitals since her husband Bill had died there from a heart failure some time ago, Josh managed to convince her that she needed to be admitted for treatment. She accepted and trusted Josh's medical knowledge and expertise. Therefore, agreed to be admitted into hospital to do the relevant tests and get the treatment that she needed. Josh had to prescribe her some morphine as he knew that although she was trying to hide it, she was in extreme agony.

In order to reassure her, he found himself promising to accompany her to the hospital to ensure that she got settled in and the relevant tests and treatment was in place for her. Mrs Jones expressed her gratitude and he then called the ambulance to transport her to the hospital. The paramedics arrived shortly afterwards. Mrs Jones' blood pressure was significantly high. Even though she was given a morphine injection the pain was still intense because she had a fractured hip bone. Being the first on call to arrive at the scene, Josh gave a handover to the ambulance crew.

They strapped Mrs Jones to the stretcher and wheeled her out to the parked ambulance. Making sure to be cautious not to hurt her any more than necessary. Once she was securely strapped in, Josh turned around and spoke to Grace,

"I will follow the ambulance in my car, darling. So, I will see you when we get to the hospital."

"Okay doc, I will see you shortly," responded Grace as she winced through the pain.

Josh followed on whilst the ambulance sped along as quickly as possible to the hospital. When they arrived, Grace was wheeled inside where handovers were done and she was sent for an x-ray, followed by other tests. After she was transferred to the ward, Josh told her that he needed to go, so wished her well and took his leave.

The pager went off again, so he made a call using the phone at the nurses' station, wrote the details on a paper then bolted down the corridor towards the main entrance. Getting into his car he zoomed down the road to the next emergency call. The night was filled with emergencies including two vehicle collisions. There were emergencies he handled on his own without the need for intervention but on both occasions, he had to get the victims of the vehicle collisions air lifted via air ambulance to a nearby hospital. By the time his on call shift was over he was absolutely shattered. He kicked off his shoes as soon as he entered his home, and stripped off his clothes one by one, and threw them into the wash basket.

Desperately, he needed a shower, breakfast and a good sleep. But getting home, showering and eating wasn't the hard part for Josh. It was the shutting down when he climbed into bed. His brain was still in doctor mode. He rang the hospital to check in on Mrs Jones and was told that she was in surgery. With that confirmed he was able to close his eyes for the first time in hours. Falling into a deep sleep at last, his body exhausted but completely relaxed, the image of those big 'I need you' eyes came before him. He dreamt of her and he shouldn't have. He didn't want to, or at least that's what he wanted to believe. 'Josh, please don't leave' came the familiar voice again in his dream. It did something to him. His body reacted to it. He became tense, aroused and became even more baffled as to what the next step should be. For a doctor he of all people knew that hearts are fragile things that needs to be taken good care of. Right now, he was not sure if he would be able to give that as much as he would want to. He had always cared for her deeply as a friend, but lately through all the stress and strains, his emotional state was going haywire. The dream was taunting him, teasing his heart strings, his emotional and mental stability was in tatters and his manhood strained.

Awaking to find that he had been sleeping for a mere two hours, his breathing erratic, he calmed himself down and forced himself to go back to sleep as he knew that more sleep was needed or he would become like the walking dead. When he got up again, he would check in on Laura and see if she was okay and perhaps swing by to see Claire. He grimaced at the last thought because everything that he had witnessed came flooding back to him ten-fold like a kick to the guts.

Today he had a day off because he had been on call all night. He would find something relaxing and stress free to do, hopefully. Whatever it was he didn't want it to be boring otherwise it would give him room to think and he didn't want to think. He slept continuously for another six hours. This time luckily, he didn't dream of her.

Meanwhile, Laura was at home having an in-depth conversation with her mother about the hospital visit she had when she saw Claire. Margaret seemed to sympathise with

Claire's condition as she was quite tearful at the news. Laura didn't know what to think of her mother's reaction.

Maybe mum is fond of Claire after all.

Her mother had never appeared to be too keen on Claire. When Laura first moved in with Claire, Margaret had objected very strongly. In her eyes Claire wasn't good enough to share a house with her daughter. However, despite her mother's objections Laura was defiant and disobedient and didn't listen to her mother's opinion on the matter. Not long afterwards, Margaret began dropping in unannounced on them both. Laura wasn't too keen on her mother's habits so had to warn her off. Out of the blue, her mother's attitude and behaviour towards Claire became polite and accepting but sometimes Laura couldn't help thinking that her mum was only pretending.

Claire on the other hand loved Margaret like she was her own mother. She wished that she had someone that cared that much to check on her like that. Often, she would tell Laura how lucky she was to have a mother who cared that much because it was not easy having no one. Often Laura would wonder what she meant by such a statement, but Claire refused to talk about it. She said it was too painful and depressing to talk about, so they'd always change the subject.

"Guess what mum! I thought I saw a guy resembling Freddie?" announced Laura. "Really? And where was this?" asked Margaret looking a little on edge.

"He was at the hospital mum. He came into Claire's room to complete a medical procedure." Explained Laura to her mother.

"But he's a plumber darling. Was there a leaking tap or a blocked toilet that required his services as to why he was there?" asked Margaret sarcastically as she giggled.

"Mum! I'm serious. This is no joke," shouted Laura at her mother for the first time.

Margaret was taken aback by the panic in her daughter's eyes and the fact that she had raised her voice at her.

"Okay! So did he say hello to you?" asked her mother curiously. "No, he didn't unfortunately," she said in disappointment.

"If he didn't say hello then maybe you were mistaken my dear. It may not be him," stated Margaret as she crossed her fingers behind her back, and prayed that it wasn't Freddie.

"Maybe you're right mum. But what if it turns out to be him?" asked Laura excitedly.

"Then you don't allow him in again. Remember how your life was destroyed by him?

Years of hurt and anguish. Don't make that happen again," warned Margaret.

"All I want is an explanation about why he didn't say goodbye, and why he did that to me?" replied Laura.

At this point, Laura could see the sheer panic written on her mum's face and the fear in her eyes. "Mum what's wrong?" she asked in confusion.

"Oh, it's nothing sweetie," responded her mother, not believing her own statement.

"I think that you should just avoid this Freddie character. If he approaches you, ignore him. Tell him to leave you alone as you want nothing to do with him." advised Margaret.

"I don't know if I can resist the urge to talk to him if he wants to talk. If he wants to explain himself, and I do think that I deserve an explanation, I would hear him out. I need closure, mum. I really do."

Margaret's heart galloped even quicker than normal. She was scared that her daughter would find out the truth, that Freddie came to the house to say goodbye and explain why he had to leave. Laura mustn't find out that she Margaret knew that he had written a letter and left it with her to give to Laura. She could not let her find out the truth, that each week a letter came through the post from Freddie whilst he was away. He had rung the house at least three times a day trying to catch Laura, but Margaret would always make up an excuse as to why Laura couldn't come to the phone at that moment. The worst part was that, she'd already known that Freddie was back in the country from France because not only did he call the house when he got off the plane, he also showed up at the house unannounced and she had turned him away. And then she was elated when Laura moved out of the area to live with Claire so she knew that Laura wouldn't bump into Freddie.

Never in her wildest thoughts did Margaret dream that Laura would ever bump into Freddie again. Now she was worried that he might tell Laura the truth and she would hate her for it. She recalled each and every day when her daughter would always ask her if Freddie called for her, and her response on all occasions was no. She saw how upset her daughter was for a long time as she moped around the house. She knew that she had to do something. She had to stop them from ever talking again. Now her devious brain needed to start producing ideas.

"Maybe you should stay home and rest today and I'll go to the hospital and visit Claire on your behalf," suggested Margaret.

"Oh, sorry mum, I personally have to go because I made a promise to Amie that I would spend some time with her. But thanks a lot for the offer though, mum. I appreciate it."

"Okay, then how about I spend time with Claire keeping her company and you spend time with your friend, Amie?" suggested Margaret.

"That'll be great mum. Thanks. Wait a minute! Mum what about your flower shop business? Who's looking after that?" queried Laura.

"Oh Betty, my next- door neighbour, is looking after the business for me till I get back." Margaret said.

"Well, that's settled then. Brilliant!" stated Margaret.

Margaret felt a pang of relief. She couldn't believe that Laura had accepted her suggestion. At that thought, she could rest easy knowing that she could keep them as far apart as possible, so the secret wouldn't come out.

Before long they both got themselves ready to go to the hospital. They booked a taxi to transport them to the hospital. "That reminds me. I'll meet you back at home later Laura, so don't wait for me after you see Amie."

"Okay mum."

Laura was looking forward to spending some time with Amie and find out how she was feeling after the extreme pain that she was in yesterday. It scared her seeing someone in excruciating pain and that's why she bottled it and didn't enter the room when Amie invited her inside. It didn't prevent her from thinking about Amie and wondering whether or not she was feeling much better. This somehow swung her mind back on Freddie. As she sat there around the dining table, her disbelief at seen Freddie returned. She knew it was inevitable that they would set eyes on each other again, and at some point, exchange a conversation. She needed answers and he would not escape her wrath. She was still angry, really angry at him, for leaving her, not finding her or even contacting her at all. Most of all she was hurt, her heart felt weak, broken all over again, but a part of her felt betrayed by her body and mind.

The attraction seems to still exist and he kept taking over her thoughts. A big part of her still wanted him and that angered her even more. He didn't deserve her love anymore, so why did she still want to give hers to him. She wanted to move on from that hurt and pain. Find someone who would love, cherish and appreciate her. Someone who would always be there for her through thick and thin.

Damn it! Not again. He can't do this to me again. I won't let him.

* * *

"Hey girl! How's it going? Sorry I couldn't stop yesterday. I just can't stand seeing anyone in pain. Forgive me," said Laura apologetically.

"It's cool. I figured. At least you told the nurse. Cheers." "How's your friend?" asked Amie curiously.

"Yesterday there was no change. My mum is there with her now, she told me she would come get me if there's any change in Claire's condition."

"And you trust that, do you?" asked Amie.

"I suppose that I do. I mean, why wouldn't I trust my mother?" asked Laura as if convincing herself.

"From such a statement Laura, it sounds like you are a little doubtful. Has something happened between you guys to make you be so doubtful of the trust barrier between you and your mother?" asked Amie not meaning to pry in Laura's personal life.

"Trust me, Amie girl, it's a long story and I wouldn't know where to start to be honest," responded Laura.

"All I can say is, be sure of who you trust, who you allow within as even the closest person to you can betray your trust. Something my mum and dad always say to me, advised Amie.

"Thank you I will bear that in mind." Said Laura with acceptance.

The rest of the day was spent playing games, chilling and chatting about all sorts of girly things. They giggled so much that their stomachs hurt. They ate all the goodies that Laura took to the hospital for Amie. Their stomachs were like bear pouches so crammed with food and drink that they couldn't take another bite. Later on in the afternoon, Amie became so tired that Laura excused herself and told her that she would come back another day to check in on her. "This is my number, Amie. You can call me if you need anything."

"Thank you. I will bear that in mind. I hope that I can call you even if I don't need anything."

"Of course, you can sweetie," said Laura.

"Thank you for an amazing time. It's been so long since I had such a good laugh and not have to worry about my health," said Amie.

"My pleasure. It was fun for me, also. Catch ya later," said Laura.

Spontaneously, Laura reached out and gave Amie a tight hug. To Amie that felt as if it was a goodbye forever but she returned it and dismissed the thought from her head.

"Later kiddo," she joked to Laura.

They both smiled and Laura skipped through the door with one last backwards glance at her new pal. Suddenly she hesitated half way down the corridor staring in the direction of the main entrance door. It was no longer sunny outside. The weather was gloomy and it had begun to fade into darkness as if it was going to rain. The air that forced its way through the automated doors felt humid. The crack of thunder made her jump. She recalled that she'd never liked thunder storms. The thunder cracked again and this time a flash of lightning followed. Laura was grateful that she was inside the hospital where she could cowardly hide out for a while until it had calmed down enough for her to make her way home. From the past, since hearing about so many car accidents here and there on the news, unless it was deemed necessary, Laura was always reluctant to go behind the wheel of any vehicle without someone to accompany her on the journey. Previously when her boss had begged her to go on an errand on his behalf, she travelled by public transport making it just in time. Although driving would be the key element to travelling around more quickly, instead she buried her driving license behind all her credit cards so she couldn't see it when she looked in her purse. A more lengthy, louder roll of thunder bellowed out, accompanied by a heavier downpour of rain interrupting her thoughts. Outside people ran under the nearest shelter or belted through the entrance door to shield themselves from the rain.

Oh my! I was planning to linger here till late but I don't think that I'll bother. Mum would have called me if there were any changes with Claire. All of a sudden it dawned on her, how unrested she was as she felt the fatigue holding her body to ransom. Laura decided to face the dreadful rainstorm outside where she boarded the bus at the nearby bus stop and made her way home. By the time she got inside her front door, she was completely drenched, her clothes dripping puddles of water all around her feet. She walked with a squelch with the rain water soaked shoes on. Her hair hung down her back in wet curly ringlets. Her clothes stuck to her body, showing every curve. She rushed to the bathroom, pulled off her wet things, showered and put on her comfy pyjamas, before making herself a cup of hot cocoa and plonking herself in front of the television. Not before long she made her way upstairs with the intention of having an early night. She could not sleep because the noises outside from the rainstorm kept disturbing her. So, Laura walked up to her bedroom window and sat on the window seat peering outside watching the storm do its worst. It was quite soothing to watch to be honest. She sat there deep in a trance until something caught her eye. There was someone outside. Someone in the front yard standing under the oak tree. From the outline, she couldn't figure out if it was a woman or a man. He or she was staring up at her as if he knew where her bedroom window was. It was creepy. They didn't look away. Laura fell off her window seat to the floor with a thud scared shitless as once again she felt hounded. Who was that looking up at her bedroom window staring right through her, and what did they want with her? Was it the same person that had been watching her in the swimming pool two nights ago?

Slowly she popped her head back up and looked out to see if the person was still there and they were. Whoever it was pointed at her, and signalled for her to come outside but she slowly shook her head in a 'no' gesture. She prayed that the person wouldn't force entry into her home. She'd hoped that her mother would be back by now but unfortunately, she wasn't. Is this the person responsible for Claire's car accident? Was it him or her who was following them in the BMWx5 about a week and a half ago? Her mind was conjuring up so many questions sending her into panic mode. Someone was following her; a few days ago, on her way home from work, but she thought it was just her imagining things. Now she knew it was very real. Her heartbeat quickened to the point that she could hear the pounding of the beats in her head. It was deafening her; she couldn't think straight. Her palms were clammy and beads of cold sweat were plastered all over her forehead. She was sweating all over her body profusely. Her knees felt weak, wanting to give up on her. She forced herself to keep standing for as long as she possibly could. She could feel the warmth draining out of her body. Laura was trembling uncontrollably through fear. Grabbing hold of the window sill to sustain her balance, her knuckles were as white as a sheet. The hair strands on the back of her arms and neck were standing on end. Laura had goose bumps all over her arms. Her stomach felt nauseated. There was a large lump in her throat that felt like a tennis ball, making it difficult for Laura to swallow. Her breathing became erratic as she struggled to breathe. Suddenly, a light came from the distance as her saviour. It became brighter and brighter so the stranger darted away, running as fast as he or she could. Laura wished that she could have seen clearly enough to describe the person to a police official. Her mother wouldn't believe her, even if she did say anything. Whenever she complained about being followed or watched, Margaret would dismiss it and say she was imagining things and she needed to rest more as she was overworking herself. On the last encounter Laura got so irritated and angry at her mother for doubting her and branding her a liar, just seeking attention for herself. The police had said that unless she could describe the stalker, or if she was physically touched by the stalker then there's nothing that they could do to help her. Often Laura wondered what the point was in having police officers when they seemed to do nothing to help out anyone in danger? Laura knew that she needed to figure out how she could protect herself, although she wouldn't know where to start.

Chapter 16

Months flew by without hearing any positive news on Claire's medical progress. Josh was too busy with his work commitments to hang out with her for a while. These days he was accepting more overtime and on call jobs as if he was avoiding something. Although she wondered if it had anything to do with whatever it was that he was battling with at the hospital, there was no way of knowing. Laura knew that whenever Josh was ready to talk, he would find her. Surgery after surgery and still no results to show for them. Laura couldn't concentrate on work. She stood there in the tiny office blankly staring out of the window, a backlog of files, emails and paperwork piled upon her mahogany desk. The only thing bringing her back to reality each time was the sound of the telephone ringing, as she was always hoping that it would be the hospital with some good news. "You're no good here. Go home and we would call you if there is any change. You need rest, fresh air and you need to look after yourself, otherwise you won't be no use to your friend like this," the consultant bluntly announced to Laura each time she visited the hospital. Although she saw the point that the hospital staff were trying to make, Laura still refused to take heed. She was worried about Claire, and from time to time she wondered if Josh was okay. A while back her mother had rushed back to her home in an emergency. Laura felt scared and alone.

The image of Claire lying there helpless, strapped to so many tubes with the look of pain and discomfort was stuck in Laura's memory. Wanting to take away her friend's pain, wishing that she could magically assist in healing Claire, Laura kept wishing and hoping that she would wake up and this would all be a figment of her imagination, a dream that both of them could giggle about. How much she wanted that to be true. To hear her friend's voice, hear her laugh and Claire telling her that it was all a joke, but Laura was just fooling herself, if she believed that Claire was faking it. Her thoughts were like a runaway train at this point with no workable brakes. She could not put on the brakes long enough to sort herself out, much less to work. Every half an hour, she would call the ward to see how Claire was, but kept hearing the same old lines from the nurse on duty.

"No change I'm afraid. It's the same as I told you half an hour ago, that if there is any development, I will call you." The duty nurse would bellow down the telephone line.

Each time Laura put down the telephone another part of her died, sinking to the lowest of levels. Fright and helplessness were the only feeling that she could feel towards Claire's situation. Her body was so drained and tired, aching where it had been pushed beyond its limits. Her eyes were shadowed with dark circles and swollen, heavily laden from lack of sleep. She hadn't been able to sleep properly for so many weeks, whilst her friend laid helplessly, fighting for her life. That, alongside all those creepy episodes with this stalker following her around were making her mind venture to places it shouldn't go; she realised that it was meant to be her lying there in the hospital, not Claire. Her hand came up and cupped her mouth before she released a screech. "Oh God! I'm so, so sorry Claire. I'm so, so sorry. It was me," she kept repeating frantically.

"It really was me, but why? I don't understand," she questioned herself quizzically.

Her legs buckled under her and she fell to the floor with a thud. Tears began streaming down her face like a waterfall dripping on to the laminated floor forming a small puddle. She laid there curled up sobbing hysterically for what seemed like forever. She couldn't believe her discovery. She couldn't believe what she had done. "God! If only I had advance warning, I could have…. ," She cried out aloud letting her pleas drown out the rest of the sentence.

"I promise if you heal Claire and you let her live, I won't bring any more harm to her," Laura pleaded although she didn't really know who she was making her promise to…

At this point, Laura was wailing, her fists banging on the wooden floor, as if she was taking out her frustrations there. Shortly afterwards she sat upright and pulled her knees up and rested her chin on them as she continued crying much more quietly to prevent being overheard. Laura covered her face with her hands and cried trying to take her pain away.

Someone knocked lightly at the door and in walked Alex. Excuse me please ma'am, I was sent here to see you regarding my daughter but clearly, I can see you are somewhat pre- occupied. Is everything okay?" asked Alex with concern looking at the back of Laura's head when she turned away to dry her eyes and compose herself.

After Laura felt that she was presentable enough, she said still with her back turned, "It's okay sir, please take a seat. I'm alright now. To be honest, I forgot about our appointment, so the mistake was mine not to have been ready for you." Replied Laura much more dignified in her composure.

"Mistakes happen," came his blunt reply.

Laura walked towards her desk not giving any eye contact to the man and sat down in her black swivel chair. Swiftly she searched the pile of folders on her desk and realised that she was unsure of whose file she was trying to find. Not wanting to embarrass herself by asking for the child's name, instead, she searched her diary log to see 'Gibbons' written in as her 2pm appointment. At this point, she still hadn't made eye contact yet as she was retrieving the file from the drawer of the work desk. Laura skim read the file quickly, reminding herself of the reason for the appointment. "The reason for inviting you here today Mr Gibbons was to discuss any support that the school could provide you and your daughter, Mary, to help make the process of her learning during the times of her illness easier on the both of you. Is there anything that you would like support with, as there are options available to parents and children in your position?"

Laura looked up to await Mr Gibbon's response only to lock eyes on the very person that had been haunting her dreams. She stared wide eyed and blank faced at Alex Gibbons, shocked as the last encounter with him was in the car park at the cocktail bar in town.

I wonder if he remembered the very first time we met.

Laura subtly ran her fingers through her curly, long hair, trying to refrain from being too obvious. Alex stared at her with a smirk on his face before answering her questions. She composed herself with the professional mannerism that was required of her. "Do you mind if I take notes down to update Mary's file?"

"Please, I expect you to."

Laura smiled for the first time in a long time. It felt good to get relief from some of the stress off her shoulders. Despite the feeling in the pit of her stomach, she continued to document the relevant information that was required from Alex. She could feel his intense gaze on her every move. Her mouth felt dry, her hands felt sweaty, her pulse quickened. She took a sip of water to relieve the dryness in her throat. Automatically, she licked her lips with no pun intended. She could have sworn that his eyes darkened with desire. Laura looked down at her notepad and wrote a few more things down to distract herself from such wild hopeful thoughts. "How have you been. Laura?" asked Alex curious to know if she thought about him at all.

Laura continued the meeting, blatantly ignoring his question and continued with the task at hand as she had some important tasks to complete before she had finished for the day and she didn't want to leave the school office too late considering the weird events happening in her life at the moment. Alex took no offence to being ignored as he could see that she was troubled by something or someone. When he looked into her eyes, he could see sadness and hurt and he didn't want to add to her pressures. Her eyes were puffy and red from where she had been crying and she looked as though she could use a good night's sleep. He didn't want to pry, so he didn't ask. He was worried about what was bothering her. He wanted to know if it was because of another man. Often, he had hoped to bump into her again but little did he know that all this time she was reachable. That night they didn't get an opportunity to exchange numbers and he'd regretted it ever since. This time he wasn't going to let the opportunity pass him by. She was sitting right in front of him and he could tell that he still had an effect on her. All this time in their meeting although he was answering her questions, he was studying her body's reaction. He had noticed that Laura was struggling to maintain her professional façade and it amused him. After their conversation pertaining tp support for Mary, he extended out his hands and shook hers and whispered with gratitude, "thank you Laura."

"You're welcome, Alex. Give Mary our love. I wish her a speedy recovery."

Alex's dazzling smile almost shook her to the core. She withdrew her hand and watched him as he rose up from the chair and put on his blazer, turning to exit her office. As he walked past her desk, he dipped into his pocket and placed his business card with his personal number on the edge of her desk. Laura looked at him and smiled and continued typing up the information on her computer that Alex had given her so that it could be attached to Mary's file. When she heard the door to her office open and close, she checked to see what Alex had placed on her desk. She picked it up and saw his personal and business numbers on the card. This made her smile. Laura leant her weary head back against the back rest of her swivel chair, whilst clutching Alex's business card to her bosom. She let out a breath that she didn't realise she was holding and closed her eyes, smiling to herself as she turned the chair and she leant back so its front wheels were barely hovering off the floor.

Deep in her own thoughts the door speedily opened and zapped her out of her daydream. She snappily opened her eyes to see Alex standing there with a devilish grin across his face.

Attempting to sit up straight the chair toppled backwards and she let out a screech as the chair hit the floor with a thud, and the business card went flying through the air, landing directly in front of Alex's feet. His eyes followed the card and he bent down and retrieved it but not before looking at it to notice that it was indeed his business card. He approached Laura in a swift, fluid motion and extended his hand to help her to get up from the floor. They stared at each other for a brief moment as if in a trance. Shaking his head, he asked, "Are you okay? And do you make a habit of falling of your office chair when a parent walks in?" he chuckled. The most breathtakingly husky, deep sound that made her felt drawn in.

"Very funny but I'm fine," came her embarrassed reply with her eyes averted to the floor.

"I think that this belongs to you," said Alex with a cheeky grin as he handed the business card back to Laura.

Laura cupped her face as it reddened with embarrassment at being caught out in the act of acting like a school girl with a crush. She took a deep breath in and took the card from his hands and placed it into her handbag. "Thank you for the help, but why did you come back? Did you forget something?"

"Oh, yes, I just wanted to give you a copy of Mary's medical letters from the hospital."

Alex handed them to Laura and she scanned them on to the computer and attached them to Mary's updated file. Laura felt a little disappointed that he didn't come back for her.

Who was I kidding? He's not interested in me like that. Stop been a damn fool.

Alex watched as the flash of emotions flickered across her face during her mental battle. He reached out and held her hands and gently pulled her into his arms as he whispered in her ears, "I've wanted to do this for so long," and without another word he kissed her with a hunger like no other. At first, she stood still, in shock, her senses muddled, her body awakening rapidly to his kiss. His lips were so soft but demanding. She placed her hand on his chest feeling his heartbeats strong against her hands. If it wasn't for the solid frame of him, she wasn't sure that her feet wouldn't have buckled under the weight of her body. She leant into him, wrapping her arms around his neck, her fingers raked through his hair as he deepened the kiss between them. He groaned and whispered against her mouth, "This is even better than in my dreams."

Then he deepened the kiss again. The ringing of the telephone on her cluttered desk pulled her out of the trance he had her in. "I'm sorry Alex. I have to get this. Call me?"

She wrote her number on a sticky note pad paper and handed it to him. He took it and the medical letters, smiled and bid her farewell.

Chapter 17

Two weeks had passed since Laura had heard from Alex. Each time she picked up the phone to dial his number something stopped her from doing it. Things were getting stranger by the day and even worse in the night. Everywhere she went someone was looking at her as if something looked weird on her person. They would stare at her and when she looked in their direction they would quickly look away as if they knew something she didn't. Laura couldn't understand what was going on. So many would look at her each day so there was no way of narrowing down a list of suspects responsible for her torture. Most of the time she made sure that whenever she was out late alone, that she would get a taxi home from the hospital or from work. The supermarket was different however; it wasn't too far from home. Laura grabbed her purse from the nearby table in her bedroom and dashed out of the house to go to the supermarket to get some groceries. That day was like any other. Laura grabbed a shopping basket and went around the shop, picking up the items that she needed. After she was done, she paid at the till for her groceries. As she was headed towards the exit someone bumped into her causing her shopping bag to fall from her hand.

"I'm so sorry," came the deep, husky voice. Let me help you pick your items up."

They gathered the items one by one and put them back into the shopping bag. Laura tried so hard to see the face of the person but each time she looked in their direction they turned their head and looked in a different direction. They wore a baggy, black jogging bottoms and an oversized black hoody, black trainers, a black baseball cap pulled down over their forehead with the visor shading their eyes, and the big hood over their head that it blocked the side of their face. It was hard to capture their facial features. After the last item was placed in her shopping bag the stranger walked away without a backward glance. Laura picked up the shopping bag and walked out of the supermarket puzzled as to why the stranger didn't want her to see their face.

Oh well. At least they apologised and helped me picked up my items.

When Laura got home and was unpacking her groceries from the shopping bag she found a folded piece of scrap paper in it, and was curious to know what it was. She opened the paper to see a note constructed from magazine caption clippings that read, 'YOU ARE IN IMINENT DANGER. RUN AND DON'T LOOK BACK. TRUST NO ONE AND MAYBE YOU WILL SURVIVE.' Although she felt scared, she grabbed her keys and ran back to the supermarket to find the stranger that had help her pick up her shopping. She frantically searched the store and couldn't find them anywhere. Laura approached the security officer but he told her that he hadn't seen anyone matching the description she mentioned. He informed her that the cameras were not working as the system was down and they had only just got it up and running again. "How convenient," she muttered loud enough that the security officer could hear as she stared at him in disbelief.

The security officer dismissively walked away as he was irritated at her accusation that she was throwing in his direction. 'She must be mentally deranged or a psychopath or something. Who the hell does she think she is… accusing me of foul play?'

For a brief moment Laura stood there staring at the back of the security officer's head as he gradually disappeared out of her sight to patrol the store. She hesitantly turned and exited the store and made her way home. While she was walking home, she saw a figure in black baggy clothing standing on the farther side of the road appearing to look in her direction.

"Hey you!" she shouted.

The person turned and bolted down a side road at speed. Laura gave chase, running as fast as she could across the main road to follow the person down the side road.

"I just wanted to talk and ask you about the note." She yelled at the back of the stranger in the distance as she continued to give chase.

The stranger weaved in and out of the trees as she followed. She was adamant that she needed to know who it was and why she was in danger? But not for anything would the stranger stop to talk to her. She was becoming tired and breathless but she kept running anyway, as this was a life-or-death answer for her. "Ple… please would you stop and talk to me for a minute? I beg you. I need to know why I'm in danger. For goodness' sake would you bloody-well stop," she commanded at the back of the stranger, way in the distance.

It fell on deaf ears as the stranger didn't even stop. Clutching her chest Laura kept chasing after the stranger, only to lose them in the distance between the houses further on.

Eventually, Laura gave up running and began walking slowly back in the direction in which she had come from, but not without looking back intermittently to make sure that the stranger was not sneaking up behind her. A sharp pain shot through her chest, making her hand automatically rise up to clutch at her chest to soothe the pain.

That's the most exercise I've done in a long time.

Her throat felt parched, her body was crying out for water. She was struggling to put one foot in front of the other. Forcefully, Laura kept walking and walking even though, lactic acid was building up more and more in her tired, weary muscles. She willed herself forward until she finally made it to her front door. She unlocked the door and crawled straight to the kitchen, turning on the tap, cupping her hand under the running water forming a dip where she placed her mouth as she slurped the water gradually as the flow built up. She drank her fill and switched off the tap. Standing with her back towards the door, she stared out of the kitchen window overlooking the garden as she leant against the wet sink. Daydreaming she realised that she could have been killed. Realisation struck her hard that she had been too impulsive in chasing down the stranger who planted the warning in her shopping. Come to think of it, Laura thought that it couldn't be just pure coincidence that the stranger bumped into her at the supermarket. How the heck did the stranger know that she was going to be at the supermarket at that time?

Hmmm… I'm just thankful that nothing happened to me.

Laura took a deep breath in and exited the kitchen, going around the house double checking that all the doors and windows were tightly closed. Satisfied that they were, she sat in the lounge on the three-seat red leather recliner sofa for a while watching a film on the television. During the commercials she got up and prepared herself something to eat although she had no appetite. Laura could hear her mother's voice in her head.

This is not up for discussion young lady. You are my daughter and whether or not you are hungry, you need to make sure that you eat to keep your strength up and you need to take better care of yourself despite you feeling sad for your friend. Do you hear me child? Don't make me have to repeat myself again otherwise there'd be consequences and they won't be good ones. No matter how old you get those consequences would still apply.

Doing as she was told Laura took her simple meal to the lounge where she curled up on the leather recliner and forced herself to eat her meal. Although she knew that her mother had returned to her own home, it still felt as though she was watching her every move. It was a creepy feeling to be honest. Maybe worse than creepy. Being home alone had this weird, eerie, uneasy feeling. Sometimes Laura could swear that there was someone in the house with her. She didn't see them but she could smell various different fragrances from time to time.

None seemed familiar so as per usual she brushed it off like it was just her imagination playing tricks on her. She knew that she hadn't been sleeping properly since Claire's accident but she still tried to get on with it. There were times where she would feel dizzy like she was going to pass out but she kept pushing her body over its limits. No matter how many times that she'd been warned by duty nurses, doctors, work colleagues, even her mother, Laura still haven't listened to a single word they said. It was like it went in one ear without registering, and came out the e other. She knew that they were all right but she thought that if she had stopped even for a split second the whole world would come crashing down on her like a ton of bricks and she wasn't sure if she could handle that. The emotions that wheeled through her body were rapidly tearing her apart and she had no clue what to do. She felt so helpless and useless. Everything that had gone wrong around her was beyond her control and there was nothing that she could have done to stop it. It was like a runaway freight train that had derailed off the tracks. Laura felt as though she had no support at all from anyone. Her mother wouldn't take her seriously, as she would dismiss Laura's complaints about being stalked. All she would say was, *you need to rest more. You are seeing things that are not there. Don't be silly child. You're overworked and falling into paranoia. You need to take a break.*

Laura would walk away feeling annoyed that her mother would dismiss something as serious as that.

But if the police are not taking me seriously and I have no backing from my own mother then I stand no chance, to be honest. The sooner that I realise that I'm on my own the better it would be for me, I think.

Anger and frustration were soaring through her, venting off of her body like heated waves. Laura couldn't figure out what she could have done that was so bad in her life to be treated this way and become such a target like that. People around her either beat her senseless, tricked her into submission and then broke her heart, tried to control her life actions, get hurt because of her or try to taunt her into losing her mind.

What is it about me that intrigues people so? Do I look that weak? Well not anymore.

Laura rose up from the chair and took her dishes into the kitchen and placed them in the sink. Quickly she washed, rinsed and dried each of them and packed them away. Grabbing a bottle of cold water from the refrigerator, she switched off the kitchen light and exited switching off the television and other lights downstairs as she made her way through the house on her way upstairs to bed. Laura made her way into her bedroom and removed her clothing, had a quick refreshing shower and after towelling down and putting on a big t-shirt crawled into bed feeling exhausted. Not long after Laura could barely keep her eyes open. Slowly her heavy eyelids closed as she drifted off into dreamland. The dream wasn't clear as it jumped from event to event. She tossed and turned in her sleep, tears falling down her face as she whimpers like a puppy in her sleep. Unsure as to whether she was dreaming or awake, she was looking at a familiar face in front of her at her bedside. His hands were wiping away her tears as they kept on falling. He never said a word but kept wiping away her tears and looking at her with unreadable emotions plastered across his handsome face. He gently swept the unruly curls away from her face and smiled at her in a sinister way. Laura felt uneasy, a sudden chill all over her body. He placed a finger to her lips in a silencing gesture as she stared wide eyed at him. Slowly he lowered his big, beautiful hands over her throat and at first pretended like he was gently caressing her neck but then without warning, tightened his grip on her neck, restricting the airflow. Laura was struggling to breathe; she grabbed his hand but he only tightened his grip on her neck. She scratched away at his hands but that didn't help either. Gasping she jumped out of her sleep and raised her hand to her throat gently rubbing the areas where his hands had been. She opened her eyes to see no one there at all. She was all alone in her room. But what caught her was a lingering smell that seemed familiar to her senses although she couldn't pinpoint from where. It smelt of a mixture of spice and citrus. In her dream, if she could call it that, that was the same cologne that she smelt taunt her nostrils when he approached her bedside. The same smell that soothed her for a brief moment. And the same smell that nearly suffocated her to death. How could something that smelled so alluring be the very thing that could kill you? As scared as Laura felt she discarded the experience as just a dreamy nightmare. Her heart was beating really fast and she tried her best to slow it down to its regular rhythm. Laura rubbed her throat again as the pain there felt too real, the soreness of it all. She climbed out of bed and switched on the main light in the room, to examine her neck in the mirror as the bedside light wasn't bright enough. As Laura looked closely, she noticed some red laceration marks where his hand had been.

Does that mean that he was in my room? In my house watching me as I slept. So, was I not sleeping at all? Was I awake all this time? I'm so confused. I don't understand what is going on.

If she wasn't scared enough already, well, she was absolutely terrified now.

Chapter 18

Laura's mind was in overdrive whilst her hand gently caressed her neck in a soothing motion. As soon as she switched off the main light in her bedroom again, and just leaving the bedside lamp shining, she swore that she could hear heavy footsteps in the house as if someone was downstairs. Laura quickly bolted the latch on her bedroom door so no one could re-enter to harm her again. She sat on the floor knees pulled up to her chest as she rocked back and forth hugging her knees, her eyes wide open in fear as she stared at the faint shadows in her bedroom. All she could think was *this is it for me? The note did say to run and not look back if I wanted to survive. Oh my! What should I do? I can't risk going to Josh's as I'm scared that he would get hurt too because of me. I couldn't bear that thought. I have nowhere to go. I am sure as hell I'm not going back home to mums.* The closing of the front door downstairs pulled her from her thoughts. She could hear a vehicle engine start up as it roared to life. It skidded along the drive and sped off as if in a hurry. Laura wished that she had the courage to have looked out to see what vehicle it was, even write down the number plate but she didn't. She was frozen to the floor where she sat in fear for what felt like forever. Laura finally rose from the floor and climbed into her bed as she shivered from the coldness of the bedroom and the underlying fear within her. She pulled over the covers up to her neck and laid down on her side with her knees arched up against her chest. Laura knew that it would be hard to fall back to sleep. It was nowhere in existence now. She wondered if she should call Josh just for a friendly chat, or even Alex. She couldn't afford for Alex to see her in this frightened state of mind. What would he think of her? She picked up the phone and rang Josh. Come to think of it she hadn't spoken to Josh in a long while, since the last encounter at the hospital. Laura wondered why Josh hadn't reached out to her by now? He can't be still overworking? She'd hoped that he wasn't hurt already or perhaps dead in a ditch somewhere and no one knew about it. It was unlike Josh not to have contacted her by now.

Besides she missed talking to him and hanging out. She found herself feeling anxious and desperate to hear his voice on the other end of the line. She needed to know that he was okay and to know where had he been all this time and if he was avoiding her or something? Just when she thought that he wasn't going to answer her at all and was about to hang up the phone, his voice bellowed down the line, his breathing very heavy as if he was running or something. "Hey Josh. It's me. Are you busy?"

He paused for a moment listening to her soft voice as it came through the phone. He had thought about calling her, but he was too busy with work and other commitments that he threw himself into just as a pastime. Hearing the weakened tone of her voice made him feel so guilty and tugged at his heart. He knew that he should have been a better friend and be there for her more. Deep down he was kicking himself for it, being wrapped up in his own self-pity as to why he overworked himself taking on extra shifts and other activities. Laura needed him badly and he wasn't there. He wondered what she must think of him now. Her best friend, his former girlfriend was lying in hospital in a coma fighting for her life. So many questions and thoughts began overriding his mind. Laura sighed as she waited for him to reply but got nothing. All she could hear was his heavy rugged breathing down the telephone. Josh was zoned out once again, trapped in his own inner thoughts about everything and as much as he was a general practitioner it didn't mean that he knew how to help himself. He needed her. Those big, pleading eyes kept haunting his dreams, his thoughts. He couldn't concentrate long enough to help his own sanity when he was not working. At work he couldn't make any detrimental mistakes at all so his concentration level was on point as he had patients' lives in his hands, literally. Tears welled up, as they stung at the back of her eyes, threatening to fall. She felt like she was losing Josh too. Laura couldn't bear that thought of losing both him and Claire. She refused to accept that was even possible. Stifling a cry, she took a deep breath in and exhaled heavily.

"Jo…Josh please she begged as she sniffled, whilst the tears flowed freely down her cheeks. Please, please talk to me."

The hurt in her voice and the stifled cry pulled him out of his thoughts.

Did I make her cry? Oh God no! I never wanted to hurt her. "I'm so sorry Laura. I'm so sorry. No, I'm not busy at the moment. How have you been?"

"Oh, Josh it's been a tough few months. It's awful. It's my fault Josh. All of this is my fault." She let out at a full-blown heart wrenching cry.

Josh felt a little confused as to what Laura was implying. "Laura what do you mean by it's all your fault? What was?"

Laura was weeping at this point, sniffling in between each stretch of her choking cry, her speech barely audible to understand.

"Laura, try and take a deep breath and calm down, darling. I can't understand what you're saying."

"I… I…I… Oh God! I did…arghh… I do…don… she stuttered hysterically through guilty tears. I'm… I'm so… so…rry to ta…ke her…" she choked through her deep sobs.

"I don't understand what you're trying to explain to me, Lau. I know that it's very late but, do you want me to come over and then we can talk?"

"I don… don't knooow," she cried hysterically.

"Laura, listen to me. I'm coming over right now. Do you hear me? Do you understand what I've said to you?"

Josh wanted at least a bit of reassurance that it was okay to visit despite the late hour. He lived his life by given consent requested from every patient before treating them, except of course, for those who were unconscious or nonresponsive.

"Shh… sure."

Josh kept the line open and put on his shoes and a light jacket and grabbed the keys to his car. Outside, he got into the car and started the engine, then connected the call to the Bluetooth speaker and rested the phone on the passenger seat. He drove like a madman although he knew that he shouldn't. He had to get to her quickly. Thank goodness there were no other vehicles or road users on the back roads he was driving on. For what was supposed to take half an hour, took Josh ten minutes. Finally, he pulled up in her drive and spoke through the speaker and told Laura that he was outside so she needed to let him in. Laura scrambled off the bed to the floor, unbolted her bedroom door and made her way swiftly down the stairs to unlock the front door. Before opening the door properly, she swiped the back of her hands across her cheeks and wiped away the tears, although more were threatening to fall. Fixing the draped blanket around her shoulders she pulled the front door open. Looking at a face so kind, sympathetic and familiar made her feel a little better. She tried to force a smile but Josh could see that her beautiful smile was strained.

She looked sad, depressed and extremely exhausted. The dark circles under her eyes told the stories of lack of sleep. Her body seemed a little feeble, weak and worn down from being overworked and pushed past its limits. She had lost a bit of weight and he could see that her beauty wasn't as radiant as it should be but under the circumstances, he understood the reasons. She had lost that glow, that spark that captures anyone from the moment you lay eyes on her. Despite this she was still beautiful. Her big eyes were filled with unfallen tears as she stared at him intently. Laura stepped aside and gestured for him to enter and then closed the door behind him. Laura stood there frozen just staring at him. Josh reached out and pulled her into his arms without hesitation. Her body stiffened and was quite tense under his touch. She could hear the soothing, steady beat of his heart as it lulled her into feeling safe and secure. "I'm sorry, Lau, that I haven't been there for you but I'm here now, if and when you need me."

He felt her body relaxing under his touch and this made him feel good, that he could at least have some sort of effect on her. Shortly afterwards they entered the kitchen and he made them some tea, which they then took with them into the lounge. Laura sat down on the sofa and patted the seat directly next to her for Josh to accompany her there. They sat in comfortable silence at first whilst they consumed their hot beverages. Soon after Laura broke the silence wanting to know how Josh had been coping with Claire's accident. Even though she clearly was in pain she still put others needs before her own. "Do you want the blunt honest truth, Lau?"

"Claire broke my heart and although she is in a coma, I'm angry at her for it. I know that I should sympathise with her situation but I can't bear to look at her after what she did. I loved her wholeheartedly, I trusted her and she broke it all because she couldn't be content with all I had to offer."

Silently Laura stared at the man sitting next to her in shock, as she had had her own reservations about Claire but had never confronted her about them.

"Let me guess, was she seeing someone else?"

Josh averted his eyes towards the floor but not before Laura saw the flash of pain in his eyes. This tore at her heart. She did warn Claire and clearly, she hadn't listened. Josh had a heart of gold and Laura couldn't understand why her friend would jeopardise that relationship for another man. Laura wondered if it was that man from the cocktail bar in town that Claire was drooling over months ago.

"I'm so sorry Josh that Claire did that to you. I'm sure that she loves you and didn't mean to do that to you."

A flash of anger showed in his eyes. "She meant all of it. When she had her tongue down his throat and his hands all over her body, she wasn't thinking about me and how I would have felt, so don't you dare tell me that she didn't mean to, and that she loves me. That girl doesn't know the meaning of the word even if it was to come up and bite her on the you know what."

"Can you not forgive her and try again? I know that you still love her very much, but if she survives this, please try. Life is too short to be angry at each other."

"I'm not sure if I could. I'm afraid that it might be too late to fix it."

Laura felt terrible for them both as she was caught in the middle seeing as she was a friend to them both. Claire could have saved her relationship from falling apart if she had listened and trusted in what she had with Josh, but clearly, she didn't. Automatically, Laura reached out and held his hand, squeezing it gently under her slender fingers. Josh turned and looked at her, with unreadable emotions in his face.

"So, tell me Lau, what were you trying to explain to me over the phone before I drove here like a madman?"

Laura swallowed quite loud and let out a deep breath that she hadn't realised that she had been holding. "I was trying to tell you that I did it."

"Oh God!" she muttered. "Josh, it was my fault. I was the cause of Claire's accident."

Josh stared at Laura in disbelief and shook his head, not believing that a gentle soul like Laura was capable of such evil. *No way!* "What made you believe that you were the cause of Claire's accident?"

"On the day that Claire got into the accident I was the one who was supposed to drive the car that day into town, but whilst we were sitting on the porch having a glass of lemonade and stuff, Claire received a phone call that she took in private further down the drive. She came and told me that she had an errand to run and needed to use the car urgently so I told her sure. It was her car and I wasn't going to fight her over what wasn't mine. She made me a promise that I could borrow the car that day and she broke it for that phone call. I figured maybe she was going to see you."

"That doesn't make it your fault Lau, so you need to get that silly thought out of your head."

"But…but if I had said no and been adamant that it was my turn to use the car and remind her of her promise maybe just maybe I could have prevented her from getting hurt. I really think that the accident was for me Josh." Dropping her voice to a mere whisper as if she was afraid that someone else would have overheard what she was confiding to Josh, she spoke again. "Someone had been stalking me and I was too scared to say anything. I was afraid that I would put whoever I told in danger. The person was in the house earlier on tonight as I slept. I can't help thinking that the person who is stalking me did this to Claire. Right now, to be honest I am scared that they know that I told you and do something to harm you. I really don't want anything to happen to you."

"Damn! Lau are you serious? Didn't you tell the police so they could catch this maniac?"

"Yes, I did, but the officer just dismissed it and told me that unless they have physically harm me and that, then there's nothing that they could do."

"This is crazy. And I can't believe that you were dealing with this all on your own. You know what? Either you come home with me for a while, or I move in here to protect you."

"No way Josh! I'm sorry but I cannot put you in danger too. You mean a lot to me and I'm not sure what I would do if something happened to you because of me. I will deal with this on my own. Afterall, it's me that they want."

"Although I'm not happy with your decision and I know that you are looking out for me, either way I cannot force you. I will respect your decision for now. But just know if you need me day or night, just let me know and I'll be there. Do you know why they want you?"

"I have no clue."

"Can you promise me one thing though?"

Laura hesitated before she answered Josh's question. "Anything."

She held her breath as she looked at him awaiting his response, hoping that he didn't talk about moving in with him or with her again. "Can you promise me that you would be extremely careful and if you need me, you would let me know immediately?"

Laura breathed a sigh of relief and responded with tears welling up in her eyes. "You do know that, that is two things, right? But don't worry, I promise."

Tears was falling from her eyes again and this time with no end in sight. The more they fell, the more the tear glands produced. Josh shuffled closer to her and pulled her into his arms again. This time he held her tightly, providing such warmth and comfort. As the thought hit him, holding her chin so that she was facing upwards looking directly into his eyes, he said,

"If you had managed to convince Claire to keep to her promise and let you have the car, it would have been you that would have gotten into the accident. And you would have been in the same position as Claire in a coma, or even worse, end up dead. For all we know, there could have been foul play. Although the accident happened not far from here, it doesn't rule out the possibility and remember you and Claire always drive pass that side road to get home so it could have been you. Is that what you wanted?"

"Of course not. But she would be here right now and that's what matters."

Still holding her chin, Josh gazed into her eyes as if searching for a particular answer to some kind of question he held in mind. Instead of asking her, he whispered something so softly that she barely caught his words.

"It would have destroyed me if you had been the one to be driving the car and got hurt. I would have been so devastated," he trailed off, "I can't lose you".

His eyes looked so sincere that Laura wanted to know if she was reading correctly the many emotions plastered across his face. Laura swore that he was going to kiss her on the lips but instead he softly kissed her forehead and held her in a warm embrace again. His heart rate was no longer steady; its beats were a little faster than usual. They were strong and powerful and engulfed her in a security blanket.

"Thank you, Josh, for being here for me. I really appreciate your kindness towards me. And I'm always here for you whether you work things out with Claire or not. You've always got a friend in me, that I do promise."

Automatically, his hug tightened around Laura's frame as he placed a kiss in her curly mane. Being held like this brought her a feeling of nostalgia from when Freddie was her boyfriend. Brushing the thought aside, finally, she wrapped her arms around his waist as she leant on his chest feeling the exhaustion creeping in again. Pulling the blanket that was draped around her shoulders over them both they laid back on the sofa and drifted off to sleep in each other's arms.

Chapter 19

By the time they woke up it was twelve noon. The sun was high in the sky. The birds were chirping merrily in the trees with no care in the world. Laura felt much more rested thanks to Josh. The steady rise and fall of his chest as he breathed was like a lullaby that had soothed her to sleep. Throughout the whole time they slept he never once let go of her. His embrace held her so close that she could have felt his warm breath on her shoulder. As she nuzzled her face in between his chest and chin she drank in the freshness of the scent of him. Laura felt safe. She didn't feel alone anymore and she was thankful to Josh for that. Although a lot of the guilt had been lifted off her heart, it hadn't gone entirely.

Laura lifted her head and looked at Josh's handsome face as he slept, lightly snoring.

She couldn't hold back the smile that tugged at the corners of her mouth, as it gradually formed into a beaming smile. Laura didn't realise that Josh was watching her as she surveyed his features slowly. She felt it when the rhythm of his heartbeats changed, as it beat a little faster under the warmth of her splayed palm of her hand, but didn't think much of it as his eyes were still closed. Eventually, Josh couldn't hold back the smile that formed on his face when he saw the glorious, beaming smile that was plastered on Laura's face. It had been so long since he last saw her smile like that; so breath-taking a smile that could conquer the world. It was a ray of sunshine. The only ray of sunshine that seemed to shine for him at the moment and he cherished it.

Laura was just about to get up when she realised that he was awake, but Josh begged her not too because in his mind he knew that everything would go back to normal after they got up from that sofa, from each other's embrace.

Sometimes I miss doing that with Claire, although she betrayed me and broke my heart. Damn it! Stop thinking about her, you soppy sod.

So, they lay there blabbering on about all sorts, laughing and joking about as many different things as they could think of. Sometimes Laura would catch Josh staring but she never got the chance to read the emotions in his eyes before they disappeared.

"Do you have any plans for today, Josh?" "Nah nothing at all. Why?"

"Wanna go to the local park for a picnic? We could make the day of it."

"Sure, why not. I'm game if you are, missy." playfully he tickled her and watched her as she laughed. This was who he remembered her to be. Always smiling and happy without the carrying the world on her shoulders. He knew he had to be there as much as she would allow him to be. Suddenly he stopped tickling her and was staring at her as if she was the only thing that mattered in this moment. He felt tempted to tell her what was on his mind but stopped himself from doing so, as she stopped laughing and looked at him with those beautiful, big brown eyes. Her neatly shaped lips so inviting. Her rounded face. Her black curly mane tossled in a mess from wriggling about when tickled. Slowly he was edging closer to her and then she poked him in the sides breaking the moment and leapt up off of him giggling like a happy kid. Josh just watched her and smiled. Shortly after the smile fell from Laura's face and she became more serious as if thinking about something.

Deep down Laura knew that she was looking for a distraction, for company so as not to be alone where her thoughts would overpower her. And not to mention how scared she was about being alone. She wanted to ask Josh to stay, or to ask if she could stay at his house with him for a little while, but she was scared that she'd put him in danger, too, like she did Claire. She had already turned down his offer the night before and wished she hadn't. Somehow, she needed to face this one alone and not risk anyone else getting hurt because of her. She wouldn't be able to handle it. Feeling like she wanted to change her mind and have him move in or follow him home, she shook that thought from her head. She knew that he had his work commitments and she didn't want to burden him with her problems. He had his own problems to deal with. They got up and brushed their teeth and she washed her face, sorting themselves out, before preparing and packing the picnic basket and headed out for their picnic at the local park. Some of their conversations was a little strained but they soon rectified that and quickly it began to flow smoothly without the awkward silences. They fooled around chasing each other up and down their picnic area. At one point when Laura was hiding amongst the trees and shrubs, she heard a crackling sound as footsteps sneakily approached nearby where she hid from Josh. She felt shaken up by the incident and decided that she would make her way back towards where she'd last seen Josh. The crunch of dried leaves, the cracking of dried twigs made her snap to attention. Laura darted out from behind the tree and ran quickly back to the picnic area, but Josh wasn't there. Laura wondered if it was Josh sneaking up on her when she was hiding, or if it was someone else. Either way she couldn't wait around to find out. She wondered where Josh could be. She would have called his mobile but had accidentally left hers at home on the kitchen counter so that wasn't possible. After waiting around for what seemed like a long time, Laura began packing up the picnic goodies back into the basket. When she was finished, she folded the picnic blanket and tucked it into the basket and got up and headed back the way they had come, without Josh accompanying her. She was puzzled as to what had happened to Josh as one minute, they were having fun and the next he had disappeared without a word. Why would he leave like that without saying a word? It wasn't like him to do that.

I wonder…

Laura walked up her driveway with an uneasy feeling in the pit of her stomach and no matter how much she tried to suppress it, it just got worse. As she was about to push the keys into the front door lock, Laura noticed that the door was slightly ajar. Hesitantly, she slowly pushed the door open, her eyes surveying the hallway for any movement. At first, she felt frightened as she knew that her life might be in imminent danger although the police and her mother didn't believe her, but she soldiered on cautiously through the house, room by room. Laura entered the kitchen and placed the picnic basket on the table. She noticed that some of the plates and cups were smashed on the floor when she stepped on the broken pieces under her shoes and heard the crunching noise as another shard broke under the weight of her foot. Retreating from the kitchen she was jarred by someone who dashed past her at a raging speed, and out the front door catching her off guard. She lost her balance and fell to the floor with a thud. "Oi!"

It was no use to shout because the intruder didn't look back, or even glance at her sideways. A familiar scent ambushed her senses but she couldn't think of where she had smelt it before. Then it came to her. A few nights ago, when she was asleep in her bed and there was someone in the house with her, she could recall smelling that same scent then, too. What the hell did they want and what were they looking for? Mmmhmm… Slowly, Laura rose to her feet and made her way unsteadily up the stairs after closing the front door properly. Upstairs, the smell of her mother's perfume filled Claire's room which looked like it has been ransacked, as if someone was searching for something in particular. The drawers were pulled out of place and tossed aside as if they were insignificant. Some were broken apart and some were still intact. Until now Claire's room had untouched since she that night of the accident when she was taken to hospital. Clothes were thrown everywhere, and important paperwork scattered all across the floor. Reluctantly, Laura cleaned up the room and tidied everything back in its place, putting back together the torn apart drawers as best she could. Laura then checked her own room which had also been ransacked. Her bedroom had also been vandalised with a warning sprayed in black paint. 'I TOLD YOU TO TRUST NO ONE, TO RUN AND NOT LOOK BACK AND MAYBE YOU MIGHT SURVIVE. NOW SINCE YOU HAVEN'T LISTENED THE PEOPLE ARROUND YOU WILL DIE ONE BY ONE. THEN, YOU WILL BE NEXT.'

Oh God! Laura dropped to her knees, her eyes filled with tears and she wept at how badly her life had turned out to be. Her sorrow was replaced by fear as she wasn't sure what had happened to Josh. After she tidied her bedroom, Laura realised that the warning note was missing from her bedside table drawer. She exited the room and grabbed a bucket of warm soapy water and a scrubbing brush and scrubbed away the threatening words written on her wall that stained her memory. Laura decided to check the spare room where her mother once dwelled and saw that it was untouched, but could still smell her perfume. That didn't make any sense.

Maybe I'm going crazy and I'm just exhausted, stressed and overworked.

Running her fingers through her untamed curls she turned and went straight to shower up and put on her pyjamas and have an early night, but not before calling Josh to make sure that he was okay. Laura rang Josh twice and got no answer. Night was beginning to draw in closer and closer. Just when Laura was about to climb into bed the doorbell rang impatiently. Exhaling, she picked up a pen from the nearby desk as it was the nearest thing she had as a weapon and headed downstairs towards the front door.

"Who is it," she yelled as she waited for an answer. It's me came the croaky voice from the other side of the door. Immediately Laura recognised the voice and instantly open the door. Josh was standing on the other side of the door, with his left hand stroking his jaw. Laura invited him in, her anger fuelled by his presence. "What do you want Josh? It's only now that you remember that you abandoned me in the park?"

"Laura I'm sorry. Listen to me I had my eyes closed counting whilst you hid from me and all I felt was a blow to the jaw and someone dragging me along the ground. When they got me where they wanted me, they smacked me in the head and all I remember after that was waking up by the bushes close to the park exit. I made my way here, straight way."

Sceptically, Laura stared at him. worry and disbelief going through her mind at the same time. "Do you expect me to believe that story, Josh?"

"Yes, Laura because it's the truth. I would never abandon you like that and you know it."

"Do I? You've abandoned me before so what makes today any different?"

Josh shook his head as he didn't know how to prove it to Laura. He needed her to believe him but she clearly didn't. Despite the fact that Laura was doubting Josh's story she went to the kitchen and grabbed two ice packs and gave them to Josh. Josh placed one on his head and the other on his left jaw. All she could do was to stare at him. That familiar smell mixed with another fragrance was taunting her nostrils again, so she approached Josh to see if the smell was coming from him. Inhaling closely Laura drew back realising that the reason why that smell was so familiar to her was because it was a cologne from one of the sets that she'd bought him eight months or so ago for his birthday. Laura drew back as if she was burnt by something or someone. There was another trace of a different cologne that was oozing through muddling up her sense.

Could it be? Oh God! No. But why? It couldn't be coincidental that he wears the same cologne, turns up not long after the intruder left her house. And the thing that bothered her was why he left her at the park so suddenly. Was it to come and ransack her house? What the hell was he looking for? Was it him that had been looking in at her through the window when she was in her mother's embrace? Was it Josh that had been standing under the tree calling her to come outside? Did he watch her as she swam in the pool that night? Arghh…

She had so many questions and no answer. Her mind was baffled as she didn't want to believe that it was possible for Josh to do that to her. He seemed too angelic to then tarnish his reputation. Laura refused to believe that Josh would be capable of doing this. What did he have to gain from stalking her? None of it made any sense. She tried to quell her thoughts before, it drove her insane.

Somehow, she was so lost in her train of thoughts that she didn't notice that Josh was staring intensely at her. Laura didn't hear him calling out her name until he reached out and touched her shoulder and gently shook her. Rapidly she pulled back from Josh with her eyes opened wide. Josh realised that Laura seemed afraid, but he was unsure as to why, so he approached her with his arms outstretched to wrap her in his warm embrace, only for Laura to slowly step back away from him; the more steps he took towards her the more she stepped back. Suddenly her back was against the cold wall with nowhere to go. He was in close proximity now. Even if she wanted to move, she couldn't. Josh stood face to face with her.

Her heartbeats quickened inside her chest, a noise so deafening that she wondered if he could hear it. Well, if he could, he hadn't said anything. He reached out and pulled her against his hard chest as he wrapped his arms around her the way he had done earlier that day. He felt her body stiffen under his embrace, so he quickly released her, but not before holding her by the shoulders at arm's length, and demanding to know what was wrong with her. At first, Laura just looked at Josh squarely in the eyes and then decided to respond. Ignoring the concern revealed by Laura's response, Josh informed her that he was going home as he was back to work the following morning. Laura felt relieved that she would be rid of him for at least a few days or weeks. That should be enough time for her to figure out what to do.

Forcing a smile, she bid Josh a convincing farewell after making him believe that she forgave him for abandoning her at the park earlier on that day. Deep down she felt lousy for lying to him but she also felt that he wasn't been totally honest with her either so she felt it was justified to pretend like everything was alright.

Chapter 20

Meanwhile back at the hospital doctors worked around the clock to ensure that Claire's condition remained stable. She was slowly but surely improving in her condition. Today was the day that the doctors were going to remove the breathing tube from her throat to see if she would be able to breathe without assistance and revive her. Laura hoped that this was it and that Claire would finally be able to breathe on her own which would bring her one step closer to coming home. The doctors were quite pleased with the new test results and observations that they had recorded. They felt that it was a good turning point based on how badly Claire's condition was upon admission months ago. Laura couldn't wait to get to the hospital so that she could be there for her best friend. She couldn't wait for Claire to return home as she was hoping that everything would somehow get back to normal. No more threats, no more being scared, no more sleepless nights and hopefully no more guilt. *I hope that she could forgive me at some point soon.* Well, that was what she was hoping for anyway, but that didn't mean that it would happen that way.

Laura felt super excited about the news that Claire's condition was improving. Throughout her journey in the taxi, she kept smiling to herself and mumbling her thanks to God. She politely asked the taxi driver to drive faster as she didn't want to miss the procedure. At least I can be there for her this time, just in case that she hates me because of her accident. A sudden fear gripped her stomach as she contemplated what it would mean if Claire hated her. She envisioned how boring life would be without her best friend and felt a sadness wash over her happy spirits dampening her mood.

`Snap out of it girl. Don't be so negative.'

She cheering up, but then noticed that the taxi driver had continued to drive at his own pace and this infuriated her. She wasn't sure if he was doing this on purpose, or if he was scared to accelerate the vehicle. This made her wonder if the taxi driver had heard her request, as t had made no difference to his driving speed at all. She furiously stared daggers at the back of the taxi driver's head, trying to be patient and refraining from arguing with him. Deciding to keep her cool, Laura politely asked the taxi driver again.

"Excuse me sir, could you please drive faster as I need to get to the hospital and I'm running out of time?"

The taxi driver just kept his head straight ahead. His eyes never once averted to the rear-view mirror to acknowledge her. There was no sound, no grunt, not even a nod of the head to say okay or even a no that he would or wouldn't grant her request. Laura waited patiently for a few more minutes to see if the driver would speed up but unfortunately, he didn't. The taxi driver was driving below the speed limit and didn't care.

`I wonder if he drives like this all the time. A driver like this shouldn't be working in the taxi service.'

The anger rose in her chest till she felt like she was about to explode. She felt the heat radiating off of her skin. Laura wound down the car window to let some fresh air in but when she did this, the taxi driver spoke for the first time,

"Could you not tamper with my car window? I don't want you to break it."

The driver spat the words back at her like fireballs. Laura stared at the taxi driver for a split second.

"I'm sorry," she hurled back at him in irritation.

"I don't even think that you could afford it," he mumbled under his breath, but low enough that she could hear. Laura found what he had said quite offensive. After all, he knew absolutely nothing about her. However, she refrained from responding, as she could see the development of a confrontation beginning and she refused to take part in it.

"You could argue with yourself if you want to, but just drive the car faster, so I could get there on time, you bloody idiot."

Laura was fed up with being polite to everyone and not get the same in return. She felt frustrated with everything that was going on in her life. She didn't need someone else adding to it. She wanted something to be straight forward for once. Although she wanted to avoid the confrontation, she refused to back down. She needed to be braver and more tough if she was going to survive at all.

The taxi driver gave her a dirty look through the rear-view mirror and quickly look away.

`What the hell was this man's problem? Did he wake up on the wrong side of the bed or something? He's very argumentative and rude with no customer service skills at all. My God.!'

"By the way since I seemed to finally have your attention could you flipping well drive the car faster? I've been politely and calmly asking you that for the past thirty minutes and you just ignored me. Goddamn it!"

"If you're going to be rude and disrespectful, I'll stop the car right here and ask you to get out," he responded as his bushy eyebrows creased together angrily, and with a thin, hard, crooked smile plastered upon his rough, unshaven face. Laura couldn't believe what she was hearing as she stared at the back of his head in shock. "Are you, serious right now? You can't be. You must be joking. I have not once disrespected you, or been rude for that matter, so you must be confused. I was only trying to ask you to kindly speed up the car, so that I could get to my destination on time, as it was imperative that I do but on all occasions that I asked, you blatantly disregarded my request. You tell me who was being rude huh? You or me?"

The taxi driver just kissed his teeth and continued driving for about another minute then pulled over on the hard shoulder and shouted, "Get out now."

"What?"

"I said, get out of my car right now."

He was becoming aggressive. Laura could see the anger in his face as she stared at his reflection in the rear-view mirror. She leant back in the seat and looked at him.

"I don't understand what I could have done to anger you this way sir. It doesn't make any sense at all."

"Do you need me to forcefully remove you from my car? Are you refusing to leave?"

Laura opened her hand bag and retrieved her mobile phone and dialled the taxi company, after putting the call on speaker so that the taxi driver would be able to hear the conversation. When the controller picked up the phone and answered, the taxi driver's eyes darted in her direction. This time, he was turning around to face her with a pleading look on his face. She was oblivious to the fact that the driver was on his last strike as he was on a probationary period before being employed for a full-time position. Laura gave an explanation to the controller on the other end of the line, informing him of the confrontation that she was experiencing with the driver and the problem she was facing as the driver had pulled over on the hard shoulder and was asking her to get out of his vehicle. The controller was appalled by the despicable actions of the taxi driver, so he placed Laura on hold and radioed through to the driver directly and scolded him for his actions. The taxi driver issued an apology to the controller and made a promise to complete his journey and then return to the base. "Don't make me have to report you. Do you remember the incident that you were involved in? That's all I'm saying. This is like déjà vu, mate."

The taxi driver appeared even more irritated and started up the ignition, and drove off where he narrowly missed an oncoming vehicle. Laura felt so scared that her stomach felt queasy. The controller reassured her that the driver would ensure that she got to her destination free of charge. Finally, she realised what had irritated the driver. She expressed her gratitude to the controller for his assistance and ended the call. For the remainder of the journey the driver drove at his own pace and never said another word to her or even made eye contact. At the slow pace he was driving time, time was of the essence. Laura prayed that time would slow down long enough for her to make it to the hospital on time. Her eyes averted to the digital clock on the dashboard as she watched helplessly whilst the time drew nearer and nearer. She just couldn't tear her eyes away from the clock. Although, Laura acknowledged that her journey was now free, she couldn't care less how much the original price had been to get to the hospital. All she knew was that she needed to get there on time.

She was filled with desperation. Laura decided that she'd pay the driver as her conscience would feel guilty if she withheld the money regardless of his stupidity, that could had easily cost him his career and his livelihood. Changing the direction of her glare from the digital clock on the dashboard, Laura turned her gaze to the outstretched road ahead of them and realised how much traffic there was lined up in front of them with their brake lights signalling every roll of their wheels. It was unavoidable at this point. Laura knew that if it wasn't for the slow driving, the rudeness and the pulling over, they could have evaded the traffic.

Unfortunately, it had already happened and now she had to just roll with the flow whilst counting down the minutes and the seconds as they ticked by. The traffic stretched on for about a mile or more and finally began to clear out little by little until they could turn off at the junction.

'Thank God I wasn't going straight ahead because the traffic that way was moving at a snail's pace. It's terrible.'

About five minutes later the taxi driver veered off down the slip road to get off the motorway. They continued on until the road signs for the hospital came into view. *'Finally.'* Laura looked back at the clock and realised that she had ten minutes left. There was still a quarter of a mile left to go. She crossed her fingers, and closed her eyes willing the driver to accelerate even just a little. As if hearing her thoughts, he obliged. Laura wasn't sure if it was because he wanted to get rid of her or if he felt bad, but she didn't care as she needed to get there on time. A short while later, the taxi driver finally pulled up in the hospital car park, but not before giving way to an ambulance. Laura opened her handbag and retrieved the required amount of money displayed on the payment meter. She extended her hand with the cash and gave it to the driver as she thanked him. Although the driver was shocked that Laura was still generous enough to pay him for his services despite everything, he was still angry at her hastiness in reporting him to the controller back at the taxi office. Laura briskly opened the car door and stepped out. As she was about to close the car door her opened handbag fell off her wrist and spilled the contents. A few of the items fell under the car close to the rear wheel where she now crouched down to pick up the other items after she had alerted the driver to let him know what had happened so that he wouldn't accidentally run her over. Laura hastily collected the items as quickly as she could. As she was collecting the final item from next to the rear wheel, the taxi driver drove off, making Laura snatch her hand back before the wheel rode over it, as it skidded up the gravelled dust in her face. Luckily, she managed to grab the item in time. The wheels skidded out of the parking bay so fast that Laura felt a surge of anger, as she not only could have been injured, but the fact that the driver was so impatient and drove off so fast without any warning.

'How convenient after he made me arrive near enough late.'

"Moron!" she hurled after him in contempt as she watched the taxi disappear in the distance.

Abruptly Laura stood up, snatching her handbag from the gravelled surface. Dusting the dirt from her handbag and her knees, Laura rushed towards the hospital entrance with no time to spare, almost half running. Dodging through the crowds of people going to and fro, Laura dashed towards the location of the lifts. In the distance, she saw a lift that was filling up with people so she knew that she needed to hustle if she stood a chance of catching the lift. Laura sped up, heading into a run as her eyes focussed directly on the open lift. Accidentally, as she was running for the lift Laura tripped over someone in a wheel chair falling flat on the ground. By the time she had noticed the stranger in the wheelchair it was too late to stop.

"Are you okay ma'am?"

Laura turned and glared in the direction of the voice to see a woman sat in the wheel chair looking down at her with a concerned look plastered across her face. "Arghh... I think so. Thanks for asking. But hold up, what about you? Are you alright?"

"Yes, I'm alright, thanks."

"I'm so sorry. I was rushing so much that I wasn't looking where I was going." "It's okay. It happens to the best of us."

Laura rose up from the hospital floor and wiped her hands down the sides of her jeans. She readjusted her handbag on her slim shoulder, this time ensuring that she used her thumb to keep it in place. After apologising again for the mishap with the woman in the wheel chair, Laura headed towards the lifts and pressed the buttons for the both of them. She stood in the middle of both lifts whilst she kept a very close eye on the floor number displays as the numbers went up and down as people got in and out of the lifts on the other floors.

Impatiently, Laura tapped her feet and continuously checked her watch. Letting out a grunt, she cursed quietly under her breath to herself so that no one else would hear. "Come on, come on! You, stupid lift. Please, please, please I beg you. I'm late enough as it is.

Arghh...!"

Kissing her teeth, Laura took her index finger and punched the lift buttons again and again with much more force. Not long afterwards she stared as the numbers on the lift display started to count down lower and lower. An anxious, excited feeling enveloped her as she finally acknowledged that there might be a possibility that later on, she would see her friend, Claire, open her eyes before she left the hospital to head home. Five, stop. Four, stop.

'Come on, come on, keep on coming lower.' Three, stop. Two, one stop. Ground, ping.

'It's about time. Phew! Thank goodness.'

Laura stepped into the lift and pushed the seventh-floor button. Just as the lift doors were nearly closed, Laura thought she saw a familiar face. A blast from her past. Laura tried angling her eyes through the narrow crease of the lift doors, just before it fully closed shut, but unfortunately, she couldn't see the full appearance to make sure she wasn't going paranoid. The lift closed and began ascending up to the seventh floor, but not before stopping on the fourth and the sixth floor. Finally, Laura thought, as the lift pinged and the doors opened revealing the seventh floor. She hurried out of the lift and made her way down the intensive corridor towards Claire's room. As she walked Laura felt uneasy, as if something wasn't quite right. She couldn't put a finger on it, but she continued her journey anyway. Her eyes darted around, her head on a swivel as she glanced around absorbing and observing her surroundings. Although she couldn't see anyone in particular looking in her direction, she felt like she was been watched. Pushing the thought to one side, she anxiously made her way, striding closer and closer to her final destination. "Watch it miss. Hellooo… Miss excuse me please. This is an emergency."

Zapping back to reality, Laura quickly apologised and stepped aside, so that the porter could continue his way to take the patient lying in the hospital bed towards the lift. Laura could not help herself, but look at the patient, to make sure that it wasn't Claire. Feeling satisfied that it wasn't, she released the breath that she hadn't realised that she was holding.

'Thank goodness.' When the patient's bed and the porter were finally out of her way, she continued walking down the corridor. Not before long she entered Claire's room. Suddenly, she stopped abruptly in her tracks as she could not believe her eyes. He sat there holding her hand like he was her partner.

'Why was he even here? Why was he touching her? She only met him once at the same time as I did? Wait a minute, how did he even know that she was here? He's looking too cosy.'

He stared at Laura with a coy smile on his face. She couldn't bring herself to return that smile, so she briefly looked away. But her curiosity overcame her misgivings and she enquired,

"Why are you here?"

He cocked his head to the side with a smirk on his face that then changed to irritation.

Silently, he studied her for a moment then decided to answer her ridiculous question. "I'm here to see Claire of course. Is that a problem?"

Laura stared at him for a while without uttering a word. Her answer was plaguing her conscience so she spat it out at him catching him off guard. "It's not that it's a problem. I'm just confused as to how you knew that Claire was here? Also, I'm wondering since when you two got so close?"

George cocked his head back and laughed out loud. His deep, hoarse laughter echoed in the air. Laura stared at him intently and blurted out, "I wouldn't laugh if I was you mate. If I wanted to, I would have you thrown out of here. We would see who would get the last laugh".

Instantly his smile dissipated and was replaced by anger creating a domineering facial expression that made Laura felt uncomfortable. She knew that if she wasn't in protective mode on Claire's behalf, she would have shrivelled up under the intensity of his gaze, but somehow managed to stand her ground. There was a flash of something dark and dangerous in his eyes. The atmosphere felt thick with tension but despite this, Laura maintained eye contact as she stuck her nose in the air signalling that she was not backing down. He became irritated by her gesture as he found her impossible to deal with. He never had a woman that stood up to his wrath the way Laura did. Usually, they would back off and apologise seeking his forgiveness and he would make them suffer for their insolence. "You wouldn't dare do such a thing. I dare you to try and you would live to regret…"

The door to Claire's room burst open interrupting George's threat. The medical consultant and his team walked in, accompanied by the nurse assigned to provide the relevant medical care Claire needed, wheeling a sterile trolley carrying gauzes, wound dressings and other sterile equipment designed to complete the procedure. Frightened by the unexpected noise of the door behind her, Laura shakily turned around. The appearance of those piercing oceanic blue eyes made her feel faint.

It couldn't be, could it?

There they were again looking in her direction, that icy glare of recognition that shocked her system. This was something that she couldn't deal with right now. It would open old wounds that she didn't want to deal with again, but the drive for closure pushed her further towards his direction no matter how she tried to resist the urges that rose up inside her. Those eyes were always the most captivating. They both stared at each other for a moment, the conflict of emotions flashing in both of their eyes, asking so many questions without any answers given. He appeared as though he was about to approach her, but hesitated. After preparing everything for the procedure, the other staff members stood by glancing from one to the other. Eventually realising that neither Laura, nor the man behind those eyes, intended to break eye contact with each other. Although their curiosity was piqued and they wanted to know what the connection was between these two, they knew that something more important took precedence over the display between one of their leading consultants and Laura. "Dr Laurent! Dr Laurent! Everything is ready to complete the procedure. Are you ready to start?"

This pulled him out of his daze and back to the matter at hand. He tore his eyes away from Laura with difficulty and spoke to his colleagues in medical jargon. They completed a series of tasks such as doing repeat checks of Claire's vital signs and was pleased with the results. "Alright, everyone, let's get this done and see how it goes. Stay alert for any changes," the familiar voice bellowed at his colleagues.

The team of medical staff worked efficiently side by side, making sure that the procedure was done without any mistakes. Carefully those hands, the ones she trusted with her life, her safety, her comfort extended and were slowly removing the tube from Claire's throat, whilst someone else kept a close eye on her vital signs for any changes. They revived Claire and checked her vital signs again. As if on cue, when the procedures were finally complete, Laura released a breath that she didn't realise that she'd been holding throughout the procedures, as she keenly watched every step-by-step movement, they did to remove the tube and revive Claire.

"Turn off the ventilator, so we can observe if the patient can breathe on her own," came his command.

"Okay, doctor. The ventilator has now been turned off."

"Now we wait. The rest is up to Claire and her will to survive."

The sweetness of his voice serenaded her into the warmth of the unknown. A place that she'd once felt protected, loved, special and most of all free. Laura closed her eyes and attentively listened every time he spoke. It was the closest thing she had to remembering, although it carried a great backlash to the raw wounds below the surface that she'd fought so many years to cover up. Her broken heart was never fully mended, but couldn't sustain moving on without some difficulty. She was trying to forget about him and now life threw him back in the equation so suddenly, when she was finally piecing together the last bits of her life in order to put the past behind her. If she was honest with herself, a part of her wanted him, no matter how many times she tried to convince herself that he was no good for her.

Laura struggled to maintain that decision and she hated herself for being so weak. It angered her from time to time when she reminisced on the memories of been around him. The feelings and emotion that he raised in her was exhilarating. The way her body betrayed her as it reacted to his presence, the way her heartbeat quickened back then and still did now irritated her, as she had thought that she was stronger now but he proved her wrong just by looking at her. Being bombarded by the flood of emotions that resurfaced wasn't healthy. It made Laura realised how much she'd missed him. He was the part of her that she couldn't erase, no matter how hard she'd tried. She felt confused as she couldn't figure out what to do to change that outcome.

'Stop it girl. You're just fooling yourself. He couldn't have thought about you, otherwise he would had searched the corners of the earth to find you. Besides he should never have left you without a word. Clearly, he didn't love you and… Quit it, damn it! This doesn't help the situation.'

Laura felt the rush of overwhelming emotions that were clouding her judgement and hindering her happiness as forcefully as a waterfall. As much as she fought with all her might, her emotions always got the better of her and she realised that she was fighting a losing battle. The tears stung the back of her eyes as they threatened to expose her weakness, but she couldn't give him the satisfaction of seeing the power he held over her. It was a battle of wills now and Laura knew it. She hunted for a distraction, as she needed one urgently. The emotions that clouded her judgement were ambushing her senses and she needed to think straight.

'Be strong for Claire. There's your bloody distraction. Come on girl. Is he *really worth it? Oh God! I'm losing this one really badly. I can't take this anymore. I want....'*

At this point Laura lost all control as the tears began streaming down her saddened face. It was impossible to prevent them from continually falling. She roughly wiped the tears away before anyone noticed but they kept on falling.

'Why now dammit?'

Those deep oceanic blue eyes were now turned in her direction, displaying concern and worry about her wellbeing.

'Crap! I wonder how long he'd been staring at me.'

Laura shyly looked at Freddie and realised that his eyes were filled with tears as the recognition of the emotions there held them at the edge of pain, hurt and despair. Swiftly, he blinked back the tears and focussed his attention back on his duties. Although Laura knew it was important that he focussed on ensuring that Claire was alright, she couldn't help but feel a pang of jealousy. It became too much for Laura to bear, so she ran out of the room leaving her sobs in her wake.

'Damn! Why now? I needed closure not heartache and pain. He must think that I'm a total fool.'

Running down the corridor towards the lifts, she could hear her name being called.

Even now she couldn't run away in peace.

"Please wait, Lau," came the voice again, more pleading than demanding.

Laura hesitated for a brief moment and then continued her way inside the lift. "Dr Laurent, there's a phone call for you."

"Who is it?" he said in annoyance.

"The caller said to tell you that it's your wife."

"Wife? Oh, I see. Tell her that I'll call her back. I'm just in the middle of something." And with that said he shouted, "please hold the lift."

A stranger reached out and held the button to keep the lift doors from closing. Laura felt annoyed by this, but decided to stand further back in the lift to the far-right hand corner. "Thank you, kind sir," he said calmly and stepped inside. He gazed in Laura's direction and walked toward her, standing so close to her that she could breathe him in. *'Gosh! He smells so alluringly good'.*

The scent of his citrus scented cologne, mixed with the apple scented antibacterial hand sanitizer he used, was a raunchy combination. She could only drink in the scent of him. It was making her feel light headed. He reached out his hand and touched hers, making Laura pulled back like she had been burnt. Instead of trying again, he dug his hands into his pockets.

`He has a wife. So, does that mean he has children too? He was always a family man`

The lift door closed taking them down a few floors before opening and letting out the kind stranger, who'd held the lift. As soon as it closed again, Freddie held Laura by the shoulders and turned her to face him. "I know that you have a lot of questions and I would answer them all, I promise."

"Promise is a comfort to a fool Freddie. And I was that fool, but no more will I be. Do you hear me? I am done being a fool for you. Now if you don't mind taking your hands off of me, please and thanks."

Freddie stared at Laura as though he had been stabbed in the heart. The pain streaked across his eyes. His eyes welled up with warm tears but he quickly looked away, blinking them back to where they came from. Laura felt terrible that she had spoken so abruptly to him, but she was hurting really badly and she didn't know what to do. As if sensing her inward battle Freddie quickly reached out and squeezed her hand reassuringly.

"We'll talk this through over lunch. Everything will be alright."

Laura gently nodded in acceptance. To ease the tension, he said, "your friend's vital signs are looking promising, but the next 24-48 hours will tell us more."

For the first time in a while this made Laura smile. It was the best news ever.

"So do you think that she will recover from this and be the same person that she once was?"

"Yes, it's certainly looking that way."

"Oh, thank God," Laura said with great relief streaking through her body. Without another word they both exited the hospital lift and made their way to the food court. They chose what they felt like eating and after paying the cashier, sat down opposite each other across a steel table. They ate in awkward silence and when they were finished exited the food court out into the open air. Laura suggested that they sat on the bench in the hospital gardens amongst the beautiful, scented flowers. That way she could avoid drowning in the scent of him. They sat down and took in the breath-taking view for a short time. Freddie looked at his watch and noted that he had half an hour left of his lunch break.

"Don't make me keep you from your duties, Dr Laurent," she said sarcastically.

Laura felt conflicted and contemptuous towards Freddie, but before she attempted to close that chapter again, she had to get to the bottom of why he abandoned her, and why he never showed up at their sanctuary? Why he never called? Was he faking about the way he felt towards her? Was she not good enough to meet his standards? Where did he go? And so much more.

As if reading her mind, he said, "I never meant to hurt you, my ray of sunshine. I didn't abandon you on purpose. Remember I told you that my grandmother was really ill… the whole family moved back to be nearer to her in order to take care of her. That day that we were supposed to meet, I tried to catch you at home on my way to the airport although there was limited time, I tried to let you know, Mon Cherie, as soon as I found out, but unfortunately, I had missed you. When I swung by the house, your mother answered the door as per usual and told me that you had already left. I explained to her what my dilemma was and gave her a written letter explaining everything to give to you. I swear."

"Hmm…Mmm…"

"I'm sure that you're wondering why I couldn't call you or write you letters, but guess what? I did."

"You did exactly what?"

"I wrote to you shortly after we arrived and every week thereafter. I called your house every day and kept getting the same excuses. It saddened me every time that you didn't care enough to write back and every time your mother answered the phone, she told me that you were really busy, or you were out with your new boyfriend and you didn't want to talk to me. That tore my heart to pieces, Mon Cherie. I really loved you and I felt hurt by what I presumed were your actions. I'm so sorry that I hurt you. It was unintentionally done. I care about you a lot, Lau, and still do. I was so tempted to run away and come back to find you, but that wasn't possible. Eventually, word came to me that you were engaged and pregnant. I was so torn by this as I'd hoped that it would have been you and me together forever, married and looking forward to having children of our own. It took me a while but after hearing the news, I wrote you one last letter explaining how I felt and to let you know that I finally accepted that we weren't meant to be, and how happy I was for you. All I ever wanted was for you to be happy Lau and if it meant that I wasn't included in that, then fair enough. And you never wrote back. Not even once. You never called back neither."

Once again, his eyes welled up with tears and he didn't conceal them, but allowed them to fall so that Laura could see that he was in pain. Laura stared at Freddie as if checking to see if he was faking the way he felt. She felt worse because she knew that she should have trusted that there was a valid reason for Freddie's sudden disappearance. A part of her felt guilty for the doubt.

'But why would my mother lie to me each day knowing the truth about the whole thing? Gosh! She concealed everything and comforted me like nothing happened. Why would she say that to Freddie?'

This had Laura puzzled. Laura took a deep breath and then spoke her mind as it might be her only opportunity to get things off her chest. "Freddie, I've always loved you, wanted you, but when you left, I thought that you didn't want me. I was so distraught; my heart was torn into a million pieces and I struggled to get it mended to the point it's at now. And could you believe that my own mother comforted me and told me that you were no good for me.

Although I didn't want to, as the years passed by, I began to be convinced that mum was probably right until now. I am really sorry that my mother hurt you."

As Freddie listened to Laura's confession more and more his anger rose as he could have found her a long time ago had he known that she was misled by false information from her mother's deception. Taking a deep breath in to steady his nerves he asked,

"Did you ever got engaged, pregnant or anything of the kind?"

Freddie sat on the bench keenly listening to Laura as he awaited the answer to his question, not sure what he was hoping to hear.

' What the hell are you hoping for man? But nothing springs to mind.'

"No Freddie, I didn't," she said with a little attitude. "To be honest, I tried dating again a couple times but they didn't work out because…"

Laura trailed off from what she was about to say and leant her head back running her fingers through the unruly curls on her head, as she stared up at the clear skies above. Freddie looked at her for a brief moment, smiled and then continued what he was about to say,

"Because…?"

Laura snapped her head forward and looked him in the eyes, her cheeks feeling extremely warm as she blushed. Then she smiled for the first time since they were in each other's company. "Oh, it's nothing. It wasn't important."

"It is to me."

Laura opened her mouth as if she was going to tell him what she had wanted to say earlier but instead closed her mouth tightly shut. Freddie's anticipation to hear what Laura had planned to say was short lived as she didn't continue.

`Damn.'

"The thing was when I returned to this country years ago, Mon Cherie, the first place I went from the airport was to your house to find you. I did this every day, some mornings and some evenings for a month. Then I finally gave up because I was causing myself more pain. Your mother told me in the end that you had moved away to a different country with your husband and child. Horrible woman. She promised me something in return for a favour."

He half mumbled the last line low enough to be out of earshot.

"I told myself that all I wanted from you right now was just closure, but now I've got it, the revelations made me feel worse, Freddie. Can I ask you something and you answer me truthfully?"

"Yes of course. You know that you can ask me anything and I would always be honest with you, Mon Cherie."

Laura nervously shifted on the bench. She took her hands and brushed the front of her top as if dusting it, although nothing was there. She felt as though she was sweating profusely and this made her felt uncomfortable. Freddie stared at her amazed, with a smirk on his face realising that he still had an effect on her. Finally, Laura built up the courage and said,

"I overheard something earlier when the receptionist was calling after you for the phone call and I need to know if it's true or not. Are you really married?"

It was Freddie's turn to feel nervous. He ran his hands through his black, thick hair and inhaled and exhaled deeply. His eyes widened as the question escaped Laura's beautiful lips. He couldn't believe what she was asking.

`*Does that mean she… nah forget that.*'

Laura watched on as a nervous Freddie suddenly stood up looking in a different direction, eyebrows creased together.

`I wish that I could tell you the truth but if I do everything would change between us.

You might hate me, and I can't have that.' Laura looked at Freddie as he battled with his inner thoughts. As she was about to tell him not to bother about answering her since it was that difficult to say yes or no, Freddie turned to face her. His approach was mysterious. She couldn't read his intentions. His body language was a little strange. Reaching out to her, Freddie gently pulled Laura to her feet and held her tightly in his arms for as long as she would permit him to. Nostalgia taunted his memory and his senses as he inhaled the strawberry scent of her hair, as he closed his eyes envisioning the way they used to be. Initially, Laura was very tense in his arms for a moment. Eventually, she relaxed in his warm embrace, resting her head against his hard, muscled chest whilst listening to the steady beat of his heart. "Tu me manques."

"What does that mean?"

Freddie smiled and whispered in her ear. It means "I miss you."

Laura felt the heat rush to her cheeks. She secretly smiled at Freddie's statement. Just then Freddie decided that he was going to take that leap of faith and answer Laura's question from earlier on. As soon as he opened up his mouth to confess, his pager bleep loudly displaying an emergency and a telephone number to call back on the screen. Reluctantly he broke off their embrace and said, "I'm so sorry to do this to you. We'll have to catch up another time when I have a day off work. I have to go, Lau. Duty calls I'm afraid."

Freddie took one last look at Laura and ran off with a satisfied smile.

"Okay, I'm glad that we cleared the air somewhat," Laura called after him. Freddie raised his hand in the air and put his thumb up just before he disappeared through the hospital entrance. Laura grabbed her bag and headed back into the hospital again to return to Claire's room. When Laura arrived on to the seventh floor, she saw doctors and nurses running to and from into a room that looked like Claire's. Laura's heart plummeted to the floor. Panic set in so suddenly that she ran as fast as she could down the corridor almost falling over a parked trolley on the side by the wall.

"Could you stop running in the hospital dear, before either you or someone else gets hurt?"

"Huh! Oh! I'm so sorry ma'am. I'm in a rush."

The receptionist rolled her eyes at Laura's response, and stood there watching as Laura stopped running and instead walked as fast as she could down the corridor towards the room. When she got to Claire's room huffing and puffing from shortness of breath, partly due to having run and partly due to sheer panic, she saw George standing with his back to the door at Claire's bedside, with his phone clamped to his ear as he spoke to the caller on the line. "They say that she's going to make a full recovery."

He paused as he listened to whatever the caller had to ask, and then said. "Arghh… Yes, she would remember everything."

He paused again for a brief moment and then spoke. "Yep, she's breathing on her own now. Don't worry, things will be taken care of. I haven't forgotten the job at hand."

George quickly hangs up the phone when he heard Laura's footsteps entering the room. He had a smirk on his face as if all was well. Laura stared at him with a blank expression as she controlled her emotions within, instead of throwing accusations.

Chapter 21

Laura left the hospital much later than she wanted to, as she felt concerned for Claire's safety based on the piece of the conversation that she'd overheard from George. She couldn't help but wonder who he was talking to on the phone about Claire and why? And what it was that he was going to take care of? Was he there to harm Claire and what was his motive for doing so? Eventually, after George had left, Laura waited another ten minutes before she gathered her belongings and left, alerting the night staff that she was leaving for the night.

Laura hurriedly walked towards the lifts, finger punched the button and waited patiently for the lift to arrive. Shortly afterwards when the lift doors opened, she stepped inside and pushed the ground floor button. 'Doors closing.' The lift descended to the ground floor without making a single stop. Laura found her thoughts drifting back to the conversation she'd overheard with George. Not completely dismissing it, she decided that whenever George was around, she would keep a closer eye on him to protect her friend as a preventative. 'Ping, doors opening.' Laura stepped out of the lift surveying her surroundings as she made her way across the hospital lobby, and out into the chill night's air.

Automatically, Laura rubbed her hands down her arms to warm up herself. Scanning around she looked to see if she could see any taxi parked in the taxi rank bay. Luckily when she was about to telephone the taxi company to book a driver, a taxi pulled up and parked letting out a customer. Immediately Laura approached the taxi and calmly spoke to the driver who agreed to take her to her destination. Laura opened the rear door and got in the taxi. "Thank you, sir."

The driver nodded his head in appreciation and drove off after Laura closed the car door and was fully settled in the back seat.

Her mind kept drifting all over the place but focussed on nothing in particular. In between Laura held a brief conversation with the driver on a variety of topics. After she arrived at her house, she paid the driver the asking fare. " Thank you dear for the business."

"Oh, you're welcome. But I should really be the one to tell you thank you for bringing me home, although I hadn't pre-booked."

"No need to thank me miss. I wish your friend a speedy recovery."

"Thank you, sir," she said with an appreciative smile spread across her tired face.

Gently Laura opened the car door after replacing her purse in her handbag draped over her shoulder. She stepped out and waved at the driver after closing the car door just before he drove off beeping the horn in response. Laura strode up the driveway towards the front door, opened it and walked inside the darkened house shutting and locking the door securely behind her. This had become Laura's normal routine lately because of all the strange things that had been happening around her. Now Laura extended out her hand and felt along the wall for the light switch. She grazed something and withdrew her hand instantly before taking a step forward and reaching out again; it puzzled her that despite the switch not being in an awkward place, she just couldn't find it tonight.

'Am I really that tired? I must be. Oh well I'll rest up real soon.'

Finally, she thought, as her fingers touched the outer edge of the light switch. But as she took another step forward Laura felt a solid blow to her head before she could turn on the light.

Instinctively, she raised her hand to clutch the spot and felt the warm liquid oozing from the battered area. Before she could turn around, she lost her balance and fell to the ground with a thud. The keys fell from her hand a little further away from where her body lies. Laura was in a daze, as she squinted and watched the dark coloured trousers and shoes step around her in the glare of the intruder's torch light. Then nothing. Everything went pitch black. The last noise she'd heard was the keys. Her keys in fact, as she was dragged by the legs.

As she regained consciousness her whole body was in extreme pain. Whoever it was, was still in the room. In fact, in her bedroom.

'Why does my body ache this much?'

The person sat on the side of the bed with a cold, damp flannel pressed against the injured part of her head as they wiped away the blood. Laura could barely open her eyes wide enough to try and figure out who it was. Each time that she attempted to open her eyes, the excruciating pain in her head would increase tenfold, so she kept them closed as she winced in pain. While she lay there, her mind was in flight mode. Her brain was instructing her to run but her body couldn't move no matter how badly she wanted to.

'Is this it? Is this how I'm supposed to die? But why?'

The turmoil and confusion within her mind were driving her insane. Who the hell was above her, sitting on her bedside, touching her face, invading her privacy and violated her without her permission?

'Who the heck was he anyways?'

He avoided looking at her face to hide his identity. Something about his posture, the way he sat there seemed familiar to Laura.

'Hmm... There could only be a few possibilities.'

There was that cologne scent again taunting her flared nostrils as she breathed deeply.

'I wonder. Could it be Josh?'

With that conclusion in mind Laura took the risk and called out. "Why, Josh? What did I ever do to you?"

The intruder's hand stilled against her head. Laura felt more frightened at the thought of what might happen next to her. Squinting her eyes slyly she wondered,

'Is it really him?'

Curiously, Laura stared at the person sat beside her. "Whose Josh?" the intruder queried in a low tone so as to distort their voice a little. The sound of the voice made it abundantly clear that it was definitely not Josh who sat at her bedside. As she replayed the voice in her head, somehow it vaguely reminded her of Alex although she wasn't a hundred percent certain.

'But why would Alex do this to me? It doesn't make any sense. He appeared to be such a sweet guy, so attractive and... Don't get carried away girl, now is not the bloody time for nonsense. For goodness' sake! Your life maybe in danger at the moment and you're here drooling. Don't be an idiot. Hold up, he smells like Josh with that same cologne. What's this? Are they in this together? Okay, was this *their intention to pretend to be nice and deep down turn out to be a psychopath or did I judge Josh wrongly. Only God knows.'*

The coldness of the flannel zapped her out of her confused thoughts, reminding her that she was still in danger no matter who it was that sat on her bedside. Laura rose her hand to her head instinctively and felt the warm moisture on her fingertips.

'Oh no! I'm bleeding out. Am I dying now, right here?'

Internally Laura was kicking herself for not taking heed off the warnings that she received. The intruder shifted further forward towards her where the street light could illuminate his face. Laura finally opened her eyes when she felt him come closer. The shock that shot through her body was like a lightning bolt; she was incredulous because although she had an inclination, she genuinely did not expect to be right. It was him. It was really him.

"What are you doing here?"

"I came to see you. Is that a crime?"

Laura rolled her eyes and looked away from him as she didn't believe a word he said. *'Another time without all this torment and strange happenings would have been better. I would have been flattered by the gesture but it was too much of a coincidence that he just appeared in my home immediately after I got attacked. And here he is sat on my bed like nothing's happened. My body hurts so much. What did he do to me? I can feel his eyes staring at me. Was it him?'* Laura creased her eyebrows as she returned his gaze. Her thoughts were still in overdrive. "But how…"

Interrupting her in mid-sentence, "how do I know where you live?"

Folding her arms tightly as if shielding herself, Laura just nodded in agreement and looked at Alex sceptically. "That was easy. I was thinking about you a lot since the first time that we met, so eventually I made it my business to find out where you lived so that we could have a talk about this connection between us." he said with a mischievous smile on his face as if believing his own words.

"What connection Alex?"

"Nice try, but I know that you felt it too. Even the way that you reacted when you saw me, and the way your eyes undress me, your body language spoke volumes. You may lie to me but your body language says different. It radiates this heat whenever I'm close to you.

Like now, although you are trying to conceal it. The last time I saw you in your office for the meeting about my daughter… Hmm… Don't get me started. Like I said before and I'm saying it again, although you are a bit wary of me about why I'm here, your body still betrays you."

Alex had this unmistakable self-confidence, a dominance that said he always gets what he wants. And right now, she seemed to be his target. Laura was unsure whether to be fearful or to be flattered by the revelation. Deciding not to give in although she knew that Alex was right, Laura stood her ground and denied the way she felt about Alex. She tried her best to block out her feelings as her life seemed to be hanging in the balance in a dangerous game. Feeling angry at herself for even contemplating the thought of being with Alex, Laura forcefully pushed her hands onto the mattress and pushed herself upright into a seated position, crying out at the intensity of the pain that shot through her whole body.

"Say whatever makes you feel good about yourself and believe what you want to but although I may have thought about you just a little too much in fact, I can't be with…"

Interrupting before she said anything more, his lips came crashing down on hers, so sudden, so warm, so soft, so… mmm… Laura couldn't say another word as she was so caught up in the moment. Gently she pushed at his broad, muscular chest, but there was no easing of the intensity of his searing kiss. Instead, his kiss deepened after he slightly nipped at her lower lip making her gasp and open her mouth to him. Laura was caught in a trap as a part of her was saying that it felt so wrong and the other part was saying that it felt so right. Her dreams were nothing compared to this moment of bliss. If she wasn't sitting down already, she was sure that her knees would have buckled under her at the first impact of his lips.

Alex's tongue darted into her moist mouth the moment she opened it as if searching for his lifeline. The sheer hunger she felt as his tongue entangled with hers doing a dance of pleasure in unison. mmm… Laura moaned in his mouth, echoing in the silence of her bedroom.

Eventually her hands snaked around the back of his neck, her fingers entangled in his jet- black, silky hair pulling him even closer. She held him so close as if she couldn't get enough of him. Alex groaned into her mouth as he felt the way she clung to him, her body answering his every call. Barely pulling apart to look into Laura's eyes, what he saw there made him groan again. The sexual hunger there nearly made him loose his self-control. He wanted her but he needed to restrain himself until the right time. He was confident that he would have her very soon. Taking a deep breath he kissed her again and again. He peppered her neck with hungry kisses. He kissed her collarbone as she leant back enough to give him access. He smiled against her skin, then continued to kiss her moving down to her breasts. Her peaks hard and ready for him to suckle into his mouth. He felt obligated to answer their call. Taking a peak into his mouth, he expertly sucked on it, flicking his tongue against the top of it. "Mmm… This is better than the dreams I had. You taste so good Laura."

The way he made her feel with each touch, with each kiss, sent bolts of heat to her core, building up a pool of moisture within. Instead of responding to his statement, Laura reached out and pulled him closer and kissed him again. This time she was the one in control, she hoped. She had to try all she could to stay alive for as long as physically possible.

Whatever Alex's intention was to begin with she was hoping that he would have forgotten it by now?

'Focus girl, keep him occupied long enough to work out a plan of action where you'll still be alive tomorrow, and the next day and the day after that. After all, this should be easy to do because you know that you liked him a lot and dreamt of this moment, a life that you two could share together. Maybe just maybe I can convince him forget about hurting me in replace of…'

Alex was blankly staring at her, puzzled as to what had distracted her attention away from him. "Laura baby, is everything alright? What's on your mind because you're staring at me strangely?"

Returning from her thoughts back to the scene in front of her, Laura responded as quickly as possible to avoid suspicion.

"Oh, I'm just thinking about you and how much I wanted you."

Not that it was far from the truth, but she couldn't tell him that she was trying to keep him occupied as long as possible whilst she planned her escape. Laura placed her hands both sides of his handsome face and peppered him with kisses along his neck, collarbone and face. He closed his eyes for a brief moment enjoying the moment.

"That feels so good," he said in a low, husky tone. But let me tell you a secret, "it doesn't help me to contain myself. I'm losing all my self-control when it comes down to you.

You make me want to make love to you all night, Lau. So please don't tempt me," he whispered in her ear so deep, so husky, and so damn sexy.

Laura felt the heat rise to her cheek as she blushed at his words. His voice at this very moment was doing things to her that she couldn't explain. All she knew was that it felt so good. It made her body feel so alive. All her nerve endings were alive and tingling with a blazing heat she couldn't understand. She loved the way it made her feel. In fact, she loved the way he made her come alive. He kissed her fervently again, deepening the kiss almost instantly. This time the kiss was different. It was more passionate, much more passionate, needier, more… Her mind was now scrambled till she couldn't think straight.

'Oh God! This was bliss.

She clung to him for strength as she felt her body falling into weakened state. The pleasurable experience that Laura was having made her not want the moment to end. Laura closed her eyes; the fire that burned inside became more and more unbearable as it settled at her core.

She felt the wetness from the pool of moisture there. Suddenly, Alex pulled away from her leaving her feeling empty and abandoned. Their breathing was ragged as it tried to cool them down.

"I'm so sorry Lau, but I have to go. I hope that your head feels better soon."

For a brief moment, Laura looked at Alex confused. The way he spoke as if he was not the one to hurt her. 'And if that was the case, then who did and how did Alex get inside the house?'

"Alex before you go, can I ask you something?" "Sure. What's bothering you?"

"Was it you who hurt me? I need to know."

"Of course not. Why would I do something that silly? What reason would I have to hurt you? I really like you."

"I don't know because I remember coming home, opening the front door, going inside…"

Laura massaged her temples as she tried really hard to recollect her earlier actions before the incident. She creased her eyebrows as she struggled to remember everything. Hmm… Err… She gently bit her lower lip subconsciously. Erm… And I think that I shut the front door behind me, bolted the locks in the usual way that I do and ERM…averting her eyes up towards the ceiling as she what would happen next. Suddenly she stopped talking, a fearful look drawn on her face. At this point Laura's was wide eyed as she stared at Alex who looked back at her with worry under the glare of her bedside light. "What is it Laura? What's wrong?"

You looked as though you've seen a ghost. "Ahh… Yes I remember now, then I was feeling along the wall to find the light switch when I accidentally touched someone or something. Then, then when I finally found it and I was about to click it, that's when I felt the blow to the head. But in everything that I've said, not one detail reveals that I saw you and greeted you. It's strange. How did you get inside my house Alex, and I want the truth and nothing but that? You got that?"

"Sure," he replied as he looked at her through hooded eyes.

"Well, I'm waiting Alex. Do you want me to call the police and see what they have to say about this scenario?"

Before Alex could answer Laura's question, he was typing something on his mobile that seemed to have taken his full attention. Alex was taken aback by Laura's question, so much so that he repeated it, as if he was trying to understand the words. "Do you want me to call the police?"

Laura felt confused, because she'd expected Alex to just answer the question and that would be it. "No Laura! There's no need to call the police. I have nothing to hide."

"So, if you have nothing to hide, you wouldn't mind answering my question then.

How did you get inside my house Alex?"

"You honestly don't remember letting me in baby? Just before you closed the front door you let me in. But before you ask, no I didn't see who hit you in the head otherwise they would never have stood a chance. Plus, the house was too dark. After it happened, I switched on the light and the person was already gone, so I just looked after you instead."

"So why did you not take me to the hospital?"

"I've got medical training, so I knew what to do, Hun."

"Thank you for looking after me because I'm not sure what would have happened if you weren't here."

'You would have been just fine. You wouldn't have… I want to…'

Laura could hear Alex's mobile vibrating constantly, but he did not answer. "That sounds urgent. Someone's eager to get hold of you."

With guilt riding his conscience, Alex pretended that everything was alright. "It's okay, Lau, they can wait. I'll call them back shortly. Anyway, it's extremely late so I'm going to go home now. I'll check in on you tomorrow or something. Plus you need to rest."

"I will, I will. I'll come and let you out and lock up behind you," she said with a smile as she playfully shoved him in the back.

Steadily Laura rose from her bed to her unsteady feet and led the way down the stairs to the front door, with Alex following close behind her. Eventually his long stride came alongside her as they both descended the stairs. Just before they reached the front door Alex stopped and dipped down swiftly as if picking up something from the floor, sweeping it into his hand with a satisfied grin on his face. When Laura turned to look at him, he pretended to be was finishing off tying his trainer laces. He was wearing black trainers similar to the one Laura saw before she lost all consciousness. Seeing that display Laura didn't think much of it. As Alex rose slowly to his feet, a dark figure ran quickly by, knocking Alex over to the ground as they ran towards the back door. At first Laura was frozen in fear until she saw Alex fall to the floor. His mobile slid across the floor and hit her feet. Buzz, another message came in on his mobile now. Alex rose to his feet really quickly without making eye contact with Laura and stared directly at his mobile as if hoping that somehow, he'd drum up some mystical magic powers that would automatically slide his mobile back to him. Laura swooped down and swiped the phone up from the floor and looked at the screen. She noticed that it was a text message from an unknown number asking him to meet up. It read, 'Oi mate! It's done. Meet me asap at Lavender Avenue, Stone w…'

Laura wished that she could have read the rest of the message but it was impossible unless Alex unlocked his mobile.

'But why should he? I'm nothing to him anyway.'

Bearing that in mind, Laura sulked for a bit before shaking off the feeling. She had no right to be feeling like that. And she knew it. That didn't stop her from feeling cheated though. She felt that Alex was concealing secrets from her and she didn't like that. She wanted to know what he was hiding. She wanted to read the rest of the text message.

Although she read the first part of the message it piqued her curiosity. 'Hmm…I wonder what was done. And why it wasn't a saved number? Was he doing something dodgy?'

Laura looked up and saw Alex directly in front of her with his palm outstretched waiting for her to relinquish his mobile into his opened hand. Laura saw the slightly irritated look on Alex's face and hastily handed over his mobile. She felt the urge to query what the unknown person was referring to, but she refrained from doing so. Alex took his belongings and dusted off his dark blue denim jeans and black t-shirt and headed towards the door. He stood by the front door waiting for Laura to quit her runaway thoughts and unbolt and open the door to let him out. Realising the focus of Alex's eyes, Laura quickly moved forward and slowly unbolt the door, realising that it was bolted in the usual way that she'd always done it. Laura gasps at the sight in front of her. "Huh… So strange."

"What is it?"

"Arghh… Nothing. Don't worry about it. I'll figure it out."

Laura felt bad having to lie to Alex if he wasn't her attacker, but it had to be done.

She needed to be sure. She couldn't reveal anymore, information that could be compelling in his capture. She didn't want to give him any pre-warning as it could change the way he does things. She had her reservations about what she thought of the whole situation. If Alex was the attacker, she needed to figure out how best to catch where she could provide sufficient evidence to the police to lock him away for a while. "Okay, no problem. Take care of yourself, Lau."

"Thanks, I will."

Laura pulled open the door and Alex exited the house. Calling over his shoulder he shouted, "I'll call you or something. Laters."

Laura raised up her hand and waved goodbye to Alex as he got into his black mustang and drove away. Without hesitation, she closed the door, locking it in the usual way and ran to the back door quickly to check to see if it was closed. Reaching out and closing the back door. Laura felt satisfied and breathed more at ease. Usually, she switched off the lights before going upstairs, but this time after she grabbed a bottle of water from refrigerator, she made her way upstairs, gulped about four mouthfuls of the chilled liquid and climbed into bed exhausted and still confused.

Arms outstretched as wide as they could go, with a relieved look plastered up on her weight loss face, Claire said, "Finally, I'm out of that wretched place for a few months now."

She continued, "I slept like a baby, well nicely wrapped up for a long time in my own bed, my personal space."

Laura stared at her best friend and shook her head as she leant her head against the wall and laughed to her hearts content.

"I'm happy that you're home too, girl. I've definitely missed having you around."

'Girl, you scaredy cat. Claire can't protect you from this. She needs protecting herself.'

Laura sniggered to herself, at her own thoughts.

"Hey! You going crazy without me huh? Share the joke. Don't be a Meanie." Claire nudged her shoulder playfully and collapsed in fits of laughter. "Well, I'm here now, Lau, and I promise not to be so careless again."

With that said Claire pulled her best friend, Laura, into an embrace with a smile. "Although is only been a week since I was discharged from the hospital, I want everything to get back to normal, Lau. How's things at work girl?"

"Everything's okay to be honest. Everyone sends their love."

"Aww… How sweet of them," she teased as she scowled at the thought.

She was just fed up with everybody pitying her. Laura noticed the sudden change in Claire's attitude and decided not to pry. If it was something to worry about Claire would have spoken to her about it to obtain some good advice as Laura was always her voice of reason. A brief moment later Claire was here chirpy, jolly self again although Josh no longer wanted to be with her. She didn't mind it much because her mind was set on someone else. Claire was never one to wallow in heartbreak. As she was never short on offers, Claire would move on to a new relationship really quickly. It was like she was filling a void deep within to hide her own insecurities. On the other hand, Laura was the hopeless romantic that clung on to her past relationship. She wasn't the type to move on immediately. Laura was spending some time with Alex occasionally, but it was never truly comfortable. Although he wasn't in relationship with anyone else, he was quite a secretive person. She couldn't understand what it was that felt so strange.

'Eventually I'll figure it out, I know it.'

A few weeks flew by in the blink of an eye. Claire was much stronger and was going out quite a lot. She was always having secretive phone calls, but would never reveal what the discussions were about. Most times Claire would be arguing with her mystery caller, but still refused to confide in her best friend, Laura. Although Laura was concerned about Claire, she refused to pressure Claire for any information because she knew that when Claire was ready, she would talk it out with her.

What grabbed Laura's undivided attention was the strange things that were still happening around her especially when she was alone. Although she had received death threats and warning notes against telling anyone, she ignored the warnings and informed the police. However, they kept telling her that they'd look into it, but came back with the answer of, there was nothing that they could do unless the person tried to harm her in anyway. Unfortunately, there was no way of identifying and providing an accountable description of the person or persons as she never once laid eyes upon their uncovered faces, so there was very little information for the police to go on, which made it difficult for the police to do their jobs. Laura warned Claire to be mindful of any weird, suspicious things and any random maniacs staring at her through the window or anywhere. "They could be hiding out inside the house, too, so be extremely vigilant about this." Claire furrowed her brows as she listened to her best friend's shaky voice. Laura looked terrified and kept pulling on the hem of her dress avoiding eye contact as she recalled the past few months' events. She thought that Claire might see her as a push over, a weakling and that she wasn't. Her body trembled frantically. Laura tried to steady her nerves as she inhaled deeply and exhaled sharply letting out a heavy sigh. She wanted it all to be over desperately.

As Claire listened keenly to her friend's traumatic problems, the anger welled up inside of her causing her hands to ball up tightly in a fist ready for action, her brows creased together displaying such rage. Laura warned Claire not to intervene as she didn't want her getting hurt again or worse.

After Claire heard more and more about what Laura had been experiencing for months, being stalked, threatened and her life possibly at risk, she became infuriated. What angered her most was that since she had that dreadful car crash everything had got terrifying for her friend and there was no one to support her and protect her from these idiots who got a kick out of torturing people. Now this had Claire wondering if the car crash was linked somehow to what was happening to Laura although there was no evidence to prove it. Claire defied Laura's warnings and began to secretly do her own investigation, gathering whatever useful information she could find. After a few days, Claire thought that she had figured out who the mastermind behind the stalking was and why? Before she went off to her appointment to confront the person, she wrote a note stating,

Lau, I believe that I know who was doing this to you. I think that I figured out the reason why too. I have some information that you need to see. We need to talk tonight when I get back home.' Love, you know who. 😃

Laura had left the house earlier that morning as whenever she could, she would still visit Amy at the hospital to distract herself from her traumatic life experiences. Amy was recovering slowly and was looking forward to hopefully going home soon.

Claire felt great about her accomplishment. She knew that Laura would tell her off at first and then show her gratitude for what she had done for her. Claire smiled to herself as she placed the note that she had written for Laura's attention on the refrigerator held up by a fridge magnet. Afterwards Claire exited the house and travelled to her medical appointment. When her appointment was finished, Claire decided that she was going to confront the stalker on her own. She felt that maybe she would be able to resolve this matter without involving the authorities. She had hoped that she could reassure Laura at the end that it was all over, if she could get through to the stalker and get them to cease their torment towards Laura. As the destination where Claire was supposed to meet the stalker fast approached a nervous, scared feeling possessed her body. Her breathing became a little erratic, but she tried her hardest to slow her breathing down in order to steady her nerves. Claire inhaled deeply and exhaled and managed to slow her raggedy breath as she steadily approached the stalker. She felt her hands shaking and shoved them into her pockets so that they wouldn't notice. She tried to put on a hard, brave exterior. "I know that it was you and most likely your accomplices tormenting and threatening my friend," she blurted out with rage.

The stalker leant up against the wall, crossed their arms across their chest and perched a foot onto the wall behind them in a relaxed manner. When Claire hailed the accusation at them, they laughed out loudly as if they were amused. "And what are you going to do about it?" they mused.

Claire was furious at their goading response, as if they were playing some kind of sinister game. She extracted her hands that was buried deep in her pockets and automatically balled them in to fists by her side. They studied her reaction and burst into hysterical laughter. This increased the anger welling up inside her. Claire wasn't happy with the response that they was giving her. This fuelled an argument between them both that became very heated. At first, Claire didn't want to back down but when she realized that the stalker was no longer perched against the wall in a relaxed manner and was looking at her angrily, she thought to herself that maybe this was a bad idea to approach him in the first place, and to meet alone.

'No one knows the exact location of where I am and who I was meeting. I didn't leave any indication as to my intentions. Here I go again acting without thinking.'

The thought of being alone with the stalker now was terrifying. The argument was out of control and making her feel uneasy. The stalker was slowly approaching her slyly, but Claire was vigilant enough to notice the way the distance between them was getting shorter and shorter. Slowly she took a few steps back when she thought that they weren't looking. Claire noticed the persistent look on his face and, confused that there was no way of getting through to them so she turned on her heels and began to walk away. "Where do you think that you're going? Not so fast. You're not leaving here. I can't have you wrecking things for me."

Her heart beat like it was a galloping race horse in her chest at the moment. She could hear the blood rushing through her ears. Adrenalin was her medicine, her drive. She looked at him wide-eyed as her lip quivered and her teeth chattered when she was about to speak. Despite this she pleaded with puppy dog eyes, her hands thrown in the air in a surrender,

"Please, just let me leave. No one knows I'm here so I won't tell Laura anything. She has no clue about any of this."

The stalker stared at her intently for a moment with a devilish grin and lunged after Claire. Claire quickly dodged out of the way and they slid across the gravelled pavement with enough distance for her to launch into running mode without getting caught. They looked at her and smiled but it wasn't a smile that said you are forgiven; it was a smile that hid the evil intent under its mask. This made her feel uneasy. Claire felt waves of shivers run up and down her spine. Cold sweat was plastered all over her body. The wind suddenly felt sharp causing her body to shiver although it was a hot, bright sunny day. The stalker held up a gloved covered hand and said behind their smile,

"I was just playing with you. You can leave".

There was something about the way they dragged those words like they was forced out of them unwilling. Claire didn't hesitate to see if they would change their mind. Turning in the direction in home, she began running. She darted through all the shortcuts that she knew would take her home, knowing that she wasn't far, so at least if she got inside, then she stood a chance in calling the police. She looked back and realised that there was no one chasing after her but despite this she kept on running. She had seen too many thriller movies to know that she shouldn't stop running, and hell don't fall over. Finally, she thought, as she saw her house in the distance. She was out of breath but continued running regardless. She was panting and gasping for air and her chest was tightening but she had to keep going. She speedily ran up the driveway and extracted the keys with shaky hands from her jeans pocket only to accidentally drop them. 'Shit!' Quickly she picked them up and hurried to the front door, but not before looking back to check her surroundings for danger. Satisfied that the coast was clear, she pushed the keys in the lock of the front door and tried quickly to open it. When she swung the door open, all she felt was a hard kick to the stomach, knocking the wind out of her, making her spray saliva as she staggered backwards on to the porch and fell. The attacker grabbed her and bounded her hands and feet. Claire tried to scream even louder but they taped her mouth tightly shut to stop her from the continuous screaming she had already started. Claire was then hoisted over the attacker's shoulder and was carried to the parked car that was situated next to the bushy hedges just past their drive. It was well concealed under the big oak tree. If you didn't look closely, you would never have seen it. The attacker opened the car boot and dumped her in, forcing her limbs to bend, to fit in properly.

Chapter 22

"Oh shit! Me and my big mouth. Why did I have to be jolly Miss brave talking about I'm confronting someone that dangerous. Arghh… You stupid, stupid girl. You don't think first, do you? Alright, alright just need to figure out a way to escape right? That's all."

Claire felt the vibration of the car as he started the ignition. The car was now in motion taking her away from her safe haven. Damn it felt strange been driven like this. It gave her a nauseated feeling in her painful stomach. She tucked her knees tightly against her chest to withstand the pain she was feeling. He was no longer cruising. He was now driving as if he was in a hurry to get to a set destination but without drawing any unwanted attention to the vehicle and himself. He was smart. He knew what he was doing, even though he was a little wreck less. He had no remorse when it came down to the humps on the road. The way he drove over the humps, like he didn't care if it damaged the car or not. Claire could hear and feel the impact as the car hit against the road when it went over the humps. Each time it went over another hump and the car hit the road she was bounced up and down. When he swerved, left or right, she was flung around in the trunk, knocking into whatever he had in the bags. She couldn't brace herself as she couldn't hold on. Claire hit her head on a solid object in a bag, not to mention how she had lost count of the number of times that she hit her stomach and her side. Claire would cry out through muffled noises as loud as she could. Now the radio was on to drown out her cries. Claire tightly closed her eyes each time she cried out as the intensity of the pain increased. Silently she cursed as she felt that the attacker was purposely driving like that. Unfolding her legs Claire decided that she was going to try and free herself but no amount of wriggling, twisting and tugging could help her loosen whatever was binding her wrists and legs, keeping them so tightly together. The twisting of her wrists and legs began to cause her pain. She could feel the burning sensation as it built up. She winced as the pain became unbearable. Her inner thoughts were really wild as she imagined every possible scenario that she could think of to escape, but each one Claire came up with, was not feasible enough. Claire was pondering if she was going to die or would she be saved, and by whom? To Claire this seemed pretty unlikely that she would be rescued, for the reason that no one knew that she'd been kidnapped and no one knew where she'd been taken. Claire felt her fighting spirits evaporate and her energy drain away slowly.

'It hadn't been so long since I got discharged from hospital and my body is still in recovery mode, but after that kick to the stomach it must have caused more damage to me. I was sure that he would listen to me like he always does and stop tormenting Laura, but this time I didn't expect him to retaliate like this. Silly, silly me. He was acting weird for a while, so I should have noticed the signs and braced myself for the worst. He was usually so sweet, so kind and attentive. But…'

Claire lay there half curled up, trapped, but then suddenly her eyes abruptly flew open wide open.

'It must be… There must be… Oh no! There's more than one mastermind in this, why didn't I see that before I confronting them? No wonder, they were acting so out of the ordinary and looking around so uneasy. That explains a lot. There's someone higher up than them who runs things. It's a pity, I don't know who. But what's the point in knowing when I don't know if I'm even going to make it back home to inform Laura anyway? Think girl, think, who else could be behind this and what are their motives? Where do I fit in?'

She creased her eyebrows together deep in her thought. In fact, she was so engrossed in thoughts that she didn't notice that the car had come to a stop, until she heard the slam of the car door vibrating the vehicle a little. Panic ran through her body as she trembled nervously. Her heart beat was pounding against her ribcage like it wanted to break free. Cold sweat beads dripped down the contours of her face and over her body, making her clothing damp. Her palms were clammy and sweaty. Claire could hear footsteps outside the boot of the car, walking away, then, walking back as if they were pacing up and down, second guessing their own actions.. A deep growl was let out as the person inhaled and exhaled.

Instantaneously, the footsteps were back outside the boot of the car and the loud click of the button sounded as it flew open. She gazed up at him in fear.

He was a pure tower of muscle, and looked tremendously fierce as they stared at her with sorrow, but yet still a glimpse of resentment and anger. You could tell he was battling with his emotions, trying not to let him cloud their duty. They gently shook his head trying to clear his mind. Now all that was displayed on his face was pure anger. It was the legs that he felt most, but then she saw him lift one of his hands and looked at the crimson colour that lay there. He smiled. For the first time in a long time since she met up with him, he genuinely smiled. He was dangerously handsome when he smiled but that wasn't the point. She needed a full-proof escape plan to escape from him so that she could get home and inform Laura of what she had found out. She didn't even have her mobile phone anymore. She remembered when he hoisted her over his hard, muscled shoulders that her phone had fallen from her shallow pocket.

'If only I had followed my instincts and put it in the zipper pocket, I would have had it now. Well, can't cry over spilt milk now. I'll figure out some way. I need to.'

The ringing of his mobile phone interrupted her train of thought. He stepped away from the boot and answered the call angrily.

"What the hell, man! Where the heck are you? You said you'd be here before me… Damn it, I don't have a choice, do I? I don't care, just hurry up man!" He hung up the phone whilst the person was still talking. Whatever they had to say didn't seem to interest him.

'Was he the one in charge or was it the other person who called? Maybe, I might be able to play them against each other and make my escape. Yes, that's what I'll do.'

With a determined look set on her face Claire had a plan she'd try to execute. She hoped that it would work in her favour. He stood there studying her face and said, "Cancel whatever it was that you thought you could do because it's not going to happen. I know when your brain is in overdrive," and then burst into hysterical laughter. Composing himself, he got serious again. He gave her that unmistaken look that said 'I want to hurt you'. This struck more fear into Claire as she never thought that he hated her that much.

In what felt like hours, Claire heard another vehicle pull up and a sound of a vehicle door open. "Finally, you show up." The person didn't respond as if not wanting their identity or voice to be revealed. The shutters of a place or back of a lorry went up and something was being dragged out. The object sounded wooden. The footsteps that led away were now returning back in her direction but this time accompanied by more. Her heart pounded in her chest as if wanting to escape and leave her behind. Cold chills were taking over her body causing her to tremble although the sun beat down so hot it was scorching. Claire closed her eyes for a brief moment and inhaled and exhaled a few times trying to regulate her breathing. Whilst her eyes were closed all she could feel was a cloth over her eyes to stop her from seeing the other perpetrator involved. It was tied behind her head. As soon as they had finished tying the cloth, they let go of her head so suddenly causing Claire to bump the back of her head solidly against base of the car boot. She let out a muffled cry, as her head was pounding in agony. They grabbed her legs and dragged them rapidly outwards. Claire could feel hands on her head lifting and guiding it out of the car boot. She felt the hot, blazing sun kiss her skin, the wind caressing her wounds and any exposed skin it could find. It felt like a few steps to Claire, before she was placed in a prickly container. It was the last of the wind and sun before the lid was slammed shut. She felt the container being hoisted up in the air and placed into something much higher than a car and slid alone a ridged surface. The footsteps walked away, jumped down and pulled the shutters down, after placing her there.

All Claire could do now was just listen to the person start the ignition of the vehicle and begin the journey.

* * *

Laura came home in a taxi feeling a little uneasy. She felt an inclination that something wasn't quite right as she got home. She paid the taxi driver and got out of the car closing the door behind her. As the taxi driver drove off, she stood in the same spot for a brief moment in the sunshine staring up at the house. Taking a deep breathe she nonchalantly walked up the drive towards the porch. At first nothing seemed out of the ordinary until she stepped onto the porch and saw Claire's mobile phone on the floor, the screen cracked in several places.

"OK maybe she accidentally dropped it and didn't realise again."

Retrieving her keys from her bag, Laura stopped abruptly as she saw the door was wide open with Claire's keys in the lock. Laura was scared to death that something had happened to her best friend Claire. Automatically, to stop herself from screaming, she covered her mouth with her hands tightly, until she was calm enough trust herself not to scream. Laura looked around the house not sure what to expect. Straight away she searched the house, room by room, calling out to Claire but her best friend was nowhere to be seen. Laura checked round the back of the house and by the swimming pool but still no sign of Claire. Her throat felt parched and grainy like the desert sand. She shakily grabbed a glass from the kitchen and helped herself to some water from the fridge. She gulped down the cold liquid without taking a breath. Then she saw it. A handwritten note from Claire.

Lau, I believe that I know who was doing this to you. I think that I figured out the reason why too. I have some information that you need to see. We need to talk tonight when I get back home.' Love, you know who. 😬

Laura read the note over and over and then looked at Claire's mobile phone that she'd placed on the table with Claire's keys. Something didn't add up. Where the hell was, she? Did something happen to her?

'Oh god! No. I hope Claire's okay. I'll look for clues and hunt you down, Claire, don't you worry, I got you girl.'

Laura finished the last of the glass of water and put the glass on the kitchen counter. She walked back to the table and grabbed Claire's phone and unlocked it looking for clues. There was no sense in crying, no sense in breaking down either. This time she needed to be strong for a while in order to save Claire and save herself; putting an end to this fiasco. The Police didn't believe her, anyway, so what was the point of going to them with it. They'd just reiterate the same thing, "there's nothing, we can do unless you're physically harmed." Laura frowned as she rolled her eyes at the thought. She continued to search Claire's messages and saw one that stood out from the rest that was sent today from an unknown number.

'Meet me outside the old closed down supermarket, round the back, not far from your home.'

Although, it was hours ago, Laura headed there to see if Claire was still there, even though it didn't make any sense as to why her phone was smashed and the front door was opened with her keys dangling from the lock, but she was going anyway. Laura closed the front door behind her and walked hastily down the street towards the abandoned supermarket. She got there in under ten minutes as she ran some of the way. Searching around and calling out to Claire, Laura heard nothing. She decided to go back home. When she got there Claire's phone began to ring with George's name flashing on the screen. Laura instinctively answered.

"Hey, where are you? I thought you was supposed to meet me in town. I'm still waiting."

"This is Laura. Where are you supposed to meet Claire?"

Kissing his teeth he replied, "What's that got to do with you miss nosy parker?"

Laura rolled her eyes at his response and responded, "Well Mr believe I'm perfect, I have Claire's phone and she wouldn't be meeting you anywhere. Got it?"

Laura could hear him take a deep breath in and out before he chuckled down the line so loudly it was deafening, then said,

"If you say so mum. By the way tell Claire that I will be going away for a few days and I'll call her when I get back."

He paused for a brief moment then said in a low tone loud enough for her to hear.

"I see how you look at me Laura. I see the need in you. Are you jealous of Claire? Do you want me for yourself? All you have to do is say the words."

Laura felt repulsed by the idea of what George was suggesting.

"Hell no! You crazy idiot. Why would I want someone like you? I'd rather die than be with you. Don't know what Claire saw in you in the first place. You repulse me," she said as she cringed. George huffed like a raging bull and laughed, a laugh so sinister and evil it made her hair stand on end. Abruptly Laura hung up the phone. Hugging her hands around her body. She was at a dead end and now wasn't sure what to do, or where to go or where to start. She was just fed up with it all. The fright, the blows, people around her that she cared about getting hurt or going missing, being followed around, all of it. When was it all going to end? So many times, she felt like going home to her mother's but she remembered the erratic behaviour of her mother, and the consequences that came with it and changed her mind. But this time her gut instinct was telling her that in order to be safe that's where she needed to go - home to her mother's. One thing that she could not fault was that her mother would always try to protect her whenever she was around. Laura was in two minds whether to go the now or tomorrow just in case Claire got back and wondered where she was. With that thought in mind, Laura decided to stay home until the next day, and wait for her friend to return. Whilst waiting up she searched her storage boxes looking for the house keys for her mother's house. After hours of rummaging through each box Laura found some loose keys in a smaller box. As she rummaged through, examining each key carefully, she found the old house keys hidden between some cards -with a small, blue fabric ribbon through the key ring hole. Laura held the blue ribbon in her delicate hand and watched as the old keys dangled at its edge daring her to go. Replacing the lid back on the boxes, Laura tidied up and put the key in her suitcase that she had packed earlier. Laura waited up all night but Claire never came home.

Early morning, and Laura showered and got ready. She wrote a note to Claire telling her that she was going to her mother's and to give her a call when she got in. She placed

Claire's mobile on the kitchen table on top of the note and called a taxi to take her to her mother's residence. After waiting for what felt like ages, Laura exited the house and locked it up, making her way to the taxi that awaited her at the edge of her driveway. Just before getting in Alex rang her briefly telling her that he'd be back from his trip in a few days and would like to meet. Pausing for a moment Laura told him to let her know when he got back, and they'd arrange something then and she hung up. She put her suitcase in the taxi and then she got in and closed the car door, greeting the driver a good morning and saying the address out loud. "Okay miss, I'll get you there in a jiffy."

"Thank you."

Laura sat there staring at the scenery outside through the car window.

'*What was it about my mother's address that seems so familiar other than me living there before? Something didn't feel quite right. Maybe she was just overly worried about her best friend, Claire.*

Dismissing the uneasy feeling Laura focussed her mind on something else for now. Laura was extremely tired and suffering from lack of sleep which caused her to have a pounding headache. She leant back her head and closed her eyes until the car arrived at her destination. She saw the old maisonette up the driveway. Laura inhaled deeply, and paid the driver after grabbing her suitcase. Reluctantly, she made her way up to the front door. She retrieved the keys and attempted to open the door. Unfortunately, the keys refused to turn. Laura examined the key again.

'But this was the key. Did mum change the locks or something? I wonder if she still keeps the spare key in the flower pot round the side of the house. Only one way to find out.'

Laura reached into the flower pot hanging on the hook and felt around for a key. Just when she had thought there was no hope left, she found the key, dusted it off and pushed it into the keyhole. Finally, she thought. Laura unlocked the door and went inside calling out to her mother, just in case she was home, however she got no answer. She made herself a tea and sandwich. She sipped the tea and ate the sandwich as quickly as she could while blowing the hot liquid to cool it down. After she was finished, she washed up the dishes and made her way up to her old room. Opening the door, she walked inside. Nostalgia hit her as her bedroom was exactly the same as when she left it, so many years ago. Laura unpacked the suitcase and crawled into bed exhaustedly. Not before long she was fast asleep. Laura thought that she would have woken up before her mum got home but unfortunately that didn't happen. As she turned to change positions after being in the same spot for hours, she sleepily half opened her eyes to see her mother standing there looking at her, arms folded across her chest, her eyebrows creased together as if she was angry. This made her fully open her eyes to see her mum's face in a relaxed expression and a smile slowly crosses her face. Through a forced smile Laura said,

"Hi mum."

"Hi darling. You never told me you were coming home. Is everything alright?"

"I know, I should have called you but it was a spontaneous decision. I felt the urge to come home for some reason or another. Plus, I've wanted to come for a while."

Margaret stared at her daughter wearily as she puzzled some pieces together. Laura noticed and recognised that look that her mother plastered on her face, so she burst out in fright,

"Mum, Claire's gone missing."

The look on her mother's face was much more softer now. "Lau, what do you mean Claire's gone missing?" Laura explained in as much detail as she could about the day before. Margaret hugged her daughter in a tight embrace, then held her by the shoulder at arm's length and said "you and I both know that Claire is her own person and sometimes disappear for a few days day at a time, when she finds a new interest. I'm sure that's she's okay and will be back real soon."

"I hope that your right mum and nothing's happened to her, but it doesn't explain the key that was left in the door and why her phone was smashed on the porch.

"Maybe she left in a haste and didn't realise that she didn't lock the door and dropped her phone."

"I hope you're right, mum."

"I know that I am, darling. Just wait and see."

Although, Laura still felt uneasy, she felt a bit more relaxed with her mother's reassurance, and hugged her mother again as if saying thank you without the words.

"I'll let you know when dinner is ready." "Okay mum."

Later on, Laura heard a knock at the door. "Dinner is ready darling, so come down now." "Okay I'll be there shortly mum."

Within a minute Laura was sat around the dining table eating the dinner Margaret had prepared.

"By the way Lau, I've rented the basement out since I wasn't using it anymore. So sometimes you'll see people going and coming. You also might hear loud noises, and all sorts of stuff, as they shift around their belongings, okay?"

"Okay no problem mum."

"That's why there is a lock on the basement door from the inside of the house." Laura nodded her head as she listened to whatever her mother had to say. "Thanks for telling me; I won't go down there."

Laura got up and collected the dirty dishes and took them to the kitchen. She washed up the dishes, dried them and packed them away whilst thinking about Claire and her whereabouts, and also why her mother's address seemed so familiar in relation to something else. When Laura was finished, she watched a tv show with her mother to please her, although her mind was adrift. She promised herself she'd figure it out. As soon as the television show was over

Laura excused herself and went to bed where she had better room for thoughts without disturbance. She laid there in the dark looking up at the ceiling and reflecting back on everything that has been happening to her until suddenly there it was, the answer that she was searching for. She sat up straight in bed and gasped. She cocked her head to one side creasing her eyebrows as she looked up again at the ceiling in thought.

'Finally, I figured it out. I know why the address seemed so familiar for the reason other than home. I saw it that night I was attacked. I'm 100% sure that I saw most of it on Alex's phone screen when he got pushed over in my own home. What puzzles me is why Alex had my home address and what was his reasons for needing to know it? Hmm… I wonder. Something doesn't seem to add up. Although, it could be that other road with a similar name a few roads down from here. Well, after all I couldn't see the full address.'

Chapter 23

'Oh crap! My mobile battery is dead. I wonder if Claire tried to call me.'

Laura hastily leapt out of bed and extracted her phone charger from the top drawer, slamming the drawer shut. She plugged it into the nearby socket next to the chest of drawers and impatiently waited for the battery to charge to its first five percent, so that it could be switched back on. *'Come on, come on you, stupid phone.'*

Laura was drumming her fingertips on the surface of the chest of drawers impatiently refusing to tear her eyes away from the phone screen. She stared intently as the charging circle on the screen blinked on and off signalling that the phone was being charged. A little while later, the percentage numbers slowly began to climb one by one, putting her more on edge. One percent. Okay, okay. Come on keep on climbing. Two percent. Keep it coming?

Three percent. Nearly there.' She drummed a little faster with anticipation, with sweat beads forming on her forehead. Using the back of the other hand, Laura swiftly wiped it away.

Gritting her teeth, she let out a growl and shouted aloud, "Come on you stupid thing. You're taking too long. Grrr…"

With her free hand, Laura roughly ran her fingers through her wild, curly hair. Her fingertips were becoming sore now from drumming on the solid oak furniture. 'Four percent. Okay, one more to go before you automatically switch yourself on'

"Come on! You're wasting my time."

Laura felt frustrated and she began pacing the room. However, each time she walked by the phone, she stared down at the screen. 'Nothing yet.' She bent down resting her elbows on the top of the chest of drawers and lowered her head as she glared at the phone screen with her fingers embedded in her hair, keeping the unruly mess swept back enough to hinder it from blocking her view of the phone screen. As her frustration was escalating the screen suddenly lit up. "Finally! It's about time."

Laura waited until the phone loaded up its apps and home screen. As soon as it was finished, she snatched it up whilst the message notifications kept pinging out as they were received. The first thing Laura did was go check for voicemail messages, just in case of any missed calls. 'You have three new messages. First new message sent today at eight am;

"Hey Laura, its Sarah-Jane. When you arrive in to work, could you please do me a quick favour? There's a file that I placed on your desk. Could you deal with the accounts for me and file it straight away to Mr Atkins please? Thank you in advance."

Next new message sent today at eight twenty-five am.

"Hey Lau, I know we haven't spoken since you kicked me out of your house after accusing me of wrongdoing, but I was checking in to see how you are. I've been thinking about you a lot lately, and hope that everything is okay. I've been meaning to call you for a while, but every time I picked up the phone and dialled your number, I chickened out. He took a deep breath in as if building up courage. Call me the biggest wuss if you like. You're always on my mind. I miss your company a lot. It's me, Josh, by the way, just in case you forgotten what my sweet voice sounds like. Just kidding. You can't forget me, I hope. I'm too lovely. Anyways…Even though I'll be away for a few days, please don't hesitate…to give me a call please, please."

Although some parts of Josh's message made Laura roll her eyes, it mainly made her smile and she appreciated his call, his concern and his honesty about how he felt. Laura spoke aloud, talking to herself,

"I miss you too Josh but, I have to be one hundred percent sure… But I promise that at some point I 'll call you."

Last new message sent today at eight fifty-two am. "Mon Cherie! It's been a while. I need to see you. We need to talk urgently. I'll be away for a few days, but you could still attempt to call me. I'll get back to you as soon as I can. Maybe, we could visit our sanctuary like we used to. I've never stopped loving you. Talk soon."

The background to Freddie's voicemail message was a bit noisy, although she couldn't make out what the other people were saying. A piece of a statement from what Freddie had said to another person caught Laura's attention. The last two words of his statement was the only understandable part before he severed the call. It stated, "Kill her."

'Kill who? Who was he talking about? Was it Claire?'

Laura attempted to return Freddie's phone call, but unfortunately his phone was off. She resisted the urge to leave a voicemail message for him. Laura immediately cancelled the call. Feeling queasy and light headed, Laura sat on the carpet floor with her back leant against the cold wall, staring at the dark phone screen enclosed in her hand.

'Was he capable of doing something so evil? He was always so sweet, kind and attentive ever since I've known him. He'd always listened to her and understood. What if he doesn't anymore?'

Laura replayed Freddie's message over and over again, trying to piece together the stray words like a jigsaw puzzle before "kill her" was mentioned, but no matter how many times she repeated it, even with the volume turned up to the max, even on speaker there was no added improvement. In the end, Laura gave up trying to work it out. It was a headache that she didn't need right now. Suddenly a thought conjured up in her mind, so Laura got herself ready and made her way back to the home she had shared with Claire for so many years.

Laura wanted to check to see if her friend had returned or if there were any indications as to where she might have gone. When she arrived and cautiously opened the front door, Deja vu repeats itself. There was that familiar scent of a cologne that she couldn't erase ambushing her nostrils again. Laura's senses were scrambled as nostalgia kicked in at the forefront of her mind. It was a fragrance that she had enjoyed smelling on him in the past. To be frank, comes to think of it, he still wears that fragrance now. Wow! Laura didn't think that she would have gotten a whiff of that spicy with a lace of sweetness yet masculine scent so soon. He was always on shift for the past few weeks so it had been impossible to meet up and hang out enjoying each other's company. Pausing at the entrance, Laura leant her shoulder against the door frame and stared inside what used to be her home, a safe haven, some place that she could be comfortable, but now it felt strange to her. The serenity was tarnished by traumatic events, and spiteful evil intentions.

'Wait a minute! Why would Freddie's cologne be in her house?' It doesn't make any sense. None of it did. Laura was more confused than before.

'*Freddie couldn't have changed that much, could he? His personality appeared to be sincere the last time we spoke back at the hospital.*' Laura had to admit that it had been nearly being a decade since she had seen him, so she could no longer vouch for him.

What the hell was wrong with the men around her? The men in her life all seemed to have twisted mind-sets. Somehow, they all seemed to be implicated in what she was experiencing and what was happening around her for the past months. How strange, or was it just her own paranoia?'

Inhaling deeply and slowly releasing her breath, Laura entered the house and finally closed the door behind her. Entering the kitchen in haste to check if the note and Claire's phone and keys were still where she'd left them on kitchen table. Noticing that the items were still there, clearly undisturbed, Laura decided to search the house to see if there was anything disturbed or missing. Nothing was out of place. Nothing was missing. Laura opened her filing cabinet and retrieved the file she required for work. She'd promised to do some over time at work for just a few hours daily to help occupy her mind before insanity over rid her thoughts and became the new norm. After she had done this, Laura exited the house and hastily made her way to work.

The hours flew by in the blink of an eye, which by the time Laura had a little break her work day was done. Her work day was extremely busy which meant that she had to work through all of the breaks that she was supposed to have, but that was good because having a break meant thinking, and she didn't want to think anymore. It drained her emotionally, mentally, psychologically and physically. Too many things to bombard her mind. Laura took a deep breath in and out, then got up and stretched her legs. She tidied her desk, packed away her belongings in her handbag and logged out of her computer, setting it on to standby mode. Grabbing her belongings, Laura made her way out of her office but not before double checking that everything was in its place. Satisfied that it was, she finally closed the office door behind her and made her way down the school corridor. Whilst she was walking with her mind adrift, the sound of footsteps behind her grabbed her full attention. Her senses were heightened and adrenalin rushed through her body like a fast-acting drug stimulating her muscles from being fatigued to completely energised. Every nerve ending was prickled to life in preparation for instant reaction if needed. Her heartbeats raced at a raging speed.

Automatically Laura quickened her pace, walking faster along the lengthy corridor. The sound of the footsteps had increased its pace, too. They were getting faster behind her. At one point they sounded a little too close for comfort. This made Laura break into half a run to increase the distance between her and the person behind her, but the person behind her followed suit and broke into a half run too. The corner was fast approaching that led to the exit doors designed for after office hours as everywhere else would be tightly locked. The sudden urgency to escape was paramount.

'I will not die today. I refuse.'

When she sharply turned the corner, she crashed straight into the janitor's floor buffer machine. The blood was pumping through her body so fast that it was deafening as it rushed through her veins. Somehow, she didn't hear the noise that the floor buffer machine usually makes. Laura was like a prey being hunted down by its predator. It was a terrifying feeling. When she collided with the floor buffer, the impact was so hard and fast that she stumbled greatly, but in trying to keep her feet grounded she slammed into the lockers. "Oi! Watch it. Are you blind lady?" Yelled the janitor furiously.

"I'm so sorry," she said apologetically as she clutched her shoulder from the impact.

The footsteps that Laura believed were following her became louder as they were at full running speed now. Laura faced the direction where the sound came from, only to see a tall figure dressed all in black, with a sizeable hood covering the sides of their face. As the person ran past at speed they took a quick glance in her direction, looked away and glanced at her again in recognition this time, their eyes widened. Laura shrivelled under their watchful gaze as she was trapped between the machine and the lockers. The person looked away just in time to run down the stairs at the end of the corridor that led to the fire exit doors. With sheer strength, they pushed the bar in to release the lock on the fire exit door and emerged out into the evening air. Laura stood there like a statue, still taunted by those eyes, deep oceanic blue and that familiar scent, spicy with a lace of sweetness yet masculine fragrance that taunted her senses and her ability to think logically. Her hands cupped over her mouth as she gasped in shock.

'No way! Was it him? Was it really Freddie?'

Laura felt as though her heart was smashed into pieces. "Hey lady! You are in my way. I got work to do and you're delaying me. Move damn it."

Tears filled Laura's eyes as she gazed in the janitor's direction. The janitor held up his glove- covered hands in surrender studying Laura's expression and noticed that she appeared really emotionally torn.

"Gosh! I didn't mean for you to cry miss. I'm so sorry. Please don't start the water works. I can't stand seeing people crying."

Laura stared blankly at the janitor for a brief moment, her glazed tear-kissed eyes slowly looked behind him, over his shoulder as she stared in the direction those piercing blue oceanic eyes went, then burst into full-blown sobbing.

'Was her chasing me? But I'm standing right here, so why didn't he approach me then? That's strange. I'm so confused.'

"Please stop crying miss. I never meant to shout at you."

"It's not because of you, sir. You don't have to worry. I'll be getting out of your way right now. I'm sorry once again for disturbing your work."

The janitor nodded his head in acknowledgement and restarted the machine. Laura took it as her cue to leave, and walked away towards the exit without a backwards glance. Her shoulder felt sore from the earlier impact, where she banged it against the lockers to prevent her fall. Laura went down the stairs cautiously and hesitantly pushed the bar on the exit door, entering out into the cool evening air. Shortly after getting outside, Laura surveyed her surroundings whilst she hurriedly headed towards the parked taxi awaiting her arrival. As soon as she got into the taxi and closed the door, immediately the driver drove off. Out of curiosity Laura looked back and noticed the dark clothed figure emerging from the side of the school building looking in her direction. The more distance that was created between the figure and the taxi, the lesser the focus. The figure stood there on the road watching them as the car accelerated further and further away until they were no longer visible. Facing forward, the taxi driver was caught glancing at her in the rear-view mirror, occasionally with creased eyebrows but never said a word. Laura rolled her eyes at the driver because of their nosiness. How dare they look at her like she is mentally deranged? Her eyes were puffy from crying.

She was sure that she looked a mess, but she couldn't care less what anyone's judgement was at this point.

After the taxi driver parked up in the front of her mother's address, Laura paid the driver, took her belongings and got out. She casually walked to the front door and let herself in with the spare key. The basement door was open, so she had a glimpse of the stretch of the staircase and small patch of open area. It appeared to be so different from what she could remember of her childhood ventures down there. Laura spotted movement and could hear hushed voices holding a conversation of secrecy. The inner basement door based inside the house was the one that was opened instead of the door that led to the basement from outside the house. This piqued her curiosity; it was strange as if the basement was actually rented to strangers surely, they would always use the outside access.

'Not unless my mother knows these people personally and doesn't want to reveal it. But what's with the secrecy? And how did they get inside the house? Was my mother downstairs with them?'

Her curiosity plagued her mind like a moth to lights, pushing her to call out. "Mum are you downstairs in the basement?"

Laura stood there keenly awaiting a response. All of a sudden, she heard a bit of shuffling about and then some hurried footsteps as her mother came into view. "Yes, darling I'm here. I'll be up in a minute. Just finalising a few things."

"Okay mum. I was just letting you know that I'm home." "Okay honey. Your dinner is in the kitchen."

"Thanks mum."

Margaret disappeared again and the hushed voices resumed for another ten minutes or more before she emerged out of the basement. Twenty minutes later, the front door opened and closed letting the people out. The basement door was tightly locked up as if there had been no activities there just twenty minutes before. She had no interest in knowing about the basement plans so Laura kept her mouth shut. Her mother was too short-tempered and there was no mental strength left to cope with it. She had enough of an eventful day to mentally drain her. Laura ate half of her meal and sat there for another five minutes using the fork to push the food around the plate. Not long after she put the rest of her dinner in the oven and made her way upstairs, where she got freshened up and staggered into bed exhausted and emotionally strung out. Laura wasn't aware when she had dosed off, until she was awoken by a loud bang and hushed voices. The loud bang echoed again upstairs and then her mother's stern voice ordering them around.

"Be careful before you cause damage." "Mmhmm…" came a deep response.

Sneakily Laura got out of bed avoided the creaky floor boards under her carpet floor and peeped through the window to see a lorry parked on the driveway with the shuttered back open and facing the house. There were two dark clothed figures standing with their hoods up and their backs facing the house. This irritated Laura because she was fed up with seeing dark clothed figures. No matter where she went, there they were tormenting her soul. 'Was it the new trend or something? Shishhh…'

The two figures were retrieving a big wooden trunk from the back of the lorry.

Someone glanced up at her window so she drew back as quickly as possible before getting caught out. Not feeling shielded enough, Laura decided to sit on the stairs in the darkness using the glare of the street lights and the basement light to reveal enough of the activities taking place. She watched as her mother exited the basement, and assisted with the wooden trunk.

'Why was she in the middle of this?'

"Well, this is so heavy. Bang! Be careful darn it."

Bash! Bash! "Come on, be more careful. You're going to cause damage. What's inside… Won't you damage the trunk?"

One of the figures nodded their head in agreement to what Margaret implied but not once did they speak. It was like they didn't want to be heard. The trunk was taken with ease down the stairs with Margaret following behind them. The sound of the wooden trunk being slammed to the ground impatiently echoed through the basement door. It was like they couldn't wait to put it down signifying that it was extremely heavy. The next thing she heard was dragging sounds as they pulled around the heavy wooden trunk and other items. They collected all of their boxes and crates from the lorry and took them into the basement. Then the loud shutters came down. The dark clothed individuals exited the basement and left. The lorry's ignition alongside another vehicle's was fired up and off they drove, leaving the basement door open as if they'd just delivered some things for Margaret. Laura was suspicious of these late-night activities. Fed up with concealing herself in the corner of the stairs amongst the shadows, she rose up and descended the stairs, seeing her mother hastily locking the basement door, before Laura could even put her foot on to the lowest stair.

'Wow! If there was an award for being swift, it goes to Margaret aka mother.'

Rubbing her eyes and forcefully yawning to pretend like she had just woken up and come downstairs Laura asked,

"Mum was that you making all that noise?"

"No dear. The people I rented the basement to called and asked if they could deliver some items, so I said okay."

"Oh, I see. But why this late? It's after midnight mum."

"By the way, what you doing awake at this time dear? She interrogated as she watched her daughter suspiciously.

"I was thirsty, so I wanted a glass of cold water." "Okay dear, whatever you say," she mumbled.

Laura was taken aback by that statement but chose not to respond to it. Whether it was rude or not she had no idea, but refused to aggravate her mother anymore. She retrieved the cold water from the refrigerator, said good night to her mother and headed back to bed. There was a strange feeling gripping her nerves and she couldn't shake it. Laura thought about the big, wooden trunk and the fact that they brought it in so late.

'Was there a reason for the late delivery?'

Now she needed to know what her mother's involvement with the people who rented the basement could be.

Chapter 24

A couple of days went by and Laura did the same routine repetitively. The only thing that changed was that each night close to midnight she would move around in the darkness to spy on her mother's suspicious activities with the people who rented the basement. There was something not quite right with that scenario and she intended to find out what. Around midnight every night like clockwork they would be in the basement moving things around, with their voices just a mere whisper. Laura often wondered what it was that they were talking about. Sometimes in the dead of night amongst the loud noises of the dragging, she could swear that she heard muffled screams, and lots of confrontations that led to them fighting with each other. At times Laura would stand with her ear against the basement door situated inside the house, so that she wasn't seen.

'Thank goodness the doors partly closed and they're using the outside entrance from time to time. It was imperative that she didn't get caught.'

What was strange to Laura was that every night around one am, her mother would make her way downstairs and go into the basement like a ritual. Whenever she heard Margaret's footsteps making her way downstairs, she would sneakily hide under the stairs amongst the coats, peeping to see what her mother was up to. Before Margaret entered the basement, she would always glance around to see if anyone was watching before she finally entered. Margaret had a tendency to spend a vast amount of time in the basement talking to the people until they left, whereby she would lock the basement door inside the house. *'How did the basement door inside the house got opened in the first place and at what time?'*

The next morning, Laura decided that she needed to investigate what was inside the basement to satisfy her curiosity. The question was how, as she had no idea where her mother stored the key. She sat there pondering where to look, with her elbows propped up on the table with her chin rested in the palms of her hands, her fingertips curled above her top lip as she lightly drummed them in a wave like a rhythm. Several places popped into her mind but one place stood out as the most likely, but the timing had to be perfect. The touch of a hand on her shoulder zapped her out of her thoughts. Laura jumped and her head sharply turned as she looked to see whose hand was firmly resting on her shoulder.

"Oh, hi mum! You scared me." She said with a shriek.

Margaret studied her daughter's face for a split second before responding. "Sorry dear, but just letting you know that I'll be out for the day. I won't be back tonight. I will see you tomorrow about eleven am."

Laura needed to create a diversion to distract her mother long enough for her to execute her plan. She couldn't let her mother leave just yet. She needed to eliminate finding the key for the basement in her mother's handbag. Laura hoped that it was there as it was imperative that she found it. Now, she needed to think of a brief delay that provided her with enough time to search her mother's handbag, which at that moment was placed on the chair at the head of the table. Coming up with a plan, Laura decided to secretly put her mobile on silent and set the no caller I.D so that it cannot be traced back to her. With that in place, Laura rang the house phone knowing that her mother would have to go back upstairs to her bedroom to answer it. It was a short window, so Laura knew that she had to be quick.

Margaret was a little reluctant to go back up the stairs to answer the telephone call. Kissing her teeth, she decided to go just in case it was important. Hurriedly, she climbed the stairs as fast as her feet could carry her. Laura got up and peeped around the corner and up the stairs to ensure that her mother was out of sight. Hastily she reached into her mother's handbag trying her best not to disrupt the contents too much as she searched thoroughly. Just when she thought that there was no hope, she decided to check the bunch of keys in the handbag. Extracting the keys from the bag, Laura searched through every key until she came across the basement key. `Got ya!'

Smiling to herself for her triumph, Laura removed the basement key from the brass key ring as fast as she possibly could, and replaced her mother's bunch of keys back into her handbag just in the nick of time as she heard her mother cursing under her breath as she descended the stairs. Quickly Laura put the basement key in her bra as there were no pockets in her clothing. There was no time to adjust the basement key so that it laid comfortably, so Laura had to bear the scratches and pokes from the jagged edges. Speedily she sat down in the same chair and recreated the same position that her mother left her in, so that she wouldn't look suspicious. Not long afterwards Margaret said her goodbyes and departed, leaving Laura on her own in the house. Laura had nowhere to go, so she knew that day would be the best opportunity she'd get to do her investigation since her mother wasn't returning home until the following day. Nonetheless, she wasn't going to waste too much time as her mother could change her mind and turn back up later in the day or night.

Laura ran to the nearby window and peered through the gap to see if her mother was actually gone. Satisfied with the result she rapidly completed all her tasks and freshened up. Just when she decided to get the investigation over and done with so she wouldn't get caught her mobile phone vibrated showing her work number on the display screen. "Hello."

"Laura… hello… it's me Sarah-Jane."

Laura rolled her eyes in irritation. All she was thinking was that she had no time for chit chat nor did she have anytime to be doing any more favours for this woman. She honestly didn't mind helping a colleague from time to time but this wasn't the time. She had important things to do that took precedence over anything else right now. Before responding she took a deep breath to calm herself down and then spoke.

"Oh, hi Sarah-Jane. What's up?"

"I called just to thank you for bailing me out the other day. You did an amazing job with the file. You're a star, girl. I owe you o…"

Although Laura felt guilty for feeling irritated, she abruptly interrupted what Sarah- Jane was about to say. "I'm so sorry Sarah-Jane, but I have to go now. It's important. By the way, you're welcome. Talk soon."

Soon after Laura ended the call, she heard something. Keenly she listened to the background noise again as she tried to pin point which direction it was coming from.

Suddenly the sound of loud dragging penetrated the house.

`Shit! So, they're here already. What the heck could they be dragging about so much? It's totally annoying now.'

Peering through the window again, Laura saw a BMW X5 parked on the drive with the boot open. Déjà vu struck her like a chord, as she remembered that an exact model like that was the one that followed them from the cocktail bar that night. Laura wondered if it was the same car that veered off down the dirt road not far from where they lived with the neon holiday logo sticker on it. The urge to satisfy her own curiosity was driving her forward. She grabbed her key from the side table and sneakily crept outside, being careful enough not to draw any attention. Surveying her surroundings Laura checked to see if anyone was looking in her direction before making her next move. She knew that she had to be stealthy otherwise there would most likely be dire consequences. The first time that she heard a noise she hid behind the hedge as quickly as she could to avoid getting caught in the act, although she knew that it was the territory of her arch nemeses. There was no time to spare to brush away the cobwebs otherwise she would have drawn unwanted attention to herself and she couldn't afford that. When Laura was crouched down behind the hedge, she anxiously waited for the person to go. In front of her she saw a big, brownish looking garden spider heading in her direction, and right towards her face. Laura used her hand and tightly covered her mouth to stop herself from screaming. Her heartbeats were erratic. She was so scared, her eyes wide open as she panicked, not only about the big spider, but the person on the other side of the hedge as well, she had no clue what they were capable of.

'*I can't get caught. Need to stay quiet. I can do this. I have to do this.*'

Footsteps drew nearer as the person was walking towards the hedge where she hid. Laura froze the nearer they got, her eyes darted from one side to another as she kept one eye out for the person and the other eye out for the spider. They had her trapped in a catch twenty-two situation.

'*Oh God! Oh God! Please… please, ple… please let them go away. Don't let them see me. Me and my nosy self. But you know why I have to know. I need to know if the danger is now at my mother's doorstep, so that I can warn her.*'

As if answering her inner prayer, the footsteps stopped for a short while.

'*I wonder if they can see me from where they are standing. Oh no! Don't move girl.*'

After a while the person walked away in the opposite direction and headed back inside the basement. Laura breathed a sigh of relief. Finally, she got up just before the spider crawled on to her face and made her way towards the car. As she was searching the outside of the car to find any indication of her own suspicions, her attention was drawn to the neon stickers there and the tinted glass. It was the same neon stickers she had seen that night in the rear-view mirror. Scanning her surroundings again to make sure that the coast was clear, Laura approached the driver's side window and put her hands either side of her face blocking out the extra sunlight, so she could peer inside to check for any indication as to who these people were. Absolutely nothing was there to give her any kind of information. The inside of the car was squeaky clean, so nothing was out of the ordinary. Whilst her eyes still searched inside the car anyway, she heard footsteps approaching her direction. This time she knew that she'd be more exposed.

'*Where can I hide this time? Oh, darn it. What rotten luck?*'

Edging around to the front of the car, Laura crouched down as low as possible placing her head in her lap. Luckily for her the person grabbed something from the boot, closed it and then headed back towards the basement door. "Help me! Anyone out there please help…"

The weakened voice was barely audible. The basement door was slammed shut, shutting out the captive's cries for help. There was someone trapped in the basement.

'*Could it be Claire? Or was it someone else?*' Laura was hell bent on finding out. Speedily she ran on tiptoes, avoiding any gravelled area, quietly opened the front door with the spare key and swiftly made her way inside before someone saw her. Laura released the breath caught in her chest. She exhaled heavily letting out a sigh of relief. '*Phew!*' As Laura stood there with her back leant against the door, she overheard muffled voices. But only one stood out. It sounded female. Hastily Laura took the basement key and slowly pushed it in the lock, silently turning it gradually, trying her best not to make a single sound. The lock released with a soft click and she felt relieved, although she was terrified as to what awaited her behind the basement door. Slowly she opened the door slightly lifting it to avoid the creaking that the door hinges made whenever it was opened and closed. Laura warily crept inside and closed the door behind her. Taking a deep breath in and out, Laura slowly made her down the basement stairs avoiding any creaky parts of the old wood. She stepped as lightly as she could. Adrenalin was pumping at raging speed through her body. Her senses were heightened the further down the stairs she got. Her heart beats were slamming against her chest till it was deafening. She wondered if they could hear her heart beating. There was a lump caught up in her throat making it difficult for her to swallow. She tried swallowing again but it just wouldn't budge. Her palms were clammy and sweaty. Sweat beads ran down the contours of her face and back. It made her body feel heavy and lazy. She had to use all willpower and determination to continue forward to investigate. The hairs on her arms and the back of her neck stood on edge. She could sense that danger lays ahead of her but she still pressed on. She remained very alert to her surroundings. The stairs felt never ending. Finally, she thought as she planted her feet firmly on the basement floor, even though she felt like running and not looking back. But no matter what Laura was determined to try and help whoever it was that was pleading for help.

'*Now for the decision. Do I go left or do I go right?*'

From what Laura could remember, the left led to a back room and the right led to the open space with the shelves that was used to contain storage items and equipment. Laura crept right, her eyes darting around the storage area to see if there was anything out of the ordinary. She was thorough in her search making sure that there were no signs of any captives been held there. She couldn't see any signs of a struggle in that area at all, only the drag marks made by the heavy boxes. Bracing herself she decided to check the rest of the basement. Before Laura could go in the other direction, she heard footsteps. Promptly she hid under the staircase and watched as the two dark clothed hooded figures left through the basement door and closed it after themselves. She listened carefully for a while longer to make sure that they weren't going to return. All she heard was two car doors opening and slamming shut and the kick start of the ignition when it was fired up. Laura emerged from under the staircase and went to the exit door where the hooded figures had disappeared and slightly pushed the door ajar. She peered out through the small gap and saw that the two figures were actually in the car, reassuringly, as they drove off without a backwards glance. The wheels skidded against the gravelled surface whereby a pebble flipped up and hit against the door making her jump back. The car veered off down the road as she mentally made a note of the number plate for future reference. Laura closed the door with ease and began looking around feeling a little more contented hoping that the danger was obliterated.

Walking back towards the open space where the storage items were based, she remembered catching a glimpse of a big wooden trunk, big enough to conceal a body to transport them. Approaching the trunk, Laura braced herself not knowing what to expect. All she knew was that anyone or anything could be in there. 'Thump' then came a muffled voice as she stood not too far away from the trunk. The noise caught her off guard making her hesitate for a split second through fear. Despite this, her instincts propelled her forward as quickly as she could to open the heavy lid of the trunk. When she opened it, what she saw was someone she thought that she would never see again. Laura was gobsmacked at the display in front of her. Dropping to her knees, tears filling her eyes, she covered her face with the palms of her hands and sobbed for a moment. Still in shock, she rubbed her eyes and looked again as if checking to see if she was seeing clearly. Satisfied that it wasn't an illusion, Laura outstretched her arms in pure happiness although she was concerned as to why they were locked up in the trunk. She untied the rope that bound their hands. Automatically, he rubbed the soreness around his wrists where the rope had once laid binding them into position of entrapment.

Laura helped him into a seated position and they both hugged each other and apologised to each other for everything.

Whilst they were hugging saw Alex emerged from the other side of the basement strutting with pride as he cradled a battered Claire in his arms, her hands snaked around his neck as she gazed up at him with a smile. Alex stared at the person with a smug smile on his face as if he had won something spectacular. The person stilled and looked at Alex furiously and shouted, "Put her down, you maniac."

As soon as that was said Alex began limping as though he was hurt. Claire arched her body as if she was in a lot pain. Laura quickly turned around to see who Freddie was referring to. She couldn't believe her eyes. Laura stared at Alex and Claire feeling baffled.

Although she was elated to see Claire, she was confused now even more than ever before. She needed someone to explain what was happening because she couldn't make sense of it. Laura looked to Freddie for an explanation, but not before the rope that bounded his legs together had been undone. Freddie opened his mouth in an attempt to explain what was going on to Laura, but before he could utter a word Alex interrupted and yelled,

"Get away from him Laura. He's dangerous."

Swiftly Laura rose to her feet almost stumbling backwards. Warily she reversed a few steps backwards, at least one and a half arm's length away from Freddie without taking her eyes off him. From that distance she asked,

"What does he mean by that Freddie?"

Freddie looked at Laura as though he was hurt by her reaction. Shaking his head, he closed his eyes for a split second shutting out the pain and anguish that he was feeling. All he wanted to do was to protect Laura but she shun away from him. Somehow, he knew that he needed to straighten this situation out. It desperately needed resolving and he was willing to try. All he hoped was that Laura still believed in him. `Does she still trust me with her life?

Only one way to find out.'

Snapping out of his own thoughts all eyes were on him from every direction awaiting his brave response. All he needed was one person to believe him, the only person that mattered to him at this very moment. His eyes sought Laura's as he spoke, "Mon Cherie, don't listen to him, I'm innocent. You've known me most of your life. Have I ever harmed anyone or anything?"

Freddie spoke as if pleading to her better nature. He desperately needed Laura to be on his side. He stared at her, awaiting an answer to his question. Suddenly Laura opened her mouth to speak, but before she could utter a word Alex interjected. "Laura, I saw him kidnap Claire and followed him to see where he was taking her. As I was biding my time waiting for him to leave, I got caught, so we fought. Luckily, I managed to overpower him and lock him in the trunk after knocking him out."

Believing Alex, Laura stepped completely away from Freddie feeling petrified of what he might do to her. It was a feasible explanation to explain why he was battered and tied up in the trunk. What other explanation could there be? Freddie reached out his hand to Laura, but she pulled away more from him. Freddie knew that Laura had wavered towards what Alex was saying. A burst of anger welled up inside him, threatening to explode. He lunged towards Alex who was still cradling Claire in his arms. He had to defend his reputation as he couldn't have it tarnished by such dangerous games. Noticing Freddie lunging towards him, Alex tossed Claire backwards and blocked the punch that was headed straight for his face. Claire fell with a thud, getting her hand caught in between the partitions that were behind her. Crack! Claire screamed aloud in agony. Laura tried to get to her best friend but instead got caught in the crossfire of Alex's and Freddie's wrath. A solid punch to the jaw made her wince in pain as she clutched her cheek with her hand. She lurched backwards trying to keep her footing, moving far enough away from the brutal brawl dead in front of her. There was no way that Laura could get to Claire now. The fight was out of hand and was becoming more violent by the minute. Jumping on each other, fists were exchanged without much contact before both men grabbed each other pushing and shoving before ending up on the ground. They rolled around trying to land punches and elbows into each other. The brute strength of both men was incredible. Scrambling to their feet using each other's strength as leverage to be upright neither man was backing down. Alex threw an uppercut and connected to the side of Freddie's jaw knocking him backwards, but not enough for him to lose his footing. Freddie cried out in pain but refused to back down. Freddie leant back, standing on one foot and landed a kick to Alex's gut with heavy force. Alex kneeled over from the kick, bawling out in agony. Rising back to his feet, both men continued to brawl with each other with no sign of anyone backing down. Each person was getting severely injured and Laura couldn't handle watching the men she cared for kill each other. It scared her to death so she concluded that she must call the police. After making the call, Laura tried to beg them to stop but her words fell on deaf ears. Again, she tried to get to Claire but was accidentally shoved backwards, falling flat on the ground and knocking the wind out of her for the moment. Gathering herself she hauled herself over to the corner out of harm's way. She sat there for a while sobbing her heart out because she didn't know what else to do. Building up her courage she stood up in the corner biding her time for when either she could get to her friend, both men would stop or the police would arrive just in time.

Although Freddie was furious, he tried to restrain himself from inflicting too much damage to Alex but realised that Alex didn't care when he felt a punch from Alex to his eye. Clutching his eye, he thought that any longer and he would lose control of his temper completely. He was still trying to preserve his reputation but there was no chance of that anymore. It was kill or be killed. Freddie always tried to only use his karate skills in desperate times but this was it. Feeling infuriated he took his stance and without hesitation landed Alex with a series of kicks to the head, torso and groin. Time was of the essence and he had no more time to waste. Not only was his life on the line but his career and his reputation and any possible reconciliation him and Laura. Freddie kicked Alex again to the chin when Alex sneakily tried to hit him with an object. Alex fell to the ground with a thud, vibrating the floor and crying out in agony, cursing under his breath. Not satisfied with this Freddie leapt on top of Alex and both men were exchanging punch for punch. Eventually, Freddie laid a barrage of punches into Alex's face, blood spurting everywhere. Unable to defend himself from Freddie, Alex was at his mercy. Alex attempted to put his hands up to protect his face but that just made Freddie landed the punches in his ribs instead.

Laura had never seen this side of Freddie being in such a rage before. It sent chills through her body. She feared for Alex's life and needed to get through to Freddie, but she wasn't sure how. Improvising she begged,

"Freddie, I believe you. Please stop."

Freddie turned and stared at Laura suspiciously as he connected a knee to Alex's ribs repetitively. "Please Freddie, I mean it. I believe you."

This calmed Freddie down and he leisurely got up and approached her with his arms outstretched and a relieved look on his face, his knuckles bloodied and bruised from each impact. Laura held him in a warm embrace as she watched Claire free her broken wrist from the partition and grabbed the shovel and headed towards where they stood. Claire looked at Laura for her approval. Although, Laura knew that she was deceiving Freddie, she knew that it had to be done. This made her felt heart broken and ashamed. Laura wept on Freddie's shoulder as she knew that this was really the end as he would be arrested by the police.

Freddie held her tighter trying to console her. As he completely relaxed his body, all he felt was a hard blow to the head making him feel dazed. Laura kept holding him until the police eventually arrived.

The sound of the police sirens got closer and closer until they were skidding to a halt right outside the house. The police rushed inside and took hold of Freddie out of Laura's arms placing handcuffs tightly around his bruised wrists and led him into the parked police car. The police suggested to Laura that they'd give her a lift to the hospital where her friends would be taken for medical care. And there they would take her statement. Laura took one last look at Freddie sat in the back of the other police car and looked away disappointedly.

Shortly, after the ambulance arrived to take Claire and Alex away as he insisted that he was not leaving her. Just before the paramedic closed the door to the ambulance Alex glanced up towards the attic window at the top of the house staring at dark figure with a smile and a thumbs up, like he knew who it was. Freddie noticed the exchange between Alex and the figure and knocked on the window to draw Laura's attention. When she looked at him, he tried to point in the direction of the top of the house, making Laura look up. Laura saw a figure reversing into the shadows and felt terrified. Suddenly a hand touched her shoulder startling her. "Let's go miss."

The paramedic closed the ambulance door after doing the relevant medical checks and settling Claire and Alex. Laura approached the police car, opened the car door to get in. As she put one foot inside the back of the car, she felt like she was been watched. Slowly, she peered up at the attic window and saw the figure staring down at her, and waving.